A
WORLD
WITHOUT
YOU

A

WORLD

WITHOUT

YOU

BETH REVIS

RAZORBILL

An Imprint of Penguin Random House

RAZORBILL

An Imprint of Penguin Random House
Penguin.com

ISBN: 978-1-59514-716-5

Printed in the United States of America

1 3 5 7 9 10 8 6 4 2

For Luke, the reason I started writing this book,
and
For Jack, the reason I finished.
Dei gratia.

"No doubt the universe is unfolding as it should."
—Max Ehrmann, "Desiderata"

CHAPTER 1

"It's time, Bo," Ryan says, putting his hand on my shoulder.

I shrug him off.

"Come on, buddy." He reaches for me again, but I step further away. *Buddy.* Ryan's not my friend, and it's pointless of him to pretend like he is. Ryan is no one's friend.

My feet make hollow sounds on the weathered planks of the old boardwalk, but I have to stop soon enough. The giant metal gate before me is painted green to blend into the environment, which is dumb because the environment's not really that green around here. But either way, it stops me from going forward. Not that I have anywhere to escape to anyway.

Berkshire Academy, where I live five days out of every week, is on an island. Not a tropical paradise—nope, nothing like that. It's in *Massachusetts*, of all places. Everything good about living on an island is twisted here. Islands have beaches and the ocean, yeah? Well, Pear Island has those, but good luck having fun under the sun around here. I mean, we have the sun, obviously, but it's behind clouds. And rain. And sometimes snow. A lot of times snow. And wind. Wind so strong that it blows the sand in your face like it has a personal vendetta against you. And the short summer we do have, when there is actually sun, is interrupted by, like, a month of flies swarming around. Not buzz-buzz nice flies, but greenhead flies. They sting and bite and are basically the biggest jerks of the fly population, designed specifically to ruin the day of anyone who may dare think that living on an island means you should be able to, I don't know, lie on the beach or enjoy the sun.

We don't even have a decent boardwalk. Our boardwalk was built fifty years ago, so walking on it barefoot sucks. And oh, by the way, the boardwalk goes through a *marsh*, so the only people who actually *want* to use it are old farts who look at *birds*.

Oh, how I love my island life.

"Come on, man," Ryan says again, this time with more impatience in his voice. "It's time to go."

I turn, leaning my back against the green metal gate. "There's no point."

Ryan shrugs.

I push off from the gate and follow him back toward Berkshire, the bricked mansion just visible beyond the trees in the distance.

The Doctor said Berkshire was placed here—at the end of a particularly non-paradise tropical island—because of a special grant from the government. Most of the island is a state park. The southern tip, where we are, is just the Berk and some old ruins from seventy years ago, when there was a "camp"

2

for people with polio. The top of the island is full of ice cream shops and tourists, but we hardly ever get to go there.

Ryan trudges ahead of me, keeping to himself. Good. I don't want to talk.

I'm *mad*.

This whole thing is meaningless. This whole day. There's no point to being here. To doing this.

"You have to understand," Dr. Franklin told me this morning when I informed him I wouldn't be going to the assembly. "People need closure."

"I don't," I growled.

The Doctor had given me that smarmy sympathetic smile that people do when they think they know more than you. "Come anyway," he said.

I'd hoped that if I ventured as far out into the island as I could go, he might forget about me. Or, if not forget, at least pretend to forget about me. Let *me* be the invisible one for once.

But no.

Berkshire Academy rises up from the ground before us as we round the path, all austere and formal. On paper, I guess my life is pretty sweet, living in a mansion on an island. But just like Pear Island is this twisted version of what an island should be, so is the giant brick building complete with pointy spires. It's not a Bruce Wayne palace; it's a boarding school. The Berkshire Academy for Children with Exceptional Needs.

I take a deep breath and pick up my pace so I'm walking beside Ryan instead of behind him. I'm being a jerk. I'm angry and I don't want to be here—and I don't mean on the island, I mean *here*. Now. I do want to be on this island. I want to be at the Berk. Don't get me wrong, all that stuff about the flies and the cold and all, that part sucks. But Berkshire itself . . . this place is the best thing that's ever happened to me.

But I don't want to be . . . here. Not in this moment. Not in this way. I want to be here two weeks ago, when everything was fine. Or seven months ago, when I first drove up the gravel road to the academy's open doors. Or eight months ago, before I'd even come to Berkshire or learned that it would be my new home. I want it to be then.

Not now.

Black bunting hangs over the arched walnut doors at the top of the steps, where there are still a few students hanging out. A handful of cars are parked around the circular drive, and I recognize my dad's Buick. Great. So the families have been invited. Dr. Franklin, my unit leader, hurries outside and down the brick steps. His gaze falls on me, and something in his face eases; the lines around his eyes soften, and his jaw unclenches. "Come on," he says to me, his voice gentle. Then he turns to the other students still lingering outside and gives them a stern look. "Everyone, it's time."

Dr. Franklin leads the way down the hardwood halls of Berkshire's main floor. Hardly anyone ever uses the main floor—it's formal, reserved for Family Day, scholastic banquets, graduation ceremonies, and once, after a fund-raiser, a fancy ball hosted by the board for top contributors to the school. Sofía and I snuck down to the kitchen the morning after the ball and pilfered the remains of half-drunk bottles of flat champagne that were supposed to have been thrown out.

We follow the Doctor past the main living areas, our feet barely audible on the heavy rugs that line the floors. Everything on the first floor is dark and gloomy—I much prefer the common room I share with my unit on the second floor. The cook staff is setting up a sort of buffet along one wall. I guess we're dining as a group today rather than in shifts, like we usually do. Why is it that whenever there's a hint of tragedy in life, all old people want to do is cook? It's not like a covered dish is going to solve anything. My hands clench in fists as the scent of melted cheese and roasted vegetables wafts around us.

A nice dinner isn't going to make any of this better.

The Doctor pushes open the wide doors at the back of the long hallway and holds them for us as we file into the courtyard. The rest of Berkshire's students are already waiting for us in the small arena that teachers sometimes use for outdoor lessons when the weather's not too cold. I scan the crowd quickly and notice my family standing at the back of the room, dressed in their Sunday best. My father must sense my gaze. He turns around and watches me as I follow Dr. Franklin down the steps toward the small stage at the bottom. Dad shakes his head at my ripped jeans and faded black T-shirt. Whatever—let him glare. There's a reason why I'm at boarding school and he's back at home—we're both happier when there are miles between us, and his presence does nothing but highlight just how sucky today is going to be.

The director of the school—an older, bald man whose eyebrows reach to the heavens—stands at the center of the stage in front of a table. He looks bored, but when Dr. Franklin signals to him, he nods, straightens his spine, and assumes a mask of benevolence.

"We are here today to remember the life of one of our own," he intones. His voice is low, but nearly everyone is focused on him.

Not me, though. I don't need his lies. Instead, I watch as some of the staff arrange paper lanterns on the table. After a moment, the director raises his voice. "And now, I'd like to invite Sofía Muniz's closest friends—her unit and headmaster—to say a few words."

He steps back, and for a moment he looks as if he's going to push past everyone and head back inside where the food is. But one of the teachers offers him a chair beside the table, and he sits down.

The Doctor nudges Ryan and me forward. Gwen and Harold, the other kids in our unit, are already stepping down the granite stairs toward the table with the paper lanterns. When I don't move, Dr. Franklin pushes me again.

Fine. I'll do this. Even if it's false.

The Doctor speaks first. He talks about Sofía like she was his star pupil, and I guess she kind of was. *Is.* I mean *is.* Out of all of us, Ryan has more power and control than Sofía ever did, but Sofía is the kind of quiet, attentive student that teachers like. She never causes trouble. She never messes up.

Not like me.

The Doctor's voice is tight, as if he's trying to hold back tears, and it's only now, watching as he tries to describe what Sofía meant to him—to all of us—that I feel a hard lump rising in my own throat. I blink rapidly and look away, trying to focus on the ivy clinging to the bricks on the side of the academy. I'm not the only one affected by Sofía's absence—I have to force myself to remember that. We all miss her.

When the Doctor finishes his speech, he turns to the rest of us. His eyes fall on me, and the expectation is clear: He wants me to talk. He wants me to say goodbye.

My teeth grind, and my eyes narrow, and I do not move.

Dr. Franklin sighs, and his gaze skims over the rest of us. Harold will never speak in public; he looks like he's about to throw up right now, just standing here. Since this has nothing to do with him, Ryan doesn't give a shit about being here. But Gwen trembles beside me, the words inside her boiling like water about to rattle the lid off a pot. She wants to speak, I know it. But she glances at me and then shakes her head just a little, and the Doctor nods, accepting our silence.

We move around the table that the staff set up for us. There are five paper lanterns, each a pale white. Gwen reaches forward first, her fingers sparking with light, but Dr. Franklin covers her hand with his, pulling her back. There are parents here, people not a part of the school. Can't let them see. The staff light the lanterns with the long matches they use for the fireplaces, then they hand one to each of us. Dr. Franklin looks like he's about to say something else, something poetic, but before he can break out into a full-on dirge, I let my lantern slip from my fingers, and it rises into the gray sky without any more ceremony. The others follow suit, Dr. Franklin releasing his lantern only after he mumbles something to himself, his eyes closed and his head bent. Everyone looks up. A gust of wind knocks Harold's lantern down, punching at the inflating paper balloon, but it staggers back, following the others as they drift in the direction of the ocean.

No one notices me as I leave.

That's something I learned from Sofía. Being invisible is easy.

I step further into the garden—which is basically just some stubby trees and scraggly bushes—and then round the academy and head back out to the edges of the property. Not toward the ocean—not where the lanterns are fighting through the winds to float higher—but back toward the gate and the ruins on the edge of Berkshire's grounds.

Back to the last place I last saw her.

It's such bullshit, this memorial with its empty words and fragile lanterns. All of this mourning is totally pointless.

Because Sofía's not dead.

CHAPTER 2

I hear her before I see her. I'm not surprised that she's the only one who bothered to find me after the memorial service.

"Hey, Gwen," I say, as she plops down beside me.

She gives me a sullen look. She's pissed I left the ceremony. "You're not the only one who misses her, you know."

"I know."

She glares at me, but then the fight leaves her. "This was my place first," she says, her voice softer now. "I'm the one who showed it to Sofía."

I didn't know that. I'd always sort of thought of the chimney as *my* place on the island. I discovered it my first week here, after doing some research on Berkshire and finding out that the island held one of the oldest remaining houses built by the colonists. My eyes drift to the black-and-bronze plaque adhered to the crumbling bricks near the border of the academy's grounds: REMAINS OF THE CEDRIC MOOREHEADE HOUSE. DESTROYED IN A FIRE IN 1775. ORIGINALLY BUILT IN SALEM

IN THE 1660s, LIKE THE ISAAC GOODALE HOUSE OF IPSWICH, AND MOVED TO PEAR ISLAND IN 1692.

"Why'd you come out here?" I ask Gwen.

She flicks her fingers, a burst of flame dancing out. "I like chimneys."

"Oh. Right."

I like history, so of course I'd sought the ruins out, but all that was left was the chimney. Still, I like this place for what it used to be—a house built before America was a country—and for what it might have been—someone's dream, someone's birthplace, someone's safe haven. Pear Island hasn't been used for much. In the early days, settlers grazed livestock here. But at some point, a family decided that this island, with its biting flies and harsh winds and terrible weather . . . this island would make a perfect home. The chimney is all that's left of a family. Real people who stood here centuries ago, with lives lost to time.

But Gwen doesn't care about the history. She likes it simply for what it is now. She stares into the blackened center of the chimney, where hundreds of fires must have blazed over the years. Now there's just green moss and a few plants trailing up the center. Gwen cups her palm, rubbing her thumb over air, and a tiny ball of fire appears in the center of her hand. She tosses it toward the grass and plants growing in the chimney, but the ground is too wet and the foliage too young for the flame to catch. A thin wisp of smoke trails up the bricks, then dies.

That's Gwen's power. Pyrokinesis. The ability to make and control fire.

Gwen stares at the smoke. The trees' shadows reach toward us, and the air is damp and cool and slightly salty.

After a long stretch of silence, Gwen speaks. "Harold hates it out here," she says. "Says there's witches." She rolls her eyes. "That boy is *crazy*. Like, he doesn't just have problems, he is crazy-crazy."

Harold talks to the dead. His power is probably stronger than any of ours, but it's also the most useless and will likely drive him over the edge. The Doctor works with him often, trying to help him control his gift and filter out the voices so he can maybe glean some useful information from them.

Gwen stretches her legs in front of her, her eyes still on the chimney. There's an ease to the silence between us. I don't feel like I have to talk; we're both comfortable just being together.

Before I came to Berkshire, I thought I was alone. I have these powers that no one else has. I can control time—well, *control* is a strong word. I can *sometimes*, sort of control time. And sometimes it controls me, throwing me around history until I snap back to where I'm supposed to be. When the episodes first started, I thought something was wrong with me. I didn't know what was happening, so I was scared. Not anymore, though. Not unless I lose control.

I was fifteen the first time I lost control of my power. I was sitting in history class, and my teacher was giving a lecture about the Civil War. She was describing the Battle of Shiloh, one of the bloodiest battles ever, and she told a story about a little pond near the battlefield that turned red with all the blood from the wounded. She explained to us that the story was a myth, that it probably never really happened, but then I blinked.

And I was there.

Just like that. One minute I was in class, and the next minute

I was at the Battle of Freaking Shiloh in Tennessee, and it was *loud*, it was so loud, and the air was thick like fog and smelled like blood. There were people shouting and guns drawn and cannons firing, and I could see it all. And then I saw the pond. It was just as my teacher described it: small and stained red with blood.

And I don't know what happened next. I guess I just lost it. I started screaming and screaming and screaming, and then I blinked again.

And I was back in class.

Obviously I freaked everyone the hell out. The whole class was staring at me. I was gone so quick no one even noticed, so as far as they knew, I was yelling for no reason. They didn't know that I could still smell the blood and the gunpowder and the death that hung in the air.

After that, I was scared, really scared. What if I got stuck in the past? What if I spent the rest of my life bouncing around time, powerless to stop it?

Instead, Dr. Franklin found me. And I came here. Here, where Gwen can wrap fire around her hands like a glove, where Harold whispers to ghosts and they whisper back, where Ryan can move things with his mind and influence people's thoughts. We all have powers here, except for some of the staff and a few of the tutors. Even Dr. Franklin is one of us. He can heal himself and others, which is ironic because he is literally a doctor, but he's the kind of academic doctor that teaches, not the medical kind. But even with his degrees and experience, he hasn't really been able to help me progress all that much.

"What are you thinking about?" Gwen asks, breaking the silence.

I shrug. It's sort of embarrassing to admit that I don't have much control over my powers. From the moment I arrived at Berkshire, everyone else seemed to advance so much faster than me. And while the Doc is nice, I can tell that he's getting frustrated with my lack of progress.

When the Doctor found me and told my parents about the academy, we were all pretty relieved. I was glad that someone finally understood me, and I kind of hated high school anyway, so it was nice to get a change of scenery. I also liked that the Berk was a boarding school. I mean, I love my parents, but I don't really feel comfortable at home. I never have. To be honest, I think I get along better with my old man now that I'm out of the house. We can tolerate each other when we only have to be in the same building on weekends. Our relationship is built on absence.

It's little wonder that Berkshire has become my real home.

"I wish I knew what she was thinking," Gwen says, her eyes still fixed on the fireplace. She glances at me, but looks away again. "You know, before."

I don't want to talk about that, about the day Sofía went missing.

Just thinking about it makes my head hurt. Like sharp, shooting pains.

And my tongue. How weird is that? Thinking about the day Sofía got stuck in the past makes my *tongue* hurt. On the back of my tongue, near my throat, it just *aches*. It feels like that sort of burning dread rising in your throat when you know you need to cry but you just can't.

I open my mouth. I don't know what I'm going to say to Gwen, but it doesn't matter anyway, because in that moment, she disappears. The cold twilight air is replaced with morning mist and damp dew, and the shadows from the trees suddenly all point away from me.

And I am standing in front of the chimney on the day Sofía disappeared.

CHAPTER 3

My heart thumps, and I feel like I might throw up. I bend over, my hands on my knees, trying to catch my breath.

My powers have been more and more erratic since Sofía disappeared, but they've never brought me back here, to this moment. And I've tried. I've tried to get back so many times.

I gather myself, breathing in the crisp morning air. I may not have meant to snap back to this time, but that doesn't mean I can't use it.

On the day Sofía disappeared, I had gone for a walk by myself. I went north to the gate on the boardwalk and then turned around and was heading back to the school. But I veered closer to the beach and went past the old camp ruins. They're state-owned property, and we're not supposed to hang out there. But that day I ignored the Doctor's rules.

I look around and then up. You'd be surprised how adept you get at using the sun to tell time when you never know when and where you're going to end up. Judging from the position of the sun, I figure that the past me, the me on a walk about to meet Sofía and screw up her life, is probably near the polio camp ruins.

The abandoned camp is left over from the days before vaccinations, when the sick had to be quarantined. It was built in the '50s for people with polio, but it remained open through the '80s. Now, after years of neglect, it's just a bunch of rotted wooden buildings that look like a haunted summer camp. Berkshire was built when the camp closed, and no one bothers to maintain the abandoned buildings.

I still don't know why I went there that day . . . but I did.

And that's where I saw Sofía.

To be accurate, I saw her shoes first. Bright red, perched on the edge of the remains of a shallow swimming pool at the center of a circle of broken-down buildings. It's nothing but a concrete depression now, no water or anything, and Ryan keeps talking about how it should be turned into a skate ramp, but Dr. Franklin says that's disrespectful.

She was just sitting there, her legs dangling over the edge.

"Hey," I said.

Sofía didn't respond.

I walked over and sat down next to her, her red shoes between us. It seemed strange that she'd taken her shoes off. The morning was cold, the dew on the blades of grass frozen like crystals. It was no longer quite winter but close enough. I guess Sofía was in denial about the weather.

"What's up?" I asked.

Still, nothing.

And that's when I noticed she was crying.

Not, like, loud, sniffling crying that makes your shoulders hunch and your face hurt. Just quiet tears leaking from her eyes, trailing down her cheeks, and dripping from her chin. She was so lost in her sadness that I wasn't even sure she was aware of my presence until I touched her cold face, wiping away one of the tears with the pad of my thumb.

"Hey," I said as gently as I could. "What's wrong?" I moved her shoes so I could scoot closer, but she stood up abruptly, stepping back from the edge of the pool.

"Nothing," she said, and I knew it wasn't true, but she started walking away, barefoot on the cold, sandy soil. I figured if it meant that much to her not to talk about it, then she could keep her secrets.

Still, I followed her. I knew she wanted to be alone, but there was something about the way she walked, something about the little hiccup sound she made as she wiped away her tears and pretended like they never existed . . . it didn't feel right to abandon her.

Maybe I should have left her alone. Maybe then she wouldn't have gone away.

As she passed by one of the old camp buildings, she whirled around. "You can go back in time, right?"

"Yeah," I said. I watched her closely. She wasn't acting like herself, but I didn't know how to make it better.

"Can you take other people back?"

I nodded. "Do you want to go back *here*?" I asked, waving my hand toward the abandoned buildings of the polio camp. "It's just a bunch of sick kids."

She shook her head. "No, not here. But, you know, I think maybe . . . maybe this place wouldn't be so bad."

"Sick. Kids. Just, like, buckets of sick kids all around being sick. Not my idea of a fun place."

"You don't understand," Sofía said. "When you're sick with, like, a terminal illness, something you live with forever, there are very few moments you can forget about it. It's like a lead weight inside your chest, cracking your ribs. Every time you move, you can feel that weight shifting inside of you. But then there are moments when, for whatever reason, the weight goes away. You forget you're sick. I bet this camp was full of those moments. That's what I'd want to see. That's what I want to feel."

She was right. I didn't understand.

"So where do you want to go?" I asked, still unsure of this wild mood of hers.

Sofía looked off into the distance, toward the ocean and the sun and forever, but she couldn't see any of that. "I want to go somewhere far away."

She didn't bother explaining any further. She just kept walking. I don't think she was going anywhere in particular, but we headed toward the state park. I thought about running back to get her abandoned red shoes so she wouldn't have to walk on the splintery wood of the boardwalk, but she veered left, where the ground was soft.

I look around me now. Any minute, past-me and past-Sofía will come around the bend and be standing right in front of me, at the chimney. It's where Sofía took me that day, right before she whirled around, her eyes blazing, her long, dark hair whipping back, and said: "Here."

"Here?"

"Can you take me back to this place? Back when there was just one family on the island, the ones who built this house?"

"It wasn't built here," I said. "It was built in Salem."

"Fine, then when the house was moved here. To . . ." She

turned around, her eyes scanning the plaque. "Let's go back to 1692."

"I . . . um . . ."

"You can do it, right?"

"Yeah," I said immediately, wanting to impress her, to erase the doubt in her voice. "I've been back further than that. It's just . . . why?"

"I want to go away. I want to be as far away from this world as possible. Take me back further than 1692, I don't care. Let's go to the days when Native Americans were here. Let's go further. Let's go to the dinosaurs."

All my muscles were tense, and I moved very carefully, like I would if there were a wild animal in front of me. "I've never been that far back before," I said. I regretted telling her that I could take her back. I wanted to wrap her up in my arms and hold her tight, not fling her through time and space. I didn't realize it then, but a part of me sensed that she was running away, and I didn't want to let her go, even if I was going with her.

"I don't care, I just—" Her voice cracked. "I need to escape."

I took a deep breath and grabbed both her hands in mine. I didn't know what was wrong with her, but I knew I would do anything to make her happy. As I was holding her, I called up the timestream. I saw it expanding out from the two of us, strings erupting in every direction, each one linked to a different time and place. She couldn't feel it; she didn't react at all as I focused on the date engraved on the chimney, on the house that once contained it, on the island of the past.

And then we were there.

We had been standing among ruins; we were now standing in front of a chimney with bright red bricks streaked with soot. A roaring fire blazed at the bottom, casting Sofía in an orange-yellow glow and flickering shadows across the wood floor. There were herbs drying in one corner, an iron cauldron bubbling in another. The house smelled . . . warm. It wrapped around us, peaceful and beautiful.

Sofía sighed. In that moment, I think, she was happy.

Then the door behind me flung open, and I could hear a man's deep, accented voice: "Oh my God."

I started to turn.

Sofía's hands slipped from mine.

And suddenly, like a rubber band breaking, I was snapped back to the present. I gasped for air, my entire body in shock, having been thrown through more than three centuries. My arms and legs trembled, and I fell to the cold ground, my fingers clutching the sharp blades of the long sea grass.

"What happened?" I said.

But there was no answer. Just the ruins of an ancient chimney.

Since then, I've spent every waking moment trying to find a way back to Sofía. But my powers have worked sporadically at best, and never in a way that would be helpful. Now, though . . . now that I'm here, back to the time before she was trapped . . .

I have a chance.

I could save Sofía. I could stop my past self from taking her back, from leaving her stuck in a world that wasn't hers. I've tried so many times to reach this time and place again, and now that I'm here, I can fix it. I can make sure she never ends up in the past, abandoned, trapped where I can't reach her.

I hear voices down the path. It's past-me and Sofía. This is my chance. I can save her.

I stand up straighter, prepared to run to her.

I take one step forward, my voice already rising in my throat, ready to shout a warning . . .

I'm snapped back to the present.

I feel a cool hand on the back of my neck. "Hey," Gwen says softly. "You okay? You were gone there for a moment."

I nod, swallowing. I don't know why I expected this time to be different.

I can't save Sofía. I took her to the past, and I left her there, and I can't bring her back. I've tried and I've tried. Every time I get close to her, time snaps me away again.

She's trapped. And I put her there.

CHAPTER 4

Phoebe

"Where has that boy gone off to?" Dad asks. He scowls at the dispersing crowd.

Mom looks at me like I'm keeping Bo's location a secret, but I just shrug. He stormed off before the memorial service was over. How am I supposed to know where he went?

A tall black man with a thin mustache and old-fashioned waves in his hair approaches us. He holds out his hand for my dad to shake, and Mom greets him with a smile.

"I'm Dr. Franklin," he tells me. "I'm your brother's psychiatrist."

A muscle twitches in my dad's jaw at that last word, but he doesn't say anything.

"Do you know where Bo went?" Mom asks the doctor.

Dr. Franklin frowns. "He's been greatly affected by Sofía's death," he says. He glances up; the paper lanterns are still visible, tiny specks of light in the fading sky. "They were close," he adds, looking back down at my mom.

"She was so young," my mother says. "It's tragic." Her voice drops a notch. "Depression?"

Dr. Franklin's lips press together as if he's holding back a frown. "She was very sick. We're still reeling from what happened. Sofía had seemed to adjust well to our program . . ." His voice trails off, and his eyes lose focus.

When Dr. Franklin called the house to tell us that one of Bo's fellow students passed away, he hadn't mentioned that she'd committed suicide. A Google search and some newspaper articles covering the incident revealed that. But the details were limited: TROUBLED TEEN, 17, FOUND DEAD ON CAMPUS IN PRESUMED SUICIDE; AUTOPSY REVEALS INTENTIONAL OVERDOSE OF PRESCRIPTION DRUGS.

Bo had never mentioned Sofía before, but we all still nod knowingly when Dr. Franklin tells us they were close. After all, Bo was one of the four kids who lit lanterns. We figured he knew her well. Still, he never talked about her. Not at home.

Not that I'm surprised. It's not like any of us really talk about anything when Bo's home.

There's an awkward silence, and Mom shifts nervously.

"I'm sure Bo's just inside, getting a plate with his friends," Dr. Franklin says.

Dad grunts like he no longer cares where Bo is. "So, how 'bout them Patriots?"

"I'm more of a basketball fan," Dr. Franklin replies.

Dad scowls.

Dr. Franklin turns his attention to me. "And you're Bo's little sister?"

"Phoebe," I say, holding out my hand. His grip is firm, almost too strong.

"Your brother's a great kid," Dr. Franklin says.

I raise my eyebrows but don't say anything. Before Bo came to the Berkshire Academy for Children with Exceptional Needs, he and I attended the same high school, and I can guarantee that none of our teachers would have called him a "great kid." Usually late and always inattentive, he barely passed any class other than history. Most of the teachers didn't even know we were related, but the ones who did were always shocked.

"Why don't we go inside?" Dr. Franklin says. He leads us all toward the big glass doors. Mom and Dad walk up to the main hall as if they're as comfortable here as they are at home. I trail behind, and the doctor slows his pace to walk beside me.

"This is your first time on campus." The doctor says it like a statement, but I guess it's a question.

I nod.

When my parents moved Bo to the academy, they didn't let me join them. I wanted to go, but Dad was insistent. I don't know if he was shielding me from the image of Bo at the school or if he didn't want me interacting with the other kids there, but either way, I stayed home. Now, when Dad drives to Berkshire to pick Bo up on the weekends, he goes alone.

I'd always pictured the Berkshire Academy like the asylums in horror movies: concrete walls, straightjackets, cold white tile everywhere. But this place is brick and . . . nice. The garden is perfectly landscaped, not a single leaf out of place. Pebbled paths meander through the plants, and I can hear the ocean over the sounds of people mingling. Ivy climbs up the wall, drooping elegantly over the bricks. Berkshire is like a rich old person's home. Except for the bars on some of the windows.

Inside, everything gleams, from the rich mahogany-paneled walls to the crystal chandeliers sparkling on the ceiling. Oil paintings—of the island, of the school, of past directors—look down on us. Dad veers to the right, joining the line for dinner, but Mom lingers beside me. "Go ahead," Dr. Franklin tells her. He turns to me. "Are you hungry?"

I shake my head.

"Do you want to go find your brother?"

I shrug.

"Why don't I give you a tour?"

"Okay." I don't really want a tour. I want to leave. I'm discovering that I'd rather not know the details of where my brother spends his weeks, that I prefer ignorance. Seeing this place, these people . . . it all makes Bo's situation that much more real.

But I go with Dr. Franklin as he leads me down the austere hallway with its tall ceilings and uncomfortable-looking furniture. The carpets spread out over the hardwood floors are thick and soft, and they perfectly match the long, elegant drapes that cascade over the clear glass windows that stretch floor to ceiling in the front hall. "This is our group common area," the doctor says. "We'll have Family Day set up here in a few weeks. Are you coming to that?"

"I don't know," I say.

"I'm sure Bo would appreciate you being there."

I really doubt Bo would care one way or another.

Dr. Franklin stops at the bottom of a grand staircase that sweeps up to the second-floor landing. "All the floors above are divided by units; there's an office for each psychiatrist, a common room, classrooms, and living quarters. Bo's unit is on the second floor, near the library."

"Nice setup." I peer up the stairs, but all I see is more mahogany.

The doctor takes a step up, but I hesitate. I don't really want to see more of the academy. I'm fine here on the main floor, letting the lush red carpets and heavy curtains leave me with the impression that my brother lives in an opulent mansion rather than a school for uncontrollable, borderline-crazy kids. I don't want to see the bars on his window.

"I get the impression that you're uncomfortable," Dr. Franklin says, his eyes locked on me.

I shrug.

"Think of Berkshire as any other school," Dr. Franklin continues. "It's smaller, sure—"

"It doesn't look smaller," I say.

"Well, there are only about fifty students here, divided into ten units," Dr. Franklin says. "So it's smaller in that regard. Having fewer students lets us pay closer attention than the faculty at a traditional high school. Bo's unit only has five"—he catches himself—"four students. Every session with me, every class, every meal, has no more than those three other students with Bo. Each unit is insular, so it's almost like we have ten mini-schools rather than one big one. The units become like a family."

The doctor pauses when he sees my face. He mistakes my look for one of confusion and tries to explain again. "At your high school, you move from classroom to classroom, correct?"

"Yeah."

"Here, we do the opposite. The students stay in one classroom, and our teachers go to them, shifting between units."

"So Bo has the same classmates all day? Every day?"

Dr. Franklin nods. "Isn't that nice?" he says, as if it's me he has to convince. I remember now that this was a selling point for my parents when they were considering the school. They liked that he'd have limited interaction with others, as well as "highly individualized attention."

"It is if you like the people in your class," I say. "Kind of sucks if you don't."

I want to add that Bo doesn't need this "unit family," that he has us, but then I realize: These kids probably know Bo much better than I ever have or ever will.

I shift on my feet. I'm not sure what to say, and Dr. Franklin seems to have run out of things to explain to me. He and I are two separate pieces of my brother's world, and our interaction feels like oil and water. I don't like small talk to begin with, but everything about this day has been so weird. I left my own school early to drive straight here, where I had to spend the rest of my Friday afternoon attending the memorial service for a girl I never met and then be given a tour of my brother's boarding school by the guy who prescribes him antipsychotic drugs. And it's all coming to a pinpoint of weirdness right here and now, surrounded by a thin veneer of small talk.

I catch my mother's eye across the room, and she must see the desperation on my face, because she leaves her plate of cheese and crackers and makes her way over to us at the bottom of the staircase. When she reaches us, she strokes my ponytail like I'm a pet, but I don't mind. Now she can work to fill the empty silences instead of me.

"I haven't seen Bo here, have you?" Mom asks.

Dr. Franklin frowns. "Perhaps he's in his room."

Mom's fingers twitch, tugging a bit on my hair. I pull away, but she sticks close to me. "We should probably go soon."

"As I was telling you earlier, Bo was rather close to Sofía before her passing," Dr. Franklin says. "I'd like you to consider leaving him here on the weekends for the time being. I don't think it would be wise to interrupt his therapy."

"Oh no," she says. "I would hate that."

"Hate what?" Dad asks, approaching us while holding a plate loaded with chips and dip, cheese, and slices of salami.

"He wants to keep Bo here," Mom says, her voice pitching a notch higher.

Dad's face immediately darkens. "Do we have to?" he asks the doctor aggressively.

Dr. Franklin's eyes widen, just a touch. "Well, no," he says. "But I would like to continue his therapy, and I feel like he needs a little extra focus."

"And why is that?" It's so strange to see Dad like this, trying to pick a fight with a man wearing tweed while holding a plate of charcuterie. "He's not locked up in some crazy house, we can bring him home." Dad says this more to himself than to Dr. Franklin.

"Of course you can," Dr. Franklin says. "This is in no way mandatory. It's just that Sofía's death has greatly affected him, and—"

"Didn't look affected," Dad says, his tone harsh. "He didn't even stay for the whole service. Where is that boy, anyway? I thought you ran a tight ship here, Doc, but you don't even know where Bo is, do you?"

"I think he just needed a moment to collect himself," Dr. Franklin says.

The doctor seems like someone who's pretty good at keeping his emotions under control, but I can see that he's not used to being questioned the way that Dad's grilling him now. But I also wish Dad would just shut up.

"Bo's a good boy," Mom says, taking a tiny step closer to Dad, her arm barely brushing against his. "If there's something wrong, he'd tell us. I'm sure he's okay."

Okay? *Okay?* Some girl in his class just died, and he couldn't even keep it together long enough to stay for her whole memorial service. He's clearly *not* okay. I shake my head in disgust.

Ever since it became clear that Bo needed help, it's like Dad thinks he can argue his way out of Bo being sick, and Mom thinks she can pretend her way into a different reality. They've stuck Bo in this school that looks like a mansion instead of an asylum, and that's fine, but at least don't pretend it's anything else. And certainly don't pretend it's *okay*. *Okay* is so far out of our vocabulary right now that it's practically a foreign word.

Dr. Franklin holds his hands out, palms up, as if he's pleading with my parents to see his side. "Regardless, I do think it's best that Bo stay here *this* weekend, at least. The memorial was just today, and there will be some changes in the school over the next few weeks that I'd like to help prepare him for."

"Changes?" Mom asks.

"We're having an . . . inspection of the school. Simply routine, but with any change comes some adjustment, and . . ."

"Fine, fine, we leave the boy here this weekend," Dad says. "You know, I wouldn't have driven all this way for some ceremony and paper lanterns if I'd known we weren't bringing Bo back with us."

"But—" Mom starts to protest.

"We'll get him next weekend, right, Doc?" Dad says.

"How about I call you next Thursday?" the doctor responds.

"How about I just pick him up on Friday." Dad turns around and strides off, dumping his plate in the garbage can by the front door.

Mom's stroking my hair even more aggressively now, so hard that my head is pulled back. I shift away from her.

"And how are you?" Dr. Franklin asks me, his eyes kind. "I know we're giving a lot of attention to Bo right now, but how are you doing?"

Both he and Mom stare at me, waiting for an answer.

"I'm . . . okay," I say finally.

CHAPTER 5

My parents and sister are walking out of the towering front doors of the academy when Gwen and I reach the bottom of the steps.

"There you are," Dr. Franklin says, following behind them.

"I'll go get my stuff," I say. I glance at Dad. "Sorry, I didn't realize you were in a rush."

"No rush," Dad says. "You're staying here."

Gwen bounds up the steps and disappears inside, but I'm frozen in place. "I'm staying?"

Mom nods. "Just this weekend, okay, sweetie? We'll bring you home next weekend. Is that all right?"

"Yeah, fine," I say. My mind is already churning. This isn't just fine, it's *great*. I need time to work on saving Sofía, and going home will just get in the way of that. Who knows when I'll get a chance like this again. Every weekend my parents drive up here to pick me up and take me home for "family time," something my mother hates to relinquish.

Phoebe walks a pace behind my parents as they head to their car, which is parked in the circular driveway right in front of the academy. As Mom hugs me and Dad grunts goodbye, Phoebe stands to the side, her eyes dancing over the sign in front of the school, made of brick and gleaming bronze: THE BERKSHIRE ACADEMY FOR CHILDREN WITH EXCEPTIONAL NEEDS.

Part of me wants to pull my sister aside and tell her that the sign is just a front. It's not like we can advertise what the school really is, what all of us can really do. Dr. Franklin and the rest of the unit advisors all have powers too, and they know how important secrecy is. It sort of sucks, though, the way Phoebe thinks I belong on the short bus.

Or maybe she knows the truth. I can't tell—not with her— and I'm too exhausted to try. Especially today, after watching a memorial service for someone who's not dead.

After trying to save Sofía again. After failing. Again.

"Next weekend," my mom whispers, pulling away from her tight hug. "You're okay staying here until then?"

"Yeah, yeah, I'm fine," I say.

My parents and sister get into the Buick, and my family is gone before I head back inside.

"Tomorrow I'd like to have an extra session with you," the Doctor says, holding the door open for me.

"Of course," I answer. Another session would definitely help. Even though Dr. Franklin can't control time like me, he says my emotions are causing the block, making it so I always snap back to the present when I try to reach Sofía. So if a "feelings" session with him can help me regain control of my power, I'm all for it.

When I first came to the Berk, I had no idea that so much of learning to control my powers would come from inside my head. Most of the first week was even spent in psychoanalysis. The Doctor assured me that every student goes through such rounds, to make sure they are "suitable for the special environment afforded at Berkshire Academy."

As I head upstairs, I calculate how much time I can focus on saving Sofía. We had a day off with the fake memorial service, but classes resume Monday. I may be able to negotiate some extra time from some of my teachers, though. Our classes are small and tailored to each of our strengths, paced individually. I'm several lessons behind Ryan in math, but I'm already in a different textbook from everyone else in history. Maybe a little "independent study" during that class would allow me some time to work on saving Sofía.

When we reach my floor, the Doctor tells me goodnight and reminds me of lights-out, even though it's a few hours away. He heads down a different hallway, going to the back stairs that lead all the way up to the top floor, where the staff live. It's kind of weird to think that so many people live in this one house. The way the mansion is divided and our schedules are made, I only ever see the other students here in passing. The only people I really talk to are Harold, Gwen, Ryan, Sofía, and our teachers as they rotate from unit to unit. We stay in our one big classroom all day, being served history and math and science, with a sprinkle of how-to-control-your-powers and a dash of try-not-to-explode-everything.

I haven't had control of my powers . . . ever, really. I'm like someone who never had a real driving lesson but figured out the basics on a flat road on a sunny day. I've occasionally been able to steer my time travel, but when it really matters, like with Sofía, I'm behind the wheel in the mountains with ice and fog. I keep skidding off the road, crashing into trees.

It's not going to stop me from trying, though. I was so close earlier today. Sofía was *right there*.

As soon as I'm in my room, I grab my notebook off my desk and flip it to the pages I've been using to record my efforts to save my girlfriend.

Here's what I know: Sofía Muniz, a Latina girl with an accent, dressed in modern clothing, is trapped in the very white, very strict, very conservative world of Puritan colonial Massachusetts, 1692. She also has a habit of turning invisible, and she isn't always able to control when it happens, so I'm sure the Puritans are going to think that's a swell party trick that has nothing to do with the devil. And I put her there, and I can't save her. Every time I get close, I get thrown back to the present—without her.

My eyes scan down the list. I've tried to go back to 1692. I've tried to go back to just before we left. I quickly add a few notes about today—the closest I've come to actually seeing her again.

Something was different about today. I didn't intend to go back to the day she disappeared, but there I was. If I can figure out how I got there, re-create whatever it was I did to end up there . . .

No time like the present to try. I close my eyes, calling up the timestream.

I can feel rather than see all of time stretching out around me. The timestream is made of strings extending out, swirling around as if they're resting on top of water. There are hard knots at certain points—the points where I am not allowed to go.

Woven through the strings is one bright red thread—Sofía's life.

My fingers hover over it, careful not to touch it and pull myself into her past. Not yet, anyway. I can pick out the pattern of her past—her home in Austin, her family, her friends, the Berk. Me. Her string twirls around mine like an embrace.

And then it shoots backward, violently and sharply, directly into 1692. That spot in history looks like a black hole, far darker than any other spot in the timestream. The end of Sofía's string is somewhere in there, disappearing into the void.

Beyond my reach.

I extend my hand toward that spot anyway, hoping that my fingers can feel what my eyes cannot see. I strain to get closer, and sharp pains shoot across my skin like electric bursts. I grit my teeth, ball my hand into a fist, and punch at the inky black vortex.

Bright, vivid flashes erupt into my mind's eye, speeding from one image to the next so violently that I cannot retain anything more than fragments: an ear with a diamond earring, a tree with new green leaves, the sound of crashing waves, the taste of vomit, the roofline of a house, the smell of smoke, a horse's whinnying, the feel of another hand in mine, the fingers slipping from my grasp. I cry out in frustration, groping blindly into the darkness, but the timestream repels my presence, pushing against me.

Time is fighting me, and I pull back before I lose what little control over the timestream I have. My arms flail wildly, and my fingers brush a thick string, red and blue and green and brown all wrapped together, and I see a flash of another moment in time, one I didn't intend to revisit.

My first lesson with Dr. Franklin.

Even though we all have different powers, the Doctor guides us in the basics of controlling them. The same principles apply. This has always been the point of Berkshire: to give students the control they need to blend with society. He's not training us to be superheroes or anything like that. We're not going out into the world to wear capes and masks. The Doctor just wants us to go out into the world without breaking it.

When I travel in time, I physically go into the past, but I didn't pull myself into this moment, I just brushed against it. Rather than inserting myself into the past, I see it like a movie playing in my mind.

We all sit in blue plastic chairs around the Doc's desk. Each of us is wearing a nametag, the kind that are stickers that say: HELLO, MY NAME IS . . . Harold has printed his name in such small letters that I can't read them. Gwen, on the other hand, used a glitter pen to make her name sparkle. Sofía wrote with a Sharpie, careful to add the accent mark over the *i*. She lifted the pen up with a flourish of her wrist, then looked around guiltily, as if such extravagance was something to be ashamed of.

"Now that we know each other's names," the Doctor says, "let's introduce our powers. Harold?"

Dr. Franklin turns to Harold first. Later, he would learn not to do that, to let others' voices fill the room before seeking out Harold's quiet words. Even so, Harold rises to the occasion. "I speak to ghosts." His voice is almost a whisper.

"And do they speak back?" Ryan says in a mocking voice. The Doctor shoots him a look.

"Yes," Harold says simply.

"Well, *I* can do something useful," Ryan says. He flicks his hand up, and the blue plastic chairs we're all sitting in start to float. Harold squeaks and grips the sides of his chair to keep from toppling off. Gwen kicks her feet out, swinging around.

"Thank you," Dr. Franklin says, and from the tone of his voice, it's clear he means *That's enough.* Ryan casually waves his hand, and the chairs crash back down. Sofía's off balance and almost falls; the past-me grabs her arm and catches her.

She goes completely invisible.

I jerk my arm back, shocked, but the Doc just gives her a nod and a smile. I wait for her to return to visibility, but she doesn't.

"My turn," Gwen says, and she lights her hair on fire, shaking the sparks out like glitter.

Everyone turns to look at me.

"I can move through time," I say lamely. "I mean, back in time. To the past."

Everyone waits for me to show my power. "Come on," Ryan says impatiently.

I close my eyes. I try to do something cool.

Nothing happens.

From my vantage point in the timestream, I cringe. I wanted so much to impress everyone else, but I had even less control of my powers then than I do now. So it's little wonder that when Dr. Franklin says, "We'll work on it" in that patronizing tone, I flipped from nervous to angry. I saw red—literally, I saw the world as if there were a red film over everything, and it reminded me of the bloody pond. My brain was spinning, and suddenly I was in the past, back at my grandmother's house in the mountains. It was run-down, with asbestos tiles on the outside walls and threadbare carpet inside that smelled of dust and old cigarette smoke, and it was my most favorite place in the whole world. When I opened my eyes, I was standing in her front yard, under the pecan tree, with snow falling all around. I could hear the crunch of the snow shifting under my feet, and when I stepped forward, I could taste the coldness in the air.

Now, as an observer of this moment, I see what everyone else saw. One moment I was there, the next I was gone. Ryan gets up and waves his hand in the empty space where I had been sitting. "This is cooler than your trick," he tells Sofía, who had finally returned to visibility.

"Go back to your chair," Dr. Franklin says. "You don't know when he'll—"

I burst back into existence, my arms swinging. "I'm sorry!" I shout as the Doctor steps back. The slip in time was fast and disorientating, and I hadn't meant to land a punch on Dr. Franklin's face when I returned.

The Doctor just rubs his cheek, though, and suddenly the redness disappears.

"This is something we'll all work on," he says. "Control."

I can feel the timestream slipping away from me, the moment fading. My eyes shoot to Sofía, and I beg time to let me have one last glimpse of her. Even though I know she can't see me in this memory, her face tilts just as I turn to her, giving the illusion that she's looking right at me. Her lips part to say something, and my heart surges; it feels as if she's speaking to me, impossibly, through time and space.

I blink, and all I see is my desk and the open notebook in front of me.

But I cannot get the vision of Sofía's desperate eyes out of my mind.

CHAPTER 6

Phoebe

"Adventure time!" my mother yells as she flings open my bedroom door.

I shoot up in bed. "What time is it?" I ask, but I'm not even sure I actually spoke the words aloud. It sounded more like *wharmzit.*

"It's seven in the morning on this beautiful Saturday," my mom says in a singsongy voice. "Now get up, because we are going on an adventure!"

I rub sleep out of my eyes as I start to really wake up. An adventure? Mom used to do this all the time during summer breaks when Bo and I were kids. She'd make these huge, elaborate plans and keep them totally secret from us, bursting into our rooms one random morning shouting, "Adventure!" She'd bundle us up with whatever we needed for the day and not tell us where we were going until we arrived at our destination. Sometimes it was a simple trip into the city for a duck tour of the harbor or to see a museum. Once, she packed our suitcases in the night and drove us to the airport, and it wasn't until we'd landed in Orlando that we realized we were going to Disney World.

Dad rarely went on these adventures—he had to work—but he was there for the overnight ones, and those were always the best. I look around now, but there's no suitcase in the hallway, and besides, I'd notice now if Mom were sneaking clothes to pack away. I fall back against my pillows.

Mom sits down on the bed. "I thought we could go to Faneuil Hall," she says more gently. "Hit the market, maybe get dinner in the city. A girl date."

"Yeah," I say. "Sure. Let me get dressed."

I throw on some clothes and head downstairs. Dad's home, but his office door is firmly closed. He's apparently not invited on this adventure.

We go to Bickford's for breakfast, and Mom talks about her plans for renovating the house after "the nest is finally empty." She pretends to be mad when I tell her I'd rather see the latest reboot of *Spider-Man* with my friends instead of her, even though we both know the only movies she goes to are rom-coms and anything from Disney. We make plans to get pedicures after my next report card if I make all *A*s, which is inevitable.

"I just can't remember the last time we had an adventure day!" Mom says gleefully as we get back in the car and head toward the highway.

I glance at her, but she looks sincere. Still—really? She really can't remember the last time we did a surprise adventure day? Because I remember. It was the summer before Bo started high school, and I was looking forward to having the middle school

41

all to myself. Mom had burst into our rooms on a Tuesday, and she piled us into the car, stating only that we were going to get the best meal of our lives. We drove north along the coast, and in a few hours she parked outside a lobster boat cruise in Portland, Maine.

But we never made it on the cruise. Her intent had been for us to ride in the boat, pull up some lobster traps, and eat the freshest lobster we'd ever had for dinner, bringing home an extra one for Dad.

But Bo had refused to go on the water.

It was so weird. He'd been on boats before. He used to love fishing. But he completely flipped out at the harbor, clutching his chest like he was having a heart attack and absolutely refusing to take one step onto the wood gangway. When Mom tried to talk to him, it was as if she were speaking to someone who'd gone deaf. The boat left without us, and we ate lunch at some random seafood restaurant before Mom drove us back, never mentioning Bo's meltdown again.

We never went on another "adventure" after that.

Faneuil Hall is packed. The weather's finally starting to warm up, and everyone is walking around as if they've been a prisoner of winter and can taste freedom in the air. The spaces between the market buildings are lined with kiosks and carts, a mix of crafts and clothes, snacks and souvenirs for sale. A living statue bends at the waist and offers a fake flower to Mom, trying to draw her closer. We start at the North Market building, and Mom buys me a pair of blue cat-eye sunglasses as I try to convince her to buy a pair of heart-shaped ones made of red plastic. She spends far too long trying on shoes and pushing me to join her, but even though my friend Jenny calls me a freak for it, I just don't really care about what's on my feet.

"So," Mom says as we head toward a small boutique selling sundresses. Her voice drops an octave as she imitates Dad. "How 'bout them Patriots?"

I can't help but laugh. Most people use the weather as small talk. Dad uses football. It doesn't matter that the Super Bowl happened almost two months ago; there's always next year's season to talk about.

Mom bumps my shoulder. "Come on, baby girl, tell me what's up."

"Nothing's 'up,'" I laugh, taking a dress off the rack and holding it against my shoulders even though I know I'd never wear it.

"School going well?"

I put the dress back. "Yeah, I guess. I mean, AP's harder this year."

"You're doing great, you know that?" Mom's voice is softer now, more serious. "I don't say that enough, but you are."

I shrug. "I need a scholarship."

Mom doesn't bother trying to deny it. Without a scholarship, my options are going into debt by taking out a student loan or spending a few years at a community college before transferring to a university, but neither is an appealing choice. I want to escape. I want to get as far away as possible. I don't even know where. I just want to be in a place where no one really knows me. Everyone from home already has an idea of who I am. I want to define myself on my own terms.

"I really want to go out of state," I say.

Mom frowns. "We'll see."

I sigh and turn away from the store. Shopping doesn't sound that great anymore. What's a new dress compared to a new life?

Mom jogs to catch up with me when she notices I've walked away. "So what are you thinking of majoring in?" she asks. "Any plans?"

No! I want to scream. No. I'm doing everything I know how to do—piling up AP courses and studying for the SATs while selecting extracurriculars that will look good on applications. But I have no idea what to do *after* all this work pays off. I don't have a major picked out, much less a college. I only hope that everything I'm doing means I get to get out of here. I don't care where. I just want to *go.*

"I don't know," I say.

Mom bites her lip, her face falling like she has to tell me my puppy died or something. "But sweetie, you're going to have to decide soon."

"I don't *know*," I say, much harsher than I intended. "I have time."

"Well, if you need to talk it out, or help with applications or anything, you know you can ask me or your father."

"Okay," I say noncommittally.

Mom strokes my hair. "I really am so proud of you," she says. "You're so self-reliant. I never have to worry about you." There's a slight emphasis on the last word.

When we enter Quincy Market, Mom comes up with the perfect idea for lunch: We each have to eat at least three different things from three different places. I kick it off with a pizza bagel, and she grabs Starbucks, which I say is lame since we both know she was going to get Starbucks anyway. I get a scone from a bakeshop, and she picks up some fudge at the coffee place next to it. For the main course, I call dibs on the mac-and-cheese stand, ordering a large bowl of gooey goodness.

"Oh, come *on*," she says as I dig my spoon into the bowl. "I'm going to order some too."

"You said three different things," I say, "from three different places." I lick my spoon.

Mom sticks her tongue out, but she's grinning as she leads me over to a pushcart and orders some roasted nuts.

"Not as good as mac and cheese," I say mockingly.

Mom scowls at me, but she laughs as she pulls me toward the ice cream shop.

"No more, I'm stuffed!" I say in false protest.

"You need to learn how to play the game," Mom says. "Order light so there's room for dessert."

I try not to get anything, but Mom orders me a cookies-and-cream cone anyway. I really am full, but it's kind of nice to know she remembers my favorite flavor.

"That's gross, by the way," I tell her as she licks a blueberry-flavored scoop of ice cream.

"I will never understand how a child of mine could not like berries."

"I like strawberries."

"They don't count."

After a while, we finally head home. The backseat of the car is loaded with bags—Mom went a little crazy at the candle store—and we're both full of ice cream and happiness. I start telling her all the things I always mean to tell her but somehow never do, like how I'm worried I won't be friends with Jenny and Rosemarie after high school because Rosemarie wants to stay here and I want to travel and Jenny is probably going to get a marine biology degree and move to California.

It's not like Mom gives me any life-changing advice on the ride home or anything. She mostly just listens. I may be the self-reliant kid in the family, but it's nice to pretend for at least one car ride that I don't have to be.

It's not until we're almost home that I realize: This is what life would be like all the time without Bo. I grow silent and stare out the window as Mom turns onto our street, my thoughts lingering on what the cost of such a life would be.

CHAPTER 7

I spend most of the weekend camped out in my room, examining the timestream for a way to save Sofía. To travel, I have to select moments along a string of time and pull myself into that time. To reach Sofía, I need to wrap my finger around the end of her red string—but that thread disappears into the vortex that covers Pear Island in 1692. I can see part of her string, but not the end, not where she is.

But . . . what if instead of trying to reach Sofía, I brought *her* to *me*? If I pulled the middle section of the thread, could I pull her out of the past and back to the present?

I find Sofía's red thread, my hand shaking as I reach for it. Once I touch the string, I'll have flashes of memories. Pull too hard, and I'll transport myself back to that time. But if I tug just a little and let go quickly, maybe I can loosen Sofía's thread and pull it out of the swirling black hole engulfing 1692. It won't matter that I can't go to her if I can make her come back to me.

I take a deep breath. I have to move quickly; I'll waste precious time if I let myself get sucked into the past.

I try not to think about the irony of a time traveler worried about wasting time.

I zero in on a moment in time, a portion of the string. Before I can doubt myself, I snatch the string, yanking it back and letting go as quickly as possible. I see it pucker and then—

—I *see* the past. I'm used to pulling myself physically through time, but this is different: I stay where I am, watching as the past plays out in my mind like a movie.

A session early in the year. Dr. Franklin was trying to make a game of us getting to know one another better. He'd shout out something like "If you were born before August, stand up, and if you were born in August or later, stay sitting!" or "If you'd rather go to the beach for vacation, hop up and down, but if you'd rather spend your vacation in the mountains, wave your arms." Ryan pretended like the whole thing was stupid, but everyone else had fun.

I see the Doctor now, grinning at us. It's been a while since I've seen him smile.

"If you're the oldest in your family," he says, "stand up. If you're the youngest, sit on the floor. If you're a middle child, jump up and down. And if you're an only child, stand on your chair!"

The me in this vision jumps up, looking around, eager to see what everyone else did. Ryan deigns to get up, then turns the chair around and stands on it, sighing as if it takes too much effort. Gwen plops on the floor, and Harold—little, quiet Harold—starts jumping around. Laughter breaks out in the room; none of us had seen him act so silly before.

But none of us had seen Sofía look quite that sad before either. She hadn't known how to answer because she used to be a middle child, and now she was an only child. I had merely a moment to register the deep sorrow etched into her face before she turned transparent and disappeared from sight.

I shake my head, hard, trying to clear it from the vision. Glancing at the timestream, I see that my plan has worked, at least a little. Sofía's string is looser and has moved slightly within the pattern of the timestream. But this small victory is tinged a little by melancholy—I can't help but remember how long it took Sofía to talk about her family with the group, and longer still for her to say anything more personal than their names to me in private.

The week of her family's funeral, Sofía stayed invisible and silent. Her father stayed drunk and not silent. He was angry, so angry because he'd lost his wife and daughters, but he didn't understand that even though Sofía was alive, he'd lost her too.

I'm glad Sofía lived at the academy and not with him.

Lives. Not lived. *Lives.*

I force myself to push the memories aside. There's work to do.

I select another point in the timestream where I can pluck up the red string. I brace myself, ready for the memory, as I pinch the string and yank it back as quickly as I can. I hear Gwen and Sofía's voices before I see the common room on the day Harold turned sixteen—which shocked us all because he still looked about twelve. His birthday was on a weekend, and though Gwen and I usually go home on weekends, we decided to stay because Gwen wanted to throw him a party.

Gwen, Sofía, Ryan, and I sit around the big table; Harold stands off to the side chatting with his ghosts.

"His favorite books are the Harry Potter series," Sofía says in a hushed voice.

"I can work with that," Gwen says. "Maybe we can make up a letter from Hogwarts and slip it under his door."

"Lame," Ryan drawls.

Gwen rolls her eyes at him. "Then what do you suggest?"

Ryan leans back lazily. "Hey, Harold," he calls. "Want to play Quidditch?"

Harold's whole face lights up.

The vision fades from my mind, but I'm left smiling, remembering what happened next. Ryan had been right—if we had powers, why not use them? Sofía scrounged up four brooms while Gwen found some volleyballs in the beach supply closet, and Harold, Ryan, and I went to the courtyard. Ryan used his telekinesis to make us fly on the brooms—or, more accurately, float in place or slowly move backward, since he still didn't have much control of his ability. With a little effort we got an actual Quidditch game going. Sort of. Either way, it was hilarious and fun.

When the Doctor came out to see what we were all doing, Ryan floated his gold fountain pen from his front pocket and used it as the Snitch. I think he made sure that Harold got it; Ryan wasn't so much of a dick back then. Ryan was still Ryan, though, so he made sure the ball we were using hit Harold as soon as he snatched the pen from the air. Harold collapsed onto the soft grass below, laughing his brains out.

As the vision fades, the timestream comes into sharper focus. Sofía's string is a little closer, but it's not enough. The end is still trapped in the dark spot swirling over 1692. I work quickly and select another moment along the string, striking like a cobra as I snatch it, tugging it from the weave.

Ryan, Harold, and I are hanging out by the marsh. Harold's wearing shorts; this is still at the end of summer. When Ryan starts to talk, I realize that this memory is from one of the first few days at Berkshire, when everyone was still moving in, before classes had even started.

"I've been to three of these before," Ryan says, gathering rocks into a little pile. He starts throwing them into the marsh, aiming for the birds.

"Three?" I ask.

"Schools like this." I didn't know other schools like Berkshire even existed.

"You?" he asks.

"My first."

"Me too," Harold says in a small voice, his eyes unfocused, as if he were speaking to someone other than us. "Berkshire. I like the name of it. Sounds like a place where hobbits would live."

"This place does look pretty cool," Ryan admits. "It's nicer than the last place I was at. That joint was like a prison."

"Look." Harold points down the path, toward the academy and the black van pulling into the circular drive.

"They're in our class," Ryan says. He chuckles; he'd almost hit a magpie with that last stone he threw.

I see the shorter girl first, and right away, I can tell she's the kind of girl who loves attention. It's Gwen, wearing sparkly clips in her black hair—the tips of which are dyed red—and a shirt so low-cut I can see her cleavage all the way from where

I'm standing. She's showing off her power too, sparking little fires in the palms of her hands like it's no big deal.

And just when I start to look away, I see Sofía.

And then I don't.

I almost shove Ryan in the marsh to get him to shut up about the stupid birds for two seconds as I lean forward, trying to find her again. She'd been visible for just a second, but that second was enough—she's burned into my mind. Gwen's the type of girl who demands to be noticed, but Sofía's just the opposite. She likes silent places and shadows and watching from the sidelines. She *doesn't* want me—or anyone, really—to notice her . . . so of course I notice her even more.

The memory blinks out of my mind in a flash. Seeing her like that, for the first time, reminded my heart of all the reasons why I fell in love with her in the first place. A weird, painful lump rises in my throat, and I swallow it down. I have to control my emotions, or I'll lose control of the timestream.

It looks like one more good tug will pull the end of Sofía's string from 1692. I'm not sure what this is doing to her in the past—does she feel me manipulating time around her in an effort to bring her home? But it's the only thing I can think to do.

I reach out and pluck at the red string again, already bracing for the memory that will overtake me.

Gwen bounces with excitement. "It's almost time!" she cries, pulling Sofía behind her as she leads us all outside. Dr. Franklin looks almost excited as her. We're heading to the beach well past lights-out, but he got special permission for us to view a NASA rocket shooting off from somewhere in Virginia but visible all the way up here. Gwen's not a science nerd, but she's obsessed with firepower, and she begged for the chance to watch the rocket fly by on its way to space.

The night is beyond freezing. I'm wearing my puffy coat and a hoodie and two shirts under that, and it's *still* cold.

Beside me, I notice Sofía shivering, so I pull off my hoodie and offer it to her. This was before we were, you know, a thing or whatever, but she accepts the hoodie and pulls it over her head, the sleeves dangling off her wrists. The whole thing is comically large on her, and she flaps the arms around herself.

"Thanks," she says, still twisting so the sleeves of the hoodie thwack her back.

And I don't know what to say because I'm an idiot, so I just sort of stand there and grin.

"T-minus five minutes!" Gwen shouts, glancing at her cell phone. She and Dr. Franklin stand excitedly on the beach. Harold's chattering to one of his ghosts, and Ryan's playing on his cell phone, not really caring.

Sofía and I step back from the group. Not far enough to draw attention, but enough so that we feel like we're a little bit alone.

"Thanks," she says again.

"No problem," I say, zipping up my coat.

"No, I mean . . . for being nice," she says. "Not just now, but just . . . in general."

She looks up at me, and I'm so flustered that I don't know what to say or do. As I stare at her, her pupils go transparent. That was the first time I noticed it, but I noticed it every time after. Sofía's eyes always went invisible before anything else. It wasn't like her pupils suddenly disappeared and showed her brains or whatever, it was like they became this sort of laser-focused, pinpointed reflection of the world.

And because behind her is the ocean and the sky, that's what fills her eyes.

I just keep staring, and her eyes sparkle with it all—all the stars, and then all the stars again, reflected in the waves. The transparency spreads into her irises. Moonlight dances on her eyelashes.

I grab her hand.

"Don't go," I say.

So she blinks, and the stars are gone, and she is back.

A crackle of lightning bursts behind me, and I turn to see Gwen sparking up, the strands of her hair electrified, little licks of flame sizzling on her skin.

"Tone it down a notch," Ryan complains.

"It's almost here!" Gwen shouts, ignoring him.

Sofía moves closer to me. And while everyone else's eyes are on the rocket, my lips are on hers.

CHAPTER 8

When I open my eyes, my whole body is trembling. Living through these memories again is messing with my head.

But it'll be worth it if I am able to reweave time. I stare down at the chaotic, beautiful timestream spreading out in front of me. I can see the three little puckers I've made to the red string. I reach out to try one more time, but even as I watch, the red string of Sofía's past evens out along the weave, smoothing down flat again. Any chance I had of pulling the end of Sofía's string from the vortex disappears before my eyes.

Time has a way of correcting itself, and I won't be able to save Sofía this way.

I stagger, almost falling when I get up from my desk chair. The weight of those memories drags me down and reminds me of just how much I have to lose if I lose Sofía.

And yet, like a drug addict looking for another hit, I want to dive back into the timestream and relive more memories. I almost bring it back up, but I force myself to lie down instead.

It's dangerous to dwell in the past. You don't have to be a time traveler to know that. But more than that, I can't let myself be satisfied with just memories. I need to find a way to save the *real* Sofía, not the image of her I carry around in my head.

Ugh. I need fresh air.

I used to hate Sundays. They always felt too close to Monday and to responsibilities. Since coming to the Berk, though, Sundays have become my favorite day of the week. They're the days I return from my parents' house to the place where I really belong, and to Sofía.

As I head out of my bedroom, I can hear someone, probably Ryan, playing a loud video game in the common room. A stream of curses follows a particularly loud blast on the television—definitely Ryan. I head outside. I want quiet. I need the ocean.

Growing up on the coastal side of Massachusetts, I was never too far from the Atlantic. But I didn't really appreciate being this close to the water until I moved to Berkshire. Until Sofía would take me for walks on the sand.

I arrive at the beach and kick off my shoes. Wind makes my shirt flap around as the sandy soil with stubborn clumps of grass gives way to the sand. I can taste the salt in the air, crisp and pure, and the ocean's waves drown out my dark thoughts.

The last time I was out here, Sofía came with me. It was cold that day, made bitterly so by the wind. Dark storm clouds billowed over the ocean, and although we could see lightning far out across the waves, it wasn't even raining on us. Sofía could stare at the sea for hours, but that day, there weren't any pretty blue waves, and everything was choppy and gray, as if the water was so disgusted by itself it was trying to jump out of the ocean.

We walked as far north as we could, up to the point where the sandy beach gives way to a rocky hill topped by the lighthouse. Then we turned around and walked south, past the academy, to the sharp point at the end of the island.

"My mother loved the beach but hated the sun," Sofía said, tipping her face up to the cloudy gray sky.

"Then this is the perfect place for her."

Sofía laughed. But there was a hitch in her voice, and her smile fell from her face almost immediately.

I wanted to ask her what happened to her family. She didn't talk about them often, just that they were dead. When she looked at me, I think she could see the questions I didn't ask.

"Car accident," she said.

"You don't have to—"

"It's okay. Dr. Franklin says I should talk about it. And it happened a while ago. Almost a year now."

The tide was rising; cold saltwater splashed over our feet, and Sofía gasped in surprise and pulled me further up the beach.

"Drunk driver," she added, not looking at me.

"I'm sorry," I said.

"I never know how to feel about it," she confessed. "The Doctor seems to think that I feel guilty, but I don't. It wasn't my fault. I know some people have survivor's guilt, and I guess I feel that way sometimes, like, why did I live when they didn't? But that's not how I really feel about it."

"How do you really feel?" I watched her closely, waiting to see if she'd go invisible, hoping she wouldn't.

"Empty," Sofía said.

The waves were getting higher, the air colder. There was an edge to the wind, as if it wanted to cut us.

"Let's go inside," Sofía said, rubbing her shoulders.

I checked the time on my phone. "Kitchens are closed," I groaned. After dinner, the kitchens were always open with snacks until an hour before lights-out. Usually, they were just stocked with fruit or granola, healthy stuff, but Ryan almost always talked his way into chips. He's good at getting what he wants.

"Come on," Sofía said. "I'll make you something."

Even though the kitchens weren't off-limits, it felt like we were breaking rules being there just before lights-out. I don't think students were supposed to cook, but no one came to stop us as Sofía pulled out a container of eggs and set a pot of water to boiling, adding a pinch of salt.

"My sisters and I called these 'ghost eggs,'" Sofía said.

"Harold would like them then," I replied, trying too hard to be funny.

She grinned anyway. "It's because of how they look when they cook." The water barely started to bubble, and she moved quickly. She swirled the water with a wooden spoon, making a tiny tornado in the pot, then cracked an egg with one hand. As soon as it hit the hot water, the egg twirled into the center, the clear parts immediately turning white and streaming around. It looked . . . delicate. Beautiful.

"See?" she said. "Ghost eggs."

And she was right. The poached egg did look like a little ghost floating in the water.

After a minute, she took the egg out of the hot water with a slotted spoon, dropped it on a plate, and handed it to me with salt and pepper.

"My little sister would poke the yellows and scream, 'I'm making the ghosts bleed!'" she said. "She was kind of macabre."

"Mmm, ghost blood," I said, licking my fork.

And she smiled at me, but it was a sad smile. She missed them. Not in the same way that we all missed our families while we were at Berkshire. She missed them in a deeper way, because she knew she'd never see them again. It wasn't that she was gone from them; it was that they were gone from her.

We talked a lot about family, me and Sofía. Not at first. Sofía kept her family close to her heart, like a secret, but eventually she opened up.

"Carmen was two years older than me," she told me after we hopped over the gate and were walking on the boardwalk together. A crane watched us from the marsh as we passed. "And Maria was just eleven months younger. People used to tell Mom that Maria and I were Irish twins, but she didn't understand what that phrase meant, so she'd tell them, 'No, no, we're *Latina*, not Irish.'"

She laughed, and the crane flew off, its long legs dripping water like glittering crystals.

"I miss them," Sofía said in a small voice. She moved closer to me and touched the back of my hand, as if to remind herself that I wasn't gone. Not like them.

"Carmen would always try to be my mom, even when Mom was around," she continued. "She pretended like she knew all there was to know about raising babies. And Maria—" Sofía laughed. "Maria would always try to make it harder on her, you know? Like, Carmen would say that she could get Maria to eat her vegetables, so Maria would load up all her peas in her mouth and then spit them at Carmen one at a time when Mom wasn't looking."

Sofía's face fell.

"She was only fourteen," she said, starting to turn invisible around the edges.

I pulled her down onto one of the benches on the edge of the boardwalk. It overlooked a shallow part of the marsh where the ground was dry enough to grow coneflowers and golden-rod. "I'm still here," I whispered in her ear, and I kept my arm around her until she was fully visible again.

"I just really enjoyed being a sister," she said. She snuggled deeper into my arm; it was starting to get dark and cold. "It was like being in this exclusive club, and we were the only members."

"They sound pretty amazing," I said.

"Tell me about your sister."

I shrugged, and even though the moment was nice, I got up and started walking back to the academy. "Nothing to say," I told her.

I was never really able to explain to Sofía what my family was like. For her, family was this unbreakable bond of trust and loyalty and love, and that sounds nice and all, but that's not what it's like in my home. That's not to say we didn't have those things. I'm certain if I needed my family, they'd be there. It's just that they weren't there otherwise.

Take Phoebe. You'd almost think we weren't related. We look nothing alike. We act nothing alike. We share no friends. We are as different as two people can possibly be.

Sofía doesn't really know how to live in a world where she's not a sister. But Phoebe's the exact opposite. She just doesn't think in terms of us being brother and sister. I'm just a guy who grew up with her, and we happen to share the same parents.

She was always like that, even when we were kids. She did her thing, and I did mine.

By the time I started high school and Phoebe was in middle school, there were cracks in our family. I don't think I noticed it at the time. It's only now, here, away from them, that I can see them.

Mom always talked about going back to work one day, maybe when I got to middle school. But that day came and went, and she never did. Instead, she grew increasingly . . . hover-y. When Pheebs and I were little, Mom didn't really seem to care what we did with our days, as long as we were quiet and let her do her crafts in peace. But the older we got, the nosier she got. She nagged me for details about friends I'd go out with, what I wanted to do with the day, with the weekend, with my whole damn life. After I got my powers, it just got worse.

Dad lived his job. He came home every night at the same time, but he was never really there. "Lots of work is good," he'd insist, locking the door to his office.

And Phoebe . . . she just sort of . . . she spun around so fast. She's like one of those ballerinas in the cheap music box she got for her seventh birthday. She'd spin from school to clubs to cello lessons to friends' houses, and sometimes she'd spin through the house, but she never seemed to notice anything or anyone.

And I, somehow, never really seemed to notice her.

When Pheebs entered high school, I was a sophomore. One day when I was walking down the hall, preoccupied and not really paying attention, I bumped into a girl in a bright blue sweater, her hair done up in braids, shiny pink gloss perfectly applied to her lips.

"Sorry," I mumbled, already moving away when I realized—

It was Phoebe.

She had somehow become a stranger to me. There was a moment there, brief but true, when she had legitimately been a person I did not know or recognize. Somehow while I was retreating to my room and listening to music and taking notes on history, she was spin-spin-spinning away from us all. Somehow in all this time, she had become a different person than the one I had known, a stranger.

Someone I could pass by without recognizing.

CHAPTER 9

I am so sick of memories I don't really want to have. I don't *want* to live in the past. Just give me the future, and Sofía, and a second chance.

I turn away from the ocean and plod back to the academy. Sand sticks to my feet, and I make a halfhearted effort to wipe it off before going inside the mansion. As I head up the stairs, I pass a group of students from another unit. They look a little younger than me, two guys and a girl. I wonder what their powers are. They stick together, moving to the other banister as I climb up the steps. I try to give them a friendly smile, but they hurry away. So. My reputation has preceded me. Maybe it's a good thing that the units are so self-contained and we don't interact with other students. Or maybe, if we did, they would know I'm not a monster. That losing Sofía was an accident.

I close my bedroom door and sit in the middle of my room, alone.

I blink, and the timestream stretches out around me, a

beautiful mix of opalescent light and strings. It's a chaotic mess, but it still makes a pattern I think I can almost understand.

There are the knotted places, tangles I cannot penetrate. The knots are places I've been to before. I scrutinize them, trying to see the path of my life in the scheme of time and the universe. *Here* is where I was born, *here* is where my sister broke her arm, *here* is where I got an award for history in middle school, *here* is where I discovered my powers.

And *here* . . . my fingers run over the knotted mess of where Sofía is trapped in the past. Ever since I lost her, I've been trying to find a way to reach her again. And then yesterday, I got there as easy as blinking. At least until I tried to warn her.

Time has a way of keeping itself safe and balanced. Whenever I try to alter something that has to be, whether it's punching Hitler in the face or changing my own timeline, time has kept me out. It snaps me back. It reminds me that it's in charge. So . . . maybe the reason I was able to go back to just before the moment Sofía got stuck in the past was *because* I didn't really have the intent to try to change anything.

Intent matters with time.

The real importance of this dawns on me slowly, but it's actually starting to make a lot of sense. When I've tried to go back lately, I've been focused on saving Sofía. But time doesn't *want* me to save her. It's preventing me from saving her. It knows from the start that's what I want to do.

Intent matters. If I go to the past not with the intent to change anything, but with the intent of just *seeing* Sofía . . .

I could.

I could do that.

Holy hell, I could do that.

I reach for my calendar. It's the kind that has a different page for each day. Sofía used to make fun of me all the time for using a paper calendar rather than my phone, like a normal person, but when you have the ability to slip through time, it's important to keep track of the days, and paper is more reliable.

I'm meticulous about my calendar; every day I make a special mark on it using a code that I developed. I keep track of whether or not I slipped in time that day, whether it was accidental or on purpose, where I went and when.

Now I flip through the pages, looking at the dates before I left Sofía stuck in the past. I need to find a time when she and I weren't together so I know there's no chance I'll run into my past self. *Intent matters.* I just want to see her. I just need to find a time where the me from now can go back and see her . . .

I drop the calendar on my bed, focusing on the timestream, blinking as it flows in front of me like a river of threads floating on the surface of a bubble. Strings of time and place radiate around me, blue and gold and gray and brown, each linking me to a different person, a different place, a different time. But the one tying me to Sofía is bright red and easy to find. I follow the red string with my eyes.

My hand shakes as I select the moment. A weekend, when I would be at home and Sofía would be stuck at Berkshire. Sometime after our first date, when everything was still new, but it was also starting to be comfortable. When we'd both sort of accepted the reality of the other.

October 3. A Saturday evening.

I hesitate. I won't be able to do this often—maybe not ever

again. I can lie and say I decided to stay at the Berk rather than go home, and it'll work once, but there's no way she'll believe it a second time.

But I need this now. I focus on that moment in time, the moment where I've not been before but where I could be now. I reach out with trembling hands, touching the space in the timestream, wrapping my finger around time itself.

And I'm there.

I'm in my bedroom, the sky just beginning to fade into evening. The plants outside my window are dead or dying rather than how I just left them, starting to show life. I run to my desk and read the date on my calendar.

October 3.

It worked. I'm here. She's here—somewhere in the academy.

I don't know how this is going to play out. Maybe the moment I see her, I'll be snapped back into my own time. But if my theory is right, as long as I don't try to contact her or leave her a message, a warning . . .

My stomach churns. It feels weird to spy on my girlfriend, weirder still to wish I could warn her away from me.

I just need one moment, I think to myself. I just want to see her face. Just once more. It will give me the inspiration I need to figure out how to save her.

That thought—*save her*—makes reality stutter. I feel it in my navel, a tugging, like the strings of time tightening around my stomach. My breath jerks in my lungs, and my eyes focus like lasers on a single painted concrete block on my wall. I have to shake the thought away. I can't think about saving Sofía, not while I'm here in the past. If time thinks I am going to screw with it, it'll throw me back to where I'm supposed to be.

Without her.

I bite my tongue, tasting blood but focusing on the pain. I try to clear my mind. *Intent matters.* So I won't intend to do anything other than see her. That's all. Just one look.

I sense time easing up on me, the timestream calming and accepting my presence here in the past. I stand up, my legs wobbly, but soon enough I get my bearings.

A glance at the clock tells me that it's near dinnertime. Unless we're having some sort of event, dinners are served in each unit's common room, and ours is just down the hall from my bedroom.

I creep down the hallway. I'm not sure what will happen if I'm seen. Just in case, I start thinking of excuses about why I'd be at the academy on a weekend. But I don't need them—the hallway's deserted.

There's sound and light spilling from the common room. I stand with my back against the wall, listening to the clattering of silverware on plates, the low rumble of voices. A sharp laugh—Ryan's—pierces the air. I dare to peek around the doors and look inside.

On weekends, Gwen and I both go home, leaving Harold, Ryan, and Sofía behind. They sit around the main table in the center of the common room now, eating ravioli. The table's huge even when we're all there, but it looks like it's not big enough for the three of them. They've spaced themselves out, each taking a different side of the table and sitting as far away from each other as possible.

The common room is an odd mix of old-school leather and teenaged dishevelment. Big winged chairs litter the edges of the room, interspersed with framed reproductions of famous but somewhat mismatched art—*Starry Night* beside a Renoir next to one of Picasso's broken women. But there's also a giant flat-screen connected to the latest PlayStation in one corner, and a stack of board games on the walnut table in the center of the room.

Harold sits to the right, staring at the walls and sometimes muttering. As I watch, he pauses with the fork halfway to his mouth, a distant look in his eyes. His power isn't enviable; seeing and hearing ghosts plagues him far more than it helps him. Ryan has his back to me, playing on his phone while he eats. His hulking body slouches over the table lazily.

So neither of them notice when Sofía looks up. Right at me.

A lump forms in my throat. I wasn't ready. Not for this. Not for seeing her again.

But I can't look away.

"Hi," she mouths.

"Hi," I whisper.

She moves to get up from the table, but I shake my head and raise a finger to my lips. A look of confusion crosses her face, but I can't explain. I want nothing more than to burst inside, race across the common room, grab her, and never let her go. But I can't explain why I'm here. I'd have to tell her that I'm visiting her in this past because I lost her in another. I'd have to tell her that I can't save her.

"No," I moan as the strings of time wrap around me again, squeezing, pulling. *No, I won't tell her*, I want to say. *I just want to see her. Just one more moment. Give me that. Please.*

But how am I supposed to plead with time itself?

CHAPTER 10

Intent matters. As soon as I even thought about warning Sofía, about trying to save her, time pulled me back.

I thump my head against the common room door. The windows outside are dark, far darker than the evening of October 3, and I don't have to pull out my phone to check that I'm back in the present, but I do anyway.

At least I got to see her. It wasn't much, but it was something.

I close my eyes and try to picture her in that moment when she saw me and her eyes lit up. I want to hold on to that image forever.

This is progress. My control has been weakening, but I wanted to see Sofía, and I did. Figuring out the intent thing brings me one step closer to saving her.

I turn to go back to my room, but I realize that it would actually be nice to have a distraction from all that's going on. I push open the common room door. For a moment, I see it the way it was on October 3, with Sofía at the table, and a smile plays at my lips. But I blink, and it's today, and Sofía's not here.

Ryan has the chess set out on the table, and as I step inside the room, a white bishop knocks over a black pawn of its own volition. Ryan picks up the fallen pawn, twisting it in his fingers as he stares at the board, and a black rook slides forward to take the bishop. Gwen cranks up the volume of the television across the room, ignoring everyone but the zombies she's shooting. Harold must be in bed already.

As upset as I am, I still like this place. Berkshire is a far cry from the old, rambling farmhouse where I grew up. Maybe that's why this room wraps around me like a warm blanket. That house, with its two and a half acres and pond and willow trees, is just a little too . . . provincial for me. Provincial. That's an SAT word my sister would love. But it fits. Even though the house isn't in the middle of nowhere, it's far from all my friends and within walking distance of exactly nothing. Somehow, all that space cages me in. Everything in the Berk is wrapped up in brick and contained together. It's nice.

As much as I love the academy, though, it's still a school, and the only place where Sofía and I can really just chill is the common room. It's where we eat, where we take breaks, where we hang out. Sofía first opened up to me in this room, over by the wing chairs. She was sitting on the floor, behind the chairs, reading a book and sort of fading in and out of visibility. If it hadn't been for the book, I don't think I would have noticed her.

I told her that she was reading my favorite book, but that was a lie. I'd never read it—I just wanted to talk to her. She started to tell me what she liked about it, but I was super distracted by the way she slowly turned visible, her hair illuminating gold then copper then rich brown.

I think she suspected that I didn't know the book. I mean, I knew *of* the book—it had been an option for ninth-grade reading, something about gangs in the '50s or whatever—but I'd never read it, which didn't take her long to realize. "It's about death," she said. "And it's about living after someone you love dies. And . . ." She paused, and in that moment she became completely, 100 percent visible. "And it's about not being afraid of being alone. Because in the end, we're all alone."

"Oh," I said, because I didn't know what else to say.

Books meant a lot to Sofía, and she was always reading. I didn't have many books that I liked, and I didn't really have anything eloquent that I could say to impress her, but I kind of regret not talking to her about the few books I did love. She was showing me a part of her when she told me about what book she was reading. I should have told her about a book that meant something to me the way that book meant something to her, because I can think of no better way to meet a girl than to see her through the eyes of the story she loves best.

I scowl. I don't like the way I keep thinking about Sofía, in memories and regrets as if she's gone for good. I step further into the room, torn between playing a video game with Gwen (I'd likely lose) or chess with Ryan (I'd definitely lose). But then I see Harold in the corner. I guess he didn't go to bed after all.

Harold sits as far away from everyone else as possible, his wing chair shifted so it's almost completely facing the wall. I can still see his mouth moving, though, and I can tell he's talking to spirits that only he can see.

When it comes to our powers, no one has it worse than

Harold. He sees and speaks to spirits and ghosts, but they tell him what they want to tell him, not anything he wants to hear. He can't command them. He can't do anything useful with them. He's just sort of stuck, forever listening to a bunch of dead people he can't shut up.

Maybe it's just the suckiness of this weekend, but a dark fear rises in my throat. I can't stop thinking about the black-hole feeling of where Sofía was supposed to be in the timestream. I stride across the room, scattering the chess pieces Ryan had floating beside the board. "Hey!" Ryan says indignantly, waving his hand and bringing all the chess pieces back to his side.

I start to drag another chair across from Harold, but it's heavy and loud, so I just plop down on the floor at his feet instead.

"Hello," Harold whispers, his eyes at a spot about a foot above my head. I'm not sure if he is talking to me or to a spirit I can't see. When I don't answer, Harold's gaze drifts down to mine, an expectant and curious glint to his eyes.

"Hi," I say.

Harold usually sticks to himself and spends far more time talking to his ghosts than to any of us.

"So." I press my lips together, my hands twitching with nervous energy. "I mean, so. Sofía, right? It's my fault she's gone, and obviously I need to go back and get her, but . . . I can't. I mean, I've tried. I've tried a *lot*. But for some reason, I can't save her, no matter what I do. And . . ." I swallow, almost unable to continue. "And I'm worried that maybe the reason why I can't save Sofía is because she's already too far gone, that I can't save her because it's impossible."

Harold looks at me as if I'm crazy.

"It's just that, I should be able to go back to exactly where she got stuck in time and pull her out. But . . . I can't. So maybe the reason why I can't find her in the timestream anymore is because . . . maybe she's . . ."

No. Those words can't be spoken.

"You talk to ghosts, right?" I say finally.

Harold's eyes shift, unfocused, gazing at something . . . someone . . . only he can see. "The voices speak to me," he says softly.

Creepy stuff like that is exactly the reason Harold got beat up so much at his old school.

He lets silence fall around us.

"I guess I just wanted to ask . . ."

Harold stares at me intently. Waiting.

"Do you see Sofía?"

There. I said it.

"I don't always see," Harold says, his eyes losing focus. "Often, I just hear. Whispers. Regrets. Whispers."

I lean up on my knees. I want to grab Harold, force him to give me his full attention. "But do you see or hear *Sofía*?" I ask, my voice rising. "Maybe she's gone, maybe what I did—" I swallow. "Maybe what I did killed her. And if it did, I know she'd come back. Here. To me. To all of us. Has she . . . do you see her? Do you hear her?"

Harold cocks his head like a cat about to pounce on a bird rustling in the grass. When he speaks, his voice is almost inaudible. "No. She is silent. She is not in the voices. She is just . . . gone."

I sag in relief. Gone—but not so far gone that I can't still reach her. She's not dead. She's okay. She's stuck in the past behind some sort of block that's stopping me from saving her, but she's still alive.

"Thanks, man," I say, standing up and smacking Harold on the knee. Harold jerks as if startled out of deep sleep by the touch. I'll leave him to his ghosts, then. I wander over to the cushions where Gwen is sitting, using a flamethrower on the horde approaching her character on the screen.

"You should be careful what you say," Gwen mutters, not taking her eyes off the TV.

"Huh?"

Gwen shoots me a look. "The Doctor's not here, but he is, you know?" Her voice drops an octave. "Watching." Her eyes flick to the corner where I had just been sitting, talking to Harold.

"I don't under—"

"There." Gwen's eyes linger on the ceiling, on the almost invisible black camera lens that points at exactly the spot where I had just been sitting.

"Why is the Doctor spying on us?" I ask, shifting closer to Gwen. I scan the room and notice at least three more cameras, one in each corner, pointing down on us.

Gwen shrugs. "Don't know. But he is."

"It's been like this for two weeks," Ryan calls from the table in the center of the room, his attention still on the chess game. "They installed them after the last episode." His eyes flick to Harold.

Three weeks ago, Harold was possessed by a malevolent spirit he'd been trying to talk into leaving him alone. He attacked Dr. Franklin. The Doc wasn't hurt, of course—he healed himself in seconds—but I guess the director decided to add more security after that.

To be honest, I'm just relieved that the cameras weren't installed because of *my* screw-up.

"It's probably just a precaution," I say. I can't help but wonder, though, how the director expects cameras to keep us safe.

"Sure," Ryan says, his tone flat. "Yeah, that's probably all it is."

CHAPTER 11

Sunday.

The last day of the weekend. Tomorrow, classes start again. And next weekend, I'm stuck going to my parents' house. I have to make today count.

All right, fine, let's approach this scientifically. I grab my notebook from my desk and make a list:

What I've Done Already:
- Tried to go into the past where Sofía is. Can't get there. Utterly blocked. Powers don't work.
- Tried to go to a few minutes before I sent Sofía to the past to stop myself. Didn't work. Timestream blocks me from my own timeline.
- Tried to go into the past and warn Sofía not to go with me to the 1600s. Can't get there.

Underneath the pitiful list, I add in big, bold, underlined letters: **<u>INTENT MATTERS</u>**.

Now let's try something completely different:

Attempt 1: Go back to my own past and leave myself clues to not get Sofía stuck in the first place.

I pick another weekend when I wasn't at Berkshire, so I can be sure not to meet my past self. But rather than go see Sofía, I stay in my room. I keep my mind as clear as possible, grab a piece of paper from my desk, and write a huge warning note to myself. I expect time to snap me back to the present, but it doesn't. I write the note, leave it on my bed, and return.

But it obviously doesn't work, because Sofía's still gone and the past hasn't changed.

I don't remember getting any notes in the past either, so what happened?

I carefully make a mark in my calendar, noting which day I traveled to. When I turn around, my eyes fall on my bed. When I was younger, I used to hide things from my nosy little sister between the box spring and mattress of my bed. I check, and sure enough, my note is there, but I don't know why or how.

I want to go back, I want to try again, but each weekend I travel back to creates a little divot in the timestream. The more I go back in failed attempts to leave notes, the more I run the risk of creating tangles and knots in the strings of time. If I don't play my cards right, I'll ruin my chances.

The universe doesn't want me to save Sofía.
Attempt 2: Brute force.

Sofía's vivid red string is easy to spot amid the myriad of grays and taupes and sage greens and pale blues of the other strings that represent the Berk at various different times. A lump rises in my throat as I look closely at the weave, at the way Sofía's string knots up with mine, just before it shoots off into the black hole of 1692.

The red string whirls into darkness. Trying to grab it just as it disappears into the void is crazy, like trying to grab a live electrical wire thrashing on the ground.

I do it anyway.

The string cuts into my skin—it feels like I'm trying to climb a mountain with a thread instead of a rope. The swirling vortex at the point in time and place where Sofía is threatens to throw me aside, but I don't let go. I can feel time around me, building like pressure from all sides, wanting to expel me. I strain against the forces of time trying to keep me out. Strings start to unravel, and they whip against my hand, lashing my skin.

I grit my teeth and pull harder. The string feels like barbed wire crackling with electricity. *No*, I think to myself, just that word, just *no*.

But I have to give up anyway. I can't hold on. The strings of time slip through my fingers, swirling back around the vortex where Sofía is trapped.

I go for a walk. I pace the grounds of Berkshire, from the brick steps to the sick kids' camp to the green gate blocking the boardwalk and back again. I stand in front of the burned-out brick chimney, the only link between where I am now and where Sofía is in the past. I stare at it. I argue with the blackened bricks. I argue with time. I argue with myself.

There has to be a way.

I wish I understood more about my powers. I wish I could say, "I want to be at this place, in this time," and go right back to that specific moment. Instead, I'm always sort of guessing, and everything is a little random, a little uncontrollable. It's like swimming in the ocean. You can point to a spot out in the distance where the waves aren't cresting yet, and then you can swim and swim, but you're probably not going to end up at the exact spot you were pointing to. The ocean's just too big, and the current is always moving.

By the time I make it back to Berkshire, it's almost dark. The giant lights around the brick facade are already glaring down at me, accusing me of breaking curfew. But when I slip past the big wooden doors inside the main hallway, it's mostly deserted. I half expected Dr. Franklin to be waiting on me, scowling, but instead, I'm face-to-face with one of the other unit leaders. She works with the older students, the ones who normally would have graduated by now but whose powers are either so odd or so uncontrollable that they're remaining at the academy.

"Bo," she says, nodding at me. I'm surprised she knows my name, but then I realize that the Doc probably told her to wait up for me specifically. Since Sofía's disappearance, he's been watching me more closely. I think he thinks I'm depressed, but I'm not. I'm just angry. At myself, at my powers, at the whole situation.

I nod to the unit leader, and she checks something on her phone and then proceeds to lock up the building. She sets the alarm and locks all the doors and windows to the academy with a nod of her head—she must have telekinesis like Ryan—then she smiles at me and click-clacks in her high heels toward the kitchens. Some of the staff have begun taking down the black bunting that had been spread throughout the hall for Sofía's memorial service.

I wonder what everyone else in the school thinks happened.

All the units are pretty tight-lipped. We hardly ever see other students. Mealtimes are kept small and regulated. There are very few school-wide gatherings, and when there are, we're told to keep our powers hidden and in check. Maybe they're afraid people will show off and lose control. Or maybe there's some other reason for us to be so secretive.

I bet most people thought the memorial service was real.

I wonder if they think I killed her.

It's my fault, after all, that she's not here, now.

What have they been told? Do the other unit leaders and teachers know, or does everyone here think I'm a walking tragedy?

I shake my head. It doesn't matter. Let them think whatever they want.

My footsteps as I trudge up the stairs are echoed by the unit leader's. She stays about six or seven steps behind me, but she carefully matches my pace, following me all the way to my unit's hall. She stands there, staring at me silently, until I'm in my room and the door is shut. Before she leaves, she rattles the handle of my door. It's not locked, and she doesn't enter, but the metallic rattle still sounds like a threat to me.

I am reminded of the video cameras that now watch us in the common room. I didn't think they were added because of me, but now I'm not so sure.

Before I go to bed, I creep around the corners of my room, looking for more blinking red lights hidden in the shadows. I don't find any more cameras, but I can't shake the feeling that I'm being watched.

CHAPTER 12

Phoebe

The last notes of Bach's Toccata and Fugue in D fill the orchestra room at James Jefferson High, lingering among the motivational posters and laminated pictures of long-dead composers hanging on the walls. Mr. Ramirez bows his head, eyes closed, listening as the music fades to silence. We all wait for him to respond. When he lifts his head, his eyes are alight.

"Bravo!" he shouts. "That! That was exactly it!"

The entire orchestra seems to breathe a sigh of relief. We've been practicing the piece for months, and this was the first time everything was just right. When we got about halfway through it, we could feel the tension in the room growing, waiting for someone to mess up. But no one did. We played it perfectly.

There is less than fifteen minutes left of class, so everyone starts packing away their music stands and instruments.

"Good job," Kasey says as she examines the worn strings on her bow next to me.

"You too," I say. I'm the first-chair cello, though Kasey

sometimes beats me. I think if she challenged me this week, she'd bump me down to second chair. But Kasey never cares about the rank.

"The concert is only one month away," Mr. Ramirez calls over the excited chatter of the students. "And while this piece is acceptable, we've got more work ahead of us. Cellos, don't forget to practice your suites!"

"Have a good weekend?" Kasey asks as I pack away my cello. "Where were you Friday?"

At a memorial service for some dead girl in my brother's class. "Eh, nowhere," I say. "What'd you do?"

Kasey focuses intently on snapping her cello case shut. "Mr. Ramirez wanted me to try out for this summer camp thing."

"Summer camp?"

"I guess it's more of a program. For musicians," Kasey says, still not meeting my eyes. "I told him not to bother with me, that you deserved it more, but he said I should audition."

"Dude, that's awesome," I say. I don't know why she's acting so shifty about it. Just because I'm first chair doesn't really mean I'm better than her. I have the technical side of playing the cello down—I know the notes and when to hit them. But I'm basically following directions. I have no more skill than a cook following a recipe.

But Kasey—she hardly ever looks at the music. She just *feels* it. The only reason she's second chair is because she doesn't bother with Bach. She's too busy playing the music in her head to practice the symphonies of guys who are long dead.

"Congratulations," I say again, hoping that she can see I mean it. "You're amazing. I hope you get in."

She smiles, relieved. "Thanks," she says. "I guess I'm going to shoot for Juilliard or something when I graduate. You?"

I snort. "I'm nowhere near your level, but it's sweet of you to pretend I have talent."

"You do!" Kasey protests, but she's wrong. Technical skill isn't talent. I can't play without sheet music, and I can only do what the notes tell me to do. Kasey plays a million times better when it's just her and the cello, and that's the difference.

"Besides," I add, "I don't think I'm going to keep playing once I get to college." I only signed up for orchestra because I wanted to look well-rounded for colleges, and marching band required too much extra work. They play at every game; we play two concerts a year.

My phone buzzes in my pocket. Rosemarie and Jenny are planning to grab ice cream after my orchestra practice is over and want me to hurry up.

"You should keep playing; you're really good!" Kasey says. She lugs her cello over her shoulder.

I shrug. "It's not like I'm going to major in music," I say.

"What are you going to major in?"

I readjust my own cello's strap. I wish people would quit asking me that. I'm not like Kasey. I don't have a talent. I don't have this burning passion to dedicate myself to one thing. Kasey's going to be the next Yo-Yo Ma and spend her whole life in music, and I doubt she has ever even stopped to think about how lucky she is—not just because she has talent, but because she knows exactly what she wants to do with it.

I mean, I guess I have some talents. But I don't have passion, not the way she does.

Kasey stays behind to tell Mr. Ramirez how she did at her summer program audition, and I head to my locker. I know my brother thinks I'm weird for liking school, but I do. High school is simple. I know the way things work. Just like playing the notes to Bach on the cello, I can play the teachers and the classes. It's easy to see just how to act, how to be, how to get by in high school. I understand the patterns.

I had talked to Jenny and Rosemarie at the beginning of the school year about how Bo was going to be attending a different school than me, but they didn't ask any follow-up questions, and I didn't supply any additional information. Part of me wanted to confess everything to them, to tell them that things are a mess and I can't make them right and please, please, please just listen.

But a larger part of me prefers to escape here every day. I go to school, and I pretend like everything's okay, like I'm an only child, like I live in a world without Bo. People joke with me, and I do my schoolwork, and during those hours, from eight to three, nothing's wrong. If I tell anyone about Bo, they'll treat me different. I don't want sympathy. I want to pretend that I'm just Phoebe. *Just* Phoebe. Not Phoebe, sister of Bo. Not Phoebe who can do nothing more than watch as everything falls apart around her. Just Phoebe, the junior orchestra geek who participates in too many clubs and doesn't take her eye off the prize: Graduation. College. Escape. I like that Phoebe.

But that Phoebe always goes home.

CHAPTER 13

The next morning, I'm summoned to Dr. Franklin's office before breakfast is over. I snatch an apple before I leave the common room, where the breakfast buffet is spread out. The others watch me go, no doubt wondering why the Doctor couldn't wait the fifteen minutes until the start of our group session.

"Bo," he says warmly, standing up as I enter his office.

"What's going on?" I ask. The hairs on my arms and the back of my neck prickle. I remember the dull, metallic noise of my doorknob being rattled last night by the unit leader who was waiting for me.

He sighs. "Friday was a rough day for all of us. I wanted to see how you were doing now that you've had some time to process and sort out your feelings."

I shrug. That day had been rough because he *made* it rough. I was forced to spend the entire day "mourning" Sofía when I could have been figuring out how to save her. I know we had to make it feel real for the staff who aren't in on the academy's true purpose, but it was still a waste. A pointless day that made everyone sad for no reason at all.

And it made me feel like a failure. Like Dr. Franklin and everyone else had already given up on me. On Sofía.

"I just wish I could have stopped it," I say. It would be so *simple* if I could just go back in time and stop myself from losing her. But time's not simple.

"It's not your fault, you know," Dr. Franklin says.

I shoot him an exasperated look. We both know it's *entirely* my fault. If I hadn't taken her back, she wouldn't be stuck in the past. But all I say is, "It's okay."

The Doctor frowns. "Sometimes we redirect our emotions because we're scared of them," he says slowly. "In times like these, it's important to remember that it's natural to grieve."

"Grieve?" I ask. "I'm not going to grieve. I'm going to save her."

The Doctor stands up and moves closer to me, his hand trailing across the wooden surface of his desk. His fingers tap on the edge of his desk, his face impassive but his eyes gleaming. I glance down at where he's tapping and see a small video camera on a tabletop tripod. The camera's not new; Dr. Franklin has recorded our sessions before. But this time, the light is blinking. It's recording. In the past, he'd tape us so that we could watch ourselves using our powers and learn from our mistakes. But I'm not using my power right now . . .

"Bo, I'm not sure you've fully processed what happened to Sofía," Dr. Franklin says. "It's . . . not about saving her. You *can't* save her. You know that, right?"

I rear back violently. "Why would you say that?" I ask. "I

can! I *will*. You just have to trust me. You have to give me a chance."

"Bo." The Doctor leaves the desk and stands in front of me, positioning himself between me and the camera. I search his face for answers, but I don't understand the look he's giving me. Concern and worry and . . . something else. It's like he's trying to tell me something with his eyes, but I'm not Ryan—I can't peek inside his mind and understand the thoughts he hides there.

"Bo," he repeats. "You have to understand this. You have to face the truth. Sofía is gone."

"Not forever," I protest weakly.

"Forever. She's gone. She's dead. You can't bring her back."

Bile rises in my throat. I shove Dr. Franklin away so hard that he collides with the desk. The camera shakes unevenly on its mount. I want to scream at him not to give up on me. I know I can still save her. But the word he used—*dead*—it rattles me. He knows the truth. He knows she's not dead. He knows she's stuck in the past. So why would he lie? Is this a test? Does he want to see if I can keep control of my power under stress? My mind churns. What does he want from me?

I don't realize I've started pacing until the Doctor grabs my shoulders to stop me. He gently pries my fingers away from my scalp, where I'd been clutching my hair so hard that a headache is beginning to bubble to the surface. I look down at my hands, at my curling fingers, and I force myself to take a deep breath, to let my muscles relax. That's my problem—that's always been my problem. When things go wrong, I freak.

He doesn't let go of me. His eyes lock on mine until he has my full focus.

"You're losing control," he says, the words reverberating through my head.

Control. This has always been about control. And my lack of it.

My eyes fall to the blinking light of the camera on the Doctor's desk. Before I can ask why he's recording us, the door to the Doctor's office opens. Ryan steps inside without looking at us. "Oh," he says casually when he deigns to notice us. "Want me to wait outside?" He doesn't move toward the door.

Dr. Franklin steps back from me. "No, it's fine. It's almost time to start."

As Dr. Franklin moves to the other side of his desk, Gwen enters, followed by Harold. We all take our usual seats in a semicircle around the Doc's desk. Ryan tries to get my attention, but my eyes are glued to the camera. Why is it on? What is the Doctor hoping to capture on film?

The Doctor starts speaking, but I can't focus on him. It's clear that today we're going to be talking about our feelings— about Sofía—rather than about our powers.

A knock at the door interrupts the Doctor before he can get really started. Ms. Temple, the history tutor, peeks her head inside the door. "Your guests have arrived," she tells the Doctor and then steps back out into the hallway. Dr. Franklin moves immediately to the door, speaking softly to whoever else is out there. Beside me, Gwen grows warm, sparks crackling on her clothing. She's on edge.

"Told you," Ryan says under his breath. Harold squeaks nervously.

"Told you what?" I ask Ryan, turning in my seat to face him.

"At breakfast," Gwen says, her voice low, "he said—"

The office door opens fully, and Dr. Franklin leads two people inside: a white woman with dyed auburn hair frizzy at the ends and a heavyset Asian man. The man has a large, worn briefcase in tan leather that doesn't match his black suit, and the woman carries a satchel that seems to be weighted heavily with papers.

"This is everyone?" the man asks Dr. Franklin. He nods.

The woman turns to us, holding her arm out, indicating that the Doctor can sit down with his students. It's strange to see him treated like one of us.

"Hello, all," the woman says warmly, a bright smile on her face. I give Gwen and Ryan a side-eyed glance. Gwen keeps rubbing her hands together, probably trying to hide the fire crackling under her skin. The Doctor reaches over, patting her back as if to assure her that all is well. Ryan's jaw is hard, and I think he's grinding his teeth.

"We hope to get to know each of you over the next few weeks," the woman continues. Her voice is sticky sweet. I dislike her immediately.

"Why are you here?" Ryan asks aggressively. The Doctor shoots him a look.

"Right now, we're just going to get to know you," the woman says, a false smile plastered across her face.

"That's not an answer," Gwen says.

"Gwen." Dr. Franklin's voice holds a stern, disapproving note.

"We're investigating what happened to Ms. Sofía Muniz," the man says. He doesn't move from his spot leaning against Dr. Franklin's desk, and he barely glances at the group. "And we're examining Berkshire Academy as a whole while we're at it." At this, he stares directly at the Doctor.

Rather than be intimidated, Dr. Franklin stands, reaches into his pocket, and hands the man a USB drive. "The files you requested. For some reason, the master files were all corrupt, and I wasn't able to salvage them, but I had a separate backup here."

"Thanks," the man says, slipping the drive into his pocket. "I'll review them later. They include both video and audio?"

The Doctor nods and takes his seat beside Gwen again.

My eyes dart to the camera on the Doc's desk, and suddenly everything makes sense. The Berk is under investigation. The state doesn't know what we really do here. To outsiders, it must seem as if Sofía really is dead and gone. And dead students mean government investigations. The Doctor couldn't warn me, not really, but he tried. That's why he called me into his office earlier today. He was warning me to pretend. We have to hide our powers and make these officials believe that Sofía is really gone.

I knew—of course I knew—that Sofía couldn't be gone for long before people outside Berkshire took notice, and there's only so much Dr. Franklin can do. He can't pretend forever that Sofía's okay when she's clearly missing, and he probably couldn't explain what actually happened to her. Still, does the government really need to come spy on us?

"My name is Amelia Rivers," the woman continues brightly. "And this is Carl Minh. We'll be talking to you individually later, but we just wanted to introduce ourselves since we'll be around. And if you have anything to tell us, please feel free to flag us down."

"Dr. Rivers and Mr. Minh will be staying here at Berkshire, on the sixth floor with the other staff members," Dr. Franklin

says, standing up. "And they'll be sitting in on some of our sessions together. Please pretend like they're not here; they're just
observing our methods and our classes. And when they ask
you questions about what happened to Sofía, I want you to be
honest. We have nothing to hide; no one's to blame here."

The camera light blinks on and off, on and off.

"We'll be deciding that," Mr. Minh says, dropping a small
notepad into his briefcase and snapping it shut. "Just be honest,
kids. As honest as you can be, anyway." He casts a suspicious
look among the group, then walks past the semicircle of chairs
and toward the door. "Amelia?" he calls back over his shoulder,
and his colleague hurries to follow him.

"This is bullshit," Ryan says as soon as the door closes
behind Mr. Minh.

"Ryan," Dr. Franklin says in a cautioning voice.

"They're from the government," Gwen says. "That can't be
good."

"Everyone knows Sofía's"—Ryan stops suddenly, looking
right at me—"death, it was no one's fault." But there's doubt in
his voice.

The Doctor stands. "Like the officials said, just be honest."
He moves to his desk, behind the camera.

I stare at the lens. That USB drive that the Doctor gave to
Mr. Minh . . . he had said something about audio and video.
The feed from all the cameras and tape recorders the Doctor
uses must be on that USB.

My stomach drops. *They'll see our powers.* None of us has
ever made an effort to hide our powers at the Berk—the *point*
of the academy was to train us how to use our powers, to understand and master them. At least one of us has used powers in

practically every session with the Doctor. Even the regular education teachers are powered themselves, or are related to people with powers, and they were all vetted by the academy as safe. None of them blinked an eye when Gwen lost her temper and spontaneously combusted, or when Ryan turned his homework in by floating it across the room, or when I slipped in and out of history during history lessons. We only had to hide from the waitstaff, and if that didn't work, I think Dr. Franklin or some of the other unit leaders had some failsafe methods to protect us, ways to make the staff forget anything they saw.

But these government people . . .

What the hell was Dr. Franklin thinking? He just *handed* them video evidence of our powers.

Maybe the videos have been edited. Or maybe the Doctor was going to use Ryan or one of the other telepaths to alter the officials' memories after the investigation.

Or maybe the Doctor is working with them.

I shake my head to dispel the nasty thought rising within me. The Doc had given me as much warning as he could, and he had made sure to establish the lie that Sofía's dead, not trapped in the past.

Berkshire is about learning to control our powers so we can be safe in the outside world. Powers like ours could be easily exploited, used by the highest bidder as weapons or tools. But that isn't the point of Berkshire. The academy is about education, not training. It's independent. Not a part of any government or group.

At least, that's what I thought.

"There's no point," Harold says. It's so rare for Harold to say something to the living that all of us just pause, waiting for him to continue.

"What do you mean?" the Doctor asks.

"There's no point in them investigating Sofía's disappearance," Harold says. "They'll find nothing. Nothing at all."

"They might," Dr. Franklin says. "They're not here to do anything but help."

"They can't find her. No point."

"Well, obviously there's no point," Ryan says, rolling his eyes.

"The witches took Sofía," Harold continues, ignoring him. "They took her and hid her, and there's no escape. No escape. The witches have her."

CHAPTER 14

SHIT.

Why didn't I think of this before?

What have I done? I'm so sorry, Sofía.

Witches. The answer was staring me in the face this whole time. And I love history. I love it, and I didn't even notice.

That plaque. The one on the chimney: Originally built in Salem in the 1660s, like the Isaac Goodale House of Ipswich, and moved to Pear Island in 1692.

Salem. 1692.

The Salem Witch Trials.

Berkshire is on Pear Island, just outside of Ipswich. But while they're called the Salem Witch Trials, they took place all through this area of Massachusetts.

I didn't just send Sofía to the past. I sent her to the *Salem Witch Trials.* In modern-day clothes and with the power to turn invisible. Sure, none of that will make her look like a witch.

Oh my God.

Oh my *God*.

I stuck Sofía in the worst possible past she could be stuck in.

My fingers itch to pull up the timestream, but I can't, not with the government officials here now. That black hole in the weave of time . . . the way Sofía's string disappeared into it . . .

Maybe it's already too late. Time is fluid; while I've been trying to find a way to go back to her, she's been living through the Salem Witch Trials. But maybe that's what the black hole is. Maybe it's proof that she's *not* living it.

Maybe I've already killed her.

If a tree falls in the forest, and no one's around to see it, can a time traveler still go back and prevent the tree from falling in the first place?

That's the question that has haunted me since I first discovered my powers. Because, see, that's the way time works. If something happens, it becomes an immutable fact. History is irreversible. It took me a long time to realize this. I can't change what has already happened.

I tried to do the obvious hero stuff when I first discovered my power. Stop terrorist attacks, warn people of natural disasters. I had all these elaborate plans. I just wanted to help. But time didn't want help.

Time won't let me change it. I am, at best, an observer.

I cannot rewrite history.

But not all history is written. That's my only comfort now. Sofía is trapped in a different time period, but that doesn't mean I can't save her. The unknown is my only comfort. As long as there's no proof that Sofía is gone forever, that means I still have a chance.

However . . . if I find her grave, if I see her name written in the prison records, if she's one of the witches whose death was recorded . . .

Then I will have failed. History is immutable. Once she enters history, I can't change it.

There would be no hope.

CHAPTER 15

It quickly becomes clear that all the tutors either believe Sofía's dead or are playing along for the inspecting government officials. Classes were a laughable affair today, all free time and busywork, and when I ask Ms. Temple for permission to use my free time in the library, alone, she says yes immediately.

I have my notebook in front of me, hoping that I'll come up with some brilliant plan to save Sofía, but I'm paralyzed by what Harold said, so I just keep jotting down notes about Salem, always afraid that I'll come across Sofía's name in the list of accused witches.

Witches.

I never thought witches were real, but what if there were people like us back then? The Doctor says that no one knows for sure how many of us there have been throughout history. We keep our powers hidden for a reason. But maybe the witch trials happened in part because at least some of the "witches" were just powered people like me . . . like Sofía.

If the witches have Sofía, maybe she's safe. Maybe they're hiding her. Maybe they realized what she was, and they're protecting her.

Or maybe that's just wishful thinking.

The first thing I bring up online is a list of the women who were put on trial in Salem and the surrounding areas. None of them are named Sofía Muniz, but there are at least five people who were taken prisoner whose names no one bothered to record. So either the witches are keeping Sofía safe (hopefully), or they're real, evil, magical beings and Sofía has to hide from them (unlikely), or Sofía's one of the unnamed prisoners (shit).

Or she's safe, using her power of invisibility to protect herself. Sofía's smart. And it's far better for her to be stuck in that world than, say, Harold, who'd probably be hanged on the spot, or Gwen, who'd probably welcome the burning-at-the-stake thing. I pull my notebook closer, making a rough sketch of the area of Massachusetts that was affected by the trials, marking down every name and method of death with little X's on the map. There aren't that many near Pear Island, but they could have taken her inland . . .

But even if Sofía is safe for now, she won't be okay forever. Still, Harold said Sofía's not a ghost, so for now I'm hopeful.

He also said, before, that some people die and don't come back. That was one of the first things he said, the day he introduced himself, that of all the people he sees in the afterlife, he's never seen his birth mother. But Sofía wouldn't do that. She'd come back to me.

She would.

"Hey, loser." Ryan's voice snaps me out of my dark thoughts.

"What are you doing here?" I ask, moving to close my computer screen and hide my research.

Ryan shrugs. "Temple let me skip too," he says. He stares at my notebook, and it rises in the air, landing neatly in his outstretched hand. "What the hell is this?" he says, scanning my notes. "Cake of piss?"

I try to act casual so Ryan won't think my notes are important. "I'm researching. For extra credit. Did you know that they made cake out of pee as a method to try to figure out who was a witch and who wasn't during the Salem Witch Trials?" I say as Ryan sits down across from me.

"Dude. Gross." He tosses back my notebook. "Listen," he says. "You're going to have to cool it with all the 'powers' talk. You know you can't say that shit in front of the officials, right?"

"I'm not stupid," I snap back.

"Debatable." He watches me coolly, waiting for my reaction. When I don't give him one, he says, "So if you're Mr. Time Travel, why don't you just go back to the Salem Witch Trials and do all your research in person?" he asks, leaning back in his chair as if he's proven something groundbreaking with this statement. There's a hint of mockery in his voice.

"It doesn't work like that," I say, trying to remain calm. Ryan likes to find ways to pick at people, pick, pick, pick until they break. It's part of his arsenal. The Doctor has said more than once that Ryan will develop stronger telepathy to go alongside his telekinesis. So not only can he move things with his mind, but he can read minds too. Or he'll be able to soon. It's hard to tell if that power has manifested itself yet, but what I do know is that Ryan is manipulative as hell.

"So Sofía's stuck in the past, huh?" Ryan says, throwing his head back and staring at the ceiling as if that were more enjoyable than talking to me.

"Yes. You know that."

"Yeah . . ." he says slowly. "But you're going to make sure you don't mention that in front of those government dudes."

"I won't," I say emphatically, hoping he'll leave now that he's gotten his answer.

But he doesn't take the hint; he stays right where he is. "I don't like them. Government officials sniffing around are never a good thing for a place like this. And Dr. Franklin . . ." Ryan shakes his head, his tongue pushing against his cheek. "I can't believe he actually gave them the tapes of our sessions. That's what was on that USB drive, you know. Videos. Of us. And . . ." Ryan waggles his fingers, and the pen he'd been twirling flies free, spinning toward my face until Ryan catches it with his telepathy and lets it fall harmlessly toward the table.

"The Doctor probably has a plan," I say weakly, but I can't help but share Ryan's concern. The Doc was so casual about it all, as if the cameras and their contents were no big deal, when in reality they prove everything that Berkshire is trying to help us hide.

Ryan laughs bitterly. "Well, if he doesn't have our back, I do."

I stare at him, trying to figure out what he means. Then I remember the Doctor's explanation that some files had been damaged, and he had to make the USB from a backup. Did Ryan corrupt the files? Did he alter them?

"The Berk is your first school like this, right?" Ryan asks. "I've been bouncing around special schools since sixth grade.

This one is my favorite, and I'll protect it, even if Dr. Franklin won't."

Berkshire is supposed to be our safe place. Sure, it's in a crappy location, but it's *safe*. If the Doctor is willing to work with the government, though . . . if he's willing to share our secrets, then we're in danger. Every student at the academy, most of the teachers—we'd all be put under a microscope. Tested. Used. Treated like freaks.

Just like the witches in Salem. I glance back at my computer. I can't afford this distraction. I have to focus on Sofía. But what kind of future am I bringing Sofía back to if she's going to be just as persecuted here as she might be there?

"You tell me," Ryan says. "What will those officials see when they watch those videos?"

I cringe. "They'll see Gwen summoning fire from the tips of her fingers," I say weakly. "Harold speaking to the dead. And you. Moving things with your mind."

Ryan nods slowly. "And think of the damage they can do with that information. That . . . proof."

"But why would the Doctor—?"

"I don't know," Ryan snaps. "But we have to make sure those suits don't see us using our powers on film, that they don't know what we can do, what Sofía could do. The fact that there are only two of them here—and that they seem to be rather low-rung—means they probably just have some vague suspicions, if that. If we nip this in the bud now, we can survive this and go back to being anonymous and safe."

I lean over the table. "They *have* the files, though."

"Really?" Ryan says, a smug look on his face.

My eyes widen. "What did you do?"

Ryan pulls an innocent face. "Maybe the reason I asked to be excused from class was because I saw Dr. Franklin take those two officials out for a tour of the school. Maybe I didn't come straight here. Maybe I went somewhere else instead."

"*What did you do?*" I ask again.

Ryan pulls a USB drive out of his pocket. "And I took care of the backup files too. Dr. Franklin needs a password that isn't just his cat's name."

I look around. There's a librarian in here—somewhere—but she's usually just playing solitaire on her computer near the front, only ever actually doing real work when a student calls her over. "You're going to get in so much trouble!" I say in a low voice.

My words trigger a complete change in Ryan's attitude. All playfulness and smugness disappear, replaced by harsh ferocity. "I am *not* going to get in trouble, because you're not going to tell one damn person about this, you understand?" He leans over the table, getting in my face. "And if you do, you'll regret it."

Ryan's never been exactly friendly or easygoing, but I had no idea his demeanor could flip so easily.

I raise both my hands. "I wasn't going to say anything," I say defensively. "But it's not like they're going to just be like, 'Oh well, lost all the files, no big deal.'"

Ryan leans back, a satisfied grin on his face. "Yeah, we're going to get searched for sure." He pulls out a brand new pack of gum, unwraps it, drops the cellophane on the library floor, and selects a piece to start chewing. He doesn't offer me one.

"So what're you going to do?"

Ryan appraises me. "What are *you* going to do?"

I shrug. "I dunno, dude."

Ryan rolls his eyes. "Look, even if I smash this thing with a hammer, they'll find the pieces and know that it was one of us who stole the drive. When they can't find the drive on us, they're going to search the trash and everywhere else. It'll make them even more suspicious if they find it destroyed, and besides, these things are shitastically difficult to break. The trick here is to make them think they just lost it. It was all a bad accident. I didn't delete the Doctor's backup files, I just corrupted them. It'll make it look like he formatted things wrong when he copied them to the drive. All a bad accident, no one to blame. Especially not us."

"Why don't you just alter the files?" I say.

"I did; I told you I corrupted the Doc's backup."

"No, I mean with . . ." I raise my hands near my head and waggle my fingers. "With your powers. Why not just make it look like we're normal and not powered?"

Ryan snaps his gum, thinking. "I tried that," he says. "But I haven't really done that sort of thing much. Maybe I messed up. Maybe they'll break through what I did."

"So what are you going to do with the drive?" I ask. "Throw it in the ocean or something?"

"Nope." Ryan winds the chewed gum around his finger, then bites it off. "That's where you come in."

"Me?"

"You."

I stare at him blankly.

"You and Gwen are the only two people in our unit who go home for the weekends."

"So?"

Ryan stands up, drops the USB drive on the floor, and crushes it with his heel, grinding the black plastic into the hardwood. Then he leans down, pulling out the wad of chewing gum, and sticking all the little pieces to it. "So," he says, cramming the gum and the broken drive under the table, "when you go home, stop by here first. Grab the drive and put it in your pocket. Throw it away at your house. The evidence will just disappear."

Ryan stands up. "Come on," he says cheerfully. "Time to get back to class."

CHAPTER 16

It took them just a day to notice the drive was missing. Our unit was in the Doc's office for our morning session when the woman, Dr. Rivers, knocked on the door. She motioned for Dr. Franklin to come over to her, and they stepped into the hallway to talk. I tried to look at Ryan, but he stared straight ahead, a tiny smile on his face. Moments later, Dr. Franklin had another USB plugged into his laptop, and he handed the new files to Dr. Rivers immediately and without question. I could see that Ryan was biting his lip to keep from grinning.

Before lunchtime, the officials know something is wrong. We're studying math in Ms. Okafor's class, just across the hall and two doors down from Dr. Franklin's office. Dr. Rivers and Mr. Minh storm into the office, shut the door, and soon we hear yelling. I kick Ryan under my desk, but he ignores me, his head bent over his geometry worksheet as if he was focused on it, but he's already finished all the problems.

That evening they search our rooms. We're eating in the

common room while it happens, and so none of us realize it until after. They were quiet about it—it's not like they trashed everything—but it's clear that our rooms have been searched. Our sheets are untucked, our clothing riffled through, the edges of posters on the walls are lifted up. They even flipped through my calendar, which bothers me more than anything else.

Ryan comes to my room before lights-out.

"Told you," he says, as I refold my clothes the way they're supposed to be.

But all I can think about is the haunted look on the Doctor's face. He doesn't deserve this. He's being made to look like an idiot at best and uncooperative at worst, and he's going to get in trouble. He might even get fired.

Ryan frowns and steps inside my room fully, shutting the door behind him. "You're having second thoughts," he says blankly, but there's fire behind his eyes.

I shrug. "I don't want anything to happen to the Doctor," I say.

"That asshole is the one who just turned our data over to the officials."

"Maybe he has a plan. Maybe we're messing it up."

Ryan glares at me. I can almost see that genius mind of his churning with ideas, seething with possibilities.

"You can't go to the future, can you?" he asks. "That's what you said originally, on the first day. You said you're a time traveler, but you can only go to the past."

I realize for the first time that, like Ryan, I've never really talked all that much about my powers, at least not to the group as a whole. I talked a lot about them to Sofía, in private, and everyone in my unit knows I can go back in time, but I've never really discussed details with them. It just . . . never came up.

"Yeah, no future stuff," I say. "I can see—well, I call it the timestream. It's like I'm standing in the middle of a big, flat, uh . . . it's really thin, barely visible, but it's like a rubber mat made out of a giant bubble, but with strings linking me to the different times and places. Sorry. I don't know how to describe what time looks like."

"Yeah, that must be hard," Ryan says flatly.

"And I can see sort of bright spots, big events. If I concentrate, I can figure out where I want to go, and I pull the string linking me to it, and I'm transported there."

"And it's all stuff in the past?"

"I can't go to the future. And there are limits to what I can see in the past."

"Maybe you should try."

I laugh. "You don't think I have? The timestream is like a tapestry; the past is already woven into a picture, but the future is still a tangle of strings."

"Huh." Ryan sits down on the edge of my bed, the mattress creaking under his weight. "It's really fascinating in a weird way to hear you talk about it all, like it's real."

"It is real." I stuff the rest of my clothes into my drawer and slam it shut. Ryan always says things like that. Just because something's not real to *him*, he doesn't see the value in it. He's worse with Harold. He can't see or hear Harold's ghosts, so he completely dismisses them, acts like Harold doesn't have a power at all.

Ryan's still staring at me.

"What do you want?" I ask, because I know he's not just here to chat.

"I'm . . ." Ryan fidgets on my bed. "I'm just worried," he finally says. "About the officials. What they could do. What could happen if you don't help me get rid of them."

I frown. I'm worried about that too, but . . . "I can't see the future."

"Maybe you can," Ryan says. He holds up his hands when I start to protest. "You can, uh . . . touch points in the past and go there, because they're fixed. They happened. But since the future hasn't happened yet, it could go one way or another. So maybe if you look at it that way, instead of looking for one specific thing that definitely will happen, if you look for just, uh . . . possibilities . . . maybe you can see the future that way."

All the lights in the academy flicker. Our warning that lights-out is in five minutes. Ryan gets up and turns to go to his own room, then looks back at me. "Look, just try, okay? I know you like Dr. Franklin, but maybe don't trust him. Not with this."

Ryan leaves, closing the door behind him, and I'm alone with my questions and fear. I'm still standing there when, five minutes later, the lights go off entirely.

I sit in the middle of my bed in the dark room, willing my powers to come to me. The timestream rises up, surrounding me, reminding me it's always there, whether I control it or not. The strings of time flow gently, extending out like a net floating on the surface of the ocean, and I am trapped in the center.

Before, I'd described the threads as forming a tapestry, but that's wrong. A tapestry implies organization, a clear picture.

There *is* a pattern—that much I can see—but it's not discernible at all. There are loose threads and knots and holes, and it should look like a mess, but instead, it looks beautiful.

I look first, as always, to the red thread swirling over the void of 1692. Sofía's still there. Still alive. Trapped, but not dead.

I turn, looking at the frayed, loose strings that float past the woven timestream. And I realize, I *can* see the future. Or . . . many different futures. I have to sift through the threads, find the ones that pull around behind me, almost out of sight. These threads are finer, like hair or a spider's web, barely visible. No wonder I'd never really noticed them before. Touching them leads to a sort of empty feeling, and I know instinctively that I won't be able to travel to any of these futures. Grabbing a string that leads to the past pulls me into history; merely touching it evokes the memory in my mind. But I have to wind the slender filaments of the future around my hand so tightly that I can feel my pulse in my palm in order to see just a brief scene play in my mind, and even that fades like smoke the moment my concentration wavers.

I carefully pick out the threads involving the Berk and me, right here, right now. It's like trying to select a single strand of sugar in cotton candy, but eventually I am able to lay out a dozen or so futures floating just above the palm of my hand. They're all short, slender filaments that I can barely see, but I wrap them around my palm. The further out in time they go, the less clearly I can see, but I at least get an impression of the future, and in every scenario, when I help Ryan, we succeed. When I don't, the government—or someone else—gets the USB drive and sees the videos of us using our powers.

The future gets bleaker from there.

Testing in labs. Being used as research, as a tool, as a weapon. Genetic manipulation. Shock therapy. Psychological exams. Drugs that dull the senses. Drugs that heighten them. Drugs that kill.

And behind it all, this moment. Here. Now.

All I have to do is take the drive home with me and throw it away there. No one expects it. And if I do it, then the government officials won't see our powers. They'll never know the truth. We'll all be safe.

And so will the world. The bleak dystopia in which I'm a weapon or a tool—anything but a human—disappears.

The choice is simple. I have to help Ryan. I know that for sure now.

My fingers go slack, and the futures spread out on the surface of the timestream like ripples on water. Because I've just realized something else. Not something that I saw in any of the futures, but something I *didn't* see in any of them.

Sofía.

She's not in any of my futures. Not a single one.

CHAPTER 17

Dr. Franklin and the officials have a long meeting the next day, so our morning session is cancelled. I can only imagine what's going on in the Doc's office—he's probably getting reamed not just for the missing USB drive but also for the corrupt files. As much as I hate the idea of the Doctor getting in trouble for something that Ryan did, I know I have to help. If the Doc could have seen the future, he never would have let the officials come close to the files.

I'd like to think that, anyway.

When the weekend rolls around, I find myself feeling a little bad for Harold, stuck alone with Ryan in the common room. Gwen and I live close enough to go home on the weekends. Ryan's parents live in LA; they shipped him out here, and I've never seen them before. They pay on holidays for a fancy black car to pick Ryan up and take him to the airport for visits, but that's it. Harold's parents live in Brooklyn. He could go home, and on long weekends or breaks he usually does, but I think he feels safer here. He always begs the Doctor to make some excuse to his dads to keep him here at Berkshire instead of anywhere else. I think the little dude would live behind the wallpaper and become a part of the building if he could.

But I'm betting that's about to change, and Harold will start heading home on the weekends as well. Ryan's not the sort of guy you want to hang around with when he's in a *good* mood, but the longer the officials are here, the angrier he becomes, and he seems to be focusing a lot of his rage on Harold.

I texted my mom earlier, asking to stay at the academy for another weekend, but she refused. She's determined to have "family time," something she never really cared about before I moved away. I don't know what she expects from me when I graduate. I mean, I don't think I'll go to college, but I also don't think I'm going to stick around.

Gwen and I wait together in the foyer for our parents to pick us up.

"I'm kind of glad to leave this time," Gwen says, her eyes on the window. There are a few other students from different units milling around, but we're standing off to the side. Units tend to stick together.

"Yeah, I get that," I say. It's not the same here without Sofía, and if it weren't for the chance to work on my powers more, I'd rather be home too.

"It's been super awkward."

I nod.

"I don't think I'm coming back next year," she says.

I whirl around. "What? Really? Why?"

"Isn't it obvious? Just . . . look around."

I do. I see Berkshire, far more of a home to me than the house my dad's going to drive me to. I see Gwen, a member of my unit, a part of my family. Powers are deeper than blood.

She shrugs. "This place . . . I really loved it at first. But now . . . I feel watched all the time. I feel like I can't be myself. And, no offense, but our unit kind of sucks. You're okay, but Ryan's a total dick, and Harold's practically a ghost. What's the point? The way this school sections us off into these tiny units . . . look at all these other people."

She gestures toward the ten or so kids from other units waiting for their own rides.

"We could be friends with them. Instead, I don't even know their names," Gwen says. "I spend all day with you guys and Dr. Franklin, taking the same classes from the same tutors . . . nothing changes. At least with Sofía I had a friend."

"She's coming back," I say automatically. I'm still not sure how I can save her, but I know I will.

Gwen narrows her eyes, examining me. "She's really not," she says. "You get that, right?"

"What do you mean?" There's a roaring in my ears, an ocean rising up in my brain, trying to drown out the doubt on Gwen's face. She says something else, but I don't hear her. I hate the way everyone underestimates me. They think that I'm not good enough, not strong enough, not powerful enough to save Sofía. I am. I can. *I will.*

"There's my mom." Gwen picks up her overnight bag and heads to the door. Before she can leave, though, the Doctor calls her name from the top of the stairs. She pauses, waiting for him to reach the door, and they go out together. Through the window, I see the Doctor bend down, talking to Gwen's mother with a serious look on his face. Gwen glances back at me, but I can't read her expression before she throws her bag in the backseat and drives off with her mom.

The next car to arrive is Dad's Buick. Dr. Franklin's already waiting for him, and Dad gets out so they can talk more. Even though I hustle to the car, they finish their conversation before I arrive.

"How 'bout them Patriots?" Dad asks loudly as I approach, obviously cutting off whatever conversation the Doctor was trying to have with him.

The Doc looks a little nonplussed, but he recovers quickly. "Bo's such a good student," he says. He reaches for me like he's going to ruffle my hair, but I'm not ten years old, and that's kind of a weird thing for him to do anyway, so I duck out of his reach and get into the passenger seat.

Dad doesn't speak as we drive off.

"What was that about?" I ask.

"What was what about?"

"What did Dr. Franklin say to you?"

Dad turns the blinker on well before he needs to, and he doesn't speak as he crosses the bridge, taking us off Pear Island and toward Ipswich.

"Bad business," he finally says when the car bumps from the bridge to the road.

"What do you mean?"

Dad shakes his head. "There's some bad business going on at that school."

Oh. The Doctor told him about the officials visiting.

I wonder what Dad thinks about it all. He knows I have power—he and Mom had to approve me going to Berkshire, and the Doctor told them how it's structured just for people like me, even though my particular power is super rare.

Mom was all for me going; it was Dad who hesitated.

It was Dad who called me a freak.

Not to my face. Never to my face. But I really wanted to go to the Berk. I couldn't stand my high school, even though Phoebe loves the place. And my mom wanted me to go, even though it's crazy expensive. She argued that it would help me fit in better with society after graduation and that the education was really good and could lead to future opportunities, blah, blah—she was for it.

Not Dad. Sure, the tuition was high, but I don't think he minded that. Honestly, I think he'd be pretty cool paying almost anything to get me out of the house and out of his realm of responsibility.

Dad was against Berkshire because it meant he had to admit that I wasn't normal. That I wasn't fixable. That traveling through time wasn't a "phase" I was going through.

Most people would be like, "Your kid has a superpower? Cool!" Not Dad.

I remember what he said the night Dr. Franklin came over to discuss the program. They thought I was in bed, but I wasn't.

"I don't want this place on his permanent record, Martha," Dad had said, ice clinking in his glass. "I don't want every future employee looking at his résumé to know that he's a freak."

It wasn't that he called me a freak. It was the way he said it. Like he really meant it. Like he believed it.

Things haven't been that great with Dad since then.

CHAPTER 18

Phoebe

I hear the door click open, and two sets of heavy feet stomp on the tiled floor of the kitchen. Why are boys—men—always so loud when they walk? It's like they have a need to announce their arrival.

"We're home!" Dad shouts, which, obviously.

I swing my feet over the side of the bed, tossing my book onto a pillow, but I don't get up. It's weird, but I'm not really sure what to do next. Bo's my brother, but to rush out of my room and greet him with a hug and a smile wouldn't feel right. We're not brother and sister like that. We share the same memories of growing up, but that's basically where our relationship ends.

"Phoebe!" Mom yells from the bottom of the staircase. "Come say hello to your brother!"

"Why?" He's home every weekend. There's no point in making a production of it.

"*Phoebe!*"

I roll my eyes and get up off the bed, grabbing an empty

116

glass on my way out the door. I fiddle with it as I descend the stairs.

Mom has Bo wrapped up in a hug, and I squeeze past them to refill my glass with Diet Coke from the fridge.

"Hey," I say to Bo.

"Hey," he says back.

I return to my room.

Usually, Mom lectures me about spending too much time in my bedroom. Not on the weekends, though.

I camp out on my bed with my laptop and *As I Lay Dying*—extra credit for AP lit, even though I hate Faulkner. The rest of the family pretty much follows suit. Dad hides in his office. Bo keeps his notebook in front of his face, blocking anyone from making eye contact. Only Mom flits around the house, dusting, vacuuming, straightening pictures, cleaning mirrors, going from room to room as if she can fill all the empty spaces.

At noon, there's a bang on Bo's bedroom door, across the hall from mine. For a moment, I freeze, not unlike a rabbit that's heard a predator. You can tell a lot from the sound of knuckles on a door. A tap-tap knock is friendly; a quick rap is urgent. This was the deep thud of a fist against wood. I creep off my bed, tentatively inching my own door open so I can see what's going on.

Dad stands in the hallway with a power drill in his hand.

"What?" Bo asks. He means, *What do you want?* but I hear the old sullenness in his voice, the challenge in his tone, just like he used to sound so often before he went to Berkshire. That one word—*"What?"*—holds more of a threat than his balled-up fists.

"I'm taking the door down." Dad's white-knuckled hand has a tight grip on the drill.

"*What?*" Bo repeats. "Why?"

"Dr. Franklin," Dad says, as if that's a perfectly reasonable explanation.

I take a step further back into my room, although I linger near my open door.

"The Doc wouldn't just tell you to take my bedroom door away," Bo says, his voice rising. "Stop! Why are you doing this?"

Dad stomps forward, his large presence enough to make Bo back down. Dad touches the power drill to one of the screws.

"Wait!" Bo says. "This is ridiculous!"

"We have to keep an eye on you," Dad says, his attention on the hinge. The drill whirs, and one screw is out.

"What the hell?" Bo shouts.

"Watch your language!" Dad whirls around, glaring at him.

"Treat me like a human being, then!"

"We're doing this for *your* safety," Dad growls.

"The hell you are."

"I said, watch your language!"

"If I could close my *damn door*, you wouldn't have to listen to me!"

I carefully shut my bedroom door, but I can still hear them fighting in the hallway. My phone buzzes, and I pick it up. It's a text from Rosemarie: a picture of her face with her eyes rolled into the back of her head and a slack expression. **Entertain meeeeeeeee.**

In the hallway, Dad shouts something about safety, while Bo storms into the bathroom, slamming the door shut. A second later, Bo opens the door and yells down the hall: "Is it okay to pee behind a closed door? Or do you want to remove this one too?"

What's up? I type into my phone.

"Son of a *bitch*!" Dad shouts, and then I hear the drill bang against the hardwood floor. I'm not sure if he's cursing because he dropped the drill, or if he threw the drill down because he's mad at Bo.

Can I come over? Rosemarie texts. **Super bored.**

Nah, I type. My friends know that Bo is at a special academy, but they think it's a military school or something. And they don't know that he's home every weekend. It's not really a secret; I'd just rather not discuss him at all. **Life's more boring here,** I text.

Then you come here.

I look up from my phone, at my closed bedroom door. Outside, my dad has resumed drilling, and I can hear the sound of ripping wood.

I can't. Mom wants me home.

Come onnnnnnn, Rosemarie says. **Tell your mom it's my birthday.**

Lol, that's next month.

Rosemarie sends me a shrugging emoticon. **They don't know that. And my gramps is over, so we do have cake.**

Outside, the hallway is silent. **Lololol, be right over.**

I stuff my phone into my pants pocket. I hesitate for a second, then I twist the doorknob slowly and peek outside.

Bo's door is gone. The wood at the bottom of the doorframe is splintered, as if Dad kicked it off instead of bothering with the drill. There's a huge, white gouge in the floor from where the drill fell on it. The bathroom door is still shut, and Dad's nowhere in sight.

I creep down the hall, away from my bedroom and past Dad's locked office door. I wait until I'm at the bottom of the steps before I call softly, "Mom?" She doesn't answer, so I go looking for her. I find her in the den, on her hands and knees, polishing the wide wooden legs of the coffee table so forcefully that the little brooch she's wearing on her blouse shakes. Dad gave Mom that pin after I was born: a tiny golden bee dangling from an enameled bow to represent my and Bo's names. Mom always wears it on the weekends when Bo is home, but never on the days between visits.

"Can I go over to Rosemarie's?" I ask.

"Family dinner tonight," Mom says without even looking up. Before Bo went to Berkshire, she never really cared about the idea of "family dinner." Sure, she cooked, and sometimes we ate together, but it wasn't a requirement. Now, though, she's adamant: When Bo is home, we "eat as a family." It never feels natural, though. Mom always places food on the table like it's an offering, and even though she says the point is to stay connected, she hardly talks at all.

"It's Rosemarie's birthday," I say.

Mom pauses and sits back on her heels. "Why didn't you tell me about it before?"

"I got the dates mixed up. She's really mad I'm not there already."

I can tell that Mom is wavering, though her eyes glance up at the ceiling, toward Bo's room. But rather than cave, she says, "Ask your father."

I groan. "Come on, Mom. Don't make me do that."

She's no longer polishing the coffee table, but she doesn't look up at me either.

"Please," I say. "It's not that big of a deal. It's one night, and I'll be home before nine. Come *on*."

"Fine," she tells the coffee table in a small voice.

"Thank you!" I say, bouncing on my heels. I turn to go, but then turn back, drop to my knees, and give my mom an awkward half hug.

I rush to leave, pausing before I pull the kitchen door closed behind me. Just a few minutes ago, there was nothing but shouting and the drill and slamming doors. Now there's nothing at all.

Rosemarie lives about fifteen minutes away from me if I stomp on the gas of my old clunker, but to be fair, the car barely tops fifty when I do that. This car was my reward for being the normal child. Mom didn't phrase it like that, of course she didn't, but it's the truth. Bo got sent to a fancy school, and I got a car that cost less than one month's tuition. But I love it anyway. It's mine. And it's freedom. Not that I would ever really go anywhere with it—knowing my luck, it'd break down if I tried to drive more than an hour at a time—but the car is full of potential. I *could* go. Theoretically.

It's always so unsettling, the way everything changes when Bo comes home. During the week, when he's gone, life is normal: school for me, work for Dad, whatever Mom busies herself with all day. After dinner every night, I sit in the den with Dad while he watches the Patriots or ESPN and I text Rosemarie and Jenny. Eventually, Mom makes popcorn and joins Dad on the couch. Sometimes, we each do our own separate thing, but there's still always a sense of home. Of family.

Bo's part of the family, I remind myself.

He is. He is. It's just that he's a part of a different family. When Bo's in the house, everything is so much quieter, so much heavier. Except when it isn't, like this afternoon. The family-with-Bo is like the spikes of a heart monitor—a loud burst, followed by nothing, followed by another loud burst.

To be fair, there's always been silence in the family. Before Bo went to Berkshire, it was there to protect everyone from the toxic mix of my brother and my father. But the silence filling the house now is different. It's *informed* silence. It's a silence born from the fact that we know—we all know—something is really wrong with Bo. It's not angry teenage rebellion that can be fixed by grounding him or taking his bedroom door down or whatever else Dad has tried. He can't be punished into normalcy.

We're not ignoring the problem, not really. We're all aware it's there, even Bo. We see the edges of this new Bo, this Bo who's special, different. We're not ignoring it. We're just carefully, carefully avoiding it.

The silence in our house now is born from the need for intense concentration, as we all carefully step around the truth we wish we didn't know, the person we can't help that Bo became, the future we're all afraid is collapsing around us, falling as silent and cold and crushing as snow.

CHAPTER 19

I stare at the gaping hole in my wall and wonder what Dad's going to do with the door.

I wonder *why* he took the door. Dr. Franklin definitely wouldn't tell him to do that.

Something's not right. Whatever the Doc told Dad before we left Berkshire made him feel like he couldn't trust me, but I can't figure it out. Is Dr. Franklin trying to make sure I can't work on saving Sofía?

If that was his plan, it was a stupid one. I don't need to be at school to use the timestream. But a little privacy would be nice. I rip the duvet off my bed and bunch the top sheet in my hand, pulling it closer. Grabbing a stapler from my desk, I stand up on a chair and drape the sheet over the doorframe, stapling it into place. It's not a door, but it's something.

I just don't get it. If they're not going to trust me with a door, why bother bringing me home at all? Mom kept insisting I come for the weekend, but where is she? Downstairs, cleaning. And Dad's just in his office. I sweep aside my sheet-door and step into the hallway, turning in a slow circle with my arms held wide. *Here I am*, I think. *You wanted me, so here I am.* But of course, no one sees. No one cares. My parents have no idea what to do with me.

Hell, *I* don't know what to do with me. Phoebe's room—with its door—stands right in front of me. I turn my back on it and return to my room. It'd be easier if I were like her. She's everything my parents ever wanted. Ambitious, driven, studious, and—most important of all—normal. I'm sure she has her whole life planned, just like I'm sure it's 100 percent parent-approved. Graduate, college, job. I wonder where she'll go. I bet she's already writing her application essays. But me? I doubt I could get into any college, and even if I could, I couldn't go. Not unless I knew I could control my powers. And control feels a long way off right now. The truth of the matter is that I may never have control. I may never have "normal" in my grasp.

That's the biggest difference between my sister and me. I may be able to travel through time, but she knows more about the future than I do.

I sit in the center of my bed, staring at my curtain door.

I could know the future, I realize. The timestream hides the future in thin, almost invisible filaments, but I found them before. I could do it again.

When I bring up the timestream around me, the first thing I notice is that some of the strings I'd seen before—the disastrous fates brought on by the officials if they'd found the USB drive—are gone. They're just . . . gone. Because I hid the drive, I made it impossible for the government officials to use it against us, and any future where they did no longer exists. The Berk's not safe yet—some of the futures show it being taken over by the government, some show the school closing, one even chows the school on fire—but I push aside those worries, at least for now.

The strings that tie me to my home—brown and green and blue—are more prevalent now, rising to the surface. I pick up the pale blue string, and images of Phoebe flash through my mind. I follow the string back to its beginning, sixteen years ago, to her birth, and I see the way her life is woven into time. Going into the future, the string frays, splitting off into floss-like, micro-thin threads, each a possible future for my sister.

Some things feel fairly certain—there are a few offshoots of loose strings floating away, but Phoebe's graduation is close and clear. I wrap my finger around the moment, and images of her on that day fill my mind, a movie of memories that haven't happened yet.

She's far tanner in the future than she is now, and she looks thinner, almost gaunt. She's traded her pink lip gloss for something darker, and she's swapped her contacts for winged cat-eye glasses. Even though Mom and Dad hover near her, Phoebe pretty much ignores them, chatting with her two best friends. Mom insists on taking pictures of the three girls near the fountain at the front of the school, but she doesn't notice the way Phoebe's smile doesn't reach her eyes.

Once my parents are gone, Phoebe and her friends start goofing off. She pulls them closer for a selfie, but as soon as she takes the picture, she loses her footing and falls into the fountain. Her laughter rings out as she grabs her friends and drags them in with her, completely ignoring the frowning teachers nearby. I take a moment to marvel at this Phoebe. It's only a year into the future, but I can see changes within her that I never really thought I'd see. A spontaneous Phoebe who lets her life get a little messy? One who doesn't care about what teachers think? Who would have thought.

At first, everyone's laughing and splashing, but then Phoebe pulls her wet hair back, and her hand brushes her ear.

"Hey. Hey!" Phoebe says, her voice rising when her friends don't stop playing. "I lost my earring."

Normally, Pheebs wouldn't care. She's not really much of a jewelry girl. But those earrings were our grandmother's. The three girls spend the next several minutes searching the fountain, but they don't find anything. Eventually, Phoebe has to admit defeat. She walks away from the fountain, shoulders slouched, cradling the other earring in her palm, and I know she's going to remember this day not as the day she finally achieved her dreams and graduated, but the day she lost our grandmother's earring.

The string slips from my fingers, and the image fades to nothing. These strands only show possibilities, not certainties, but I want to know more. The further into the future I go, the more potential futures I see for my family. In one, my mom gets a new job as a hotel manager, and eventually she starts an affair with the concierge and leaves Dad. In another, she starts writing a blog that gets super popular, uses it to fund a trip for her and Dad around the world, and they briefly consider adopting a baby from some third world country before they come home and resume their lives just as they were before they left.

Dad doesn't change much, not in any of the futures, even the ones where Mom leaves him. He just plods along, never adjusting his job or routine. But then, about fifteen or twenty years out, Phoebe has a baby, and she brings it to Dad, and his whole world starts to shine. It's like a lightbulb, right there in the timestream. And even though his future still doesn't seem to change much after that, all of the strings sort of glow with happiness.

Phoebe is the one with the wildly different possibilities for her future. In most of them, she goes to college, but in a few she takes time off to travel—an internship in New York, a backpacking trip in South America, a study-abroad experience in Europe. She gets different jobs too. Magazine writer, art teacher, forensic scientist for the FBI. Maybe Phoebe's futures are so varied because she's so young, or maybe it's just because Pheebs is Pheebs, and she's always been able to land on her feet, like a cat. But she's really smart, and these strings prove that she can do anything.

Including, I realize, make mistakes. Some of Phoebe's futures are . . . not good. In one path, she goes to Boston University, but then drops out for a year to travel around America. She's usually pretty safe, but at one point, near Wyoming, she hitchhikes and . . .

I don't want to think about what happens to her there. The abuse she suffers at his hands. No. I force myself to properly name it. The rape. It's terrifying. My fingers want to pull back from this thread, to find a way to cut it and make sure it never happens, but there's more to this future than that one horrific moment. There's another man, a kind one who loves her and never raises his voice at her because he can't bear to see her flinch. There's a daughter, a thin girl with dark hair like mine and clear green eyes that are all her own. There's a dog and a house and a career and friends and travel and happiness.

And it's all wrapped up together, woven into Phoebe's past and future, irrevocably and literally tied to that moment in Wyoming. I let go of this future's string, wondering if that family and that life are worth the path it takes to get them. I think, from the way Phoebe held her daughter, they are.

In some of Phoebe's futures she's rich, and in some she's not. In some she marries—in those versions, she almost always ends up with the same guy, although she meets him in different ways—and in some she doesn't. In several of her futures, she dies young—either from some stupid risk or decision, or from just blind, dumb, horrible luck. Most of her futures give her at least sixty or seventy more years, though, and in one she makes it to 103, with three kids and eight grandkids and even a great-granddaughter.

But the thing that strikes me most about Phoebe's future is that, of all the possibilities, there's not a single one that's definitively *right*. I cannot pull apart the threads and find the one that's perfect for her. They're all perfect and imperfect in different ways, even the one that includes Wyoming. They all have moments of intense joy and intense sorrow. Each decision Phoebe makes, each circumstance she can't change and must find a way to live with . . . every one ends in a life that's not really that much better or worse than any of the others. She finds just as much joy in having kids as she does in not having them; in getting a high-paying job as working for pennies in an art gallery; in traveling the world or making one place home. But she finds just as much sorrow in each life too.

After I sort through her threads, I sit back on my bed, and . . . I don't know, I feel sort of peaceful. It's weird. I was super anxious before, but this is like a perfect moment of calm.

I can't really help my parents; they're old, they've made their decisions, they made them a long time ago, before I was ever born.

But Pheebs . . . man, Phoebe has a real chance. She has the whole world, a myriad of futures, all within her reach. And it feels a little like a burden has been lifted.

I've never really known what I was supposed to do with this power of mine. Stop horrible things from happening? Ensure the right course of events? But I don't have to worry about Phoebe. There *is* no right path for her, no wrong path. They're all just . . . possibilities, and she can pick whichever one she wants. It's not up to me to change her future, to make sure the right future happens. I'm not responsible for her. I can let her spin-spin-spin away into her own future.

CHAPTER 20

Phoebe

Rosemarie's house is almost hidden by the trees in her yard. It's . . . not much. Dad's in real estate, and he was the one who sold Rosemarie's family their home three years ago. So he knew exactly what kind of loan they had (and hadn't) qualified for. On the few occasions when I couldn't drive, Dad would drop me off at her house, grumbling the whole ride there and then frowning at the trash in her yard and the car that never left the driveway because it didn't work.

Whatever. I love it here.

There are already tons of cars in Rosemarie's driveway and yard. I park near the mailbox and walk up to the house. Late wild daffodils bloom in scattered patches, filling in the spotty grass. The front door is mostly open—Rosemarie's home is always hot—and I don't bother knocking as I walk inside.

"Bee!" Rosemarie's little brother shouts, crashing into my legs.

"Hey, Peter." I rub the bristly ends of his buzz cut. "Nice hair."

"Rosie did it," he says.

Peter's nine years old and what his parents call "precocious" on good days and "annoying as hell" on bad ones. Rosemarie always calls him the latter, but she usually doesn't mean it.

"Phoebe!" Rosemarie yells from the couch. An episode of some reality show blares over the noise spilling in from the kitchen. I can see Rosemarie's mother in there, stirring a giant pot of homemade pasta sauce, flanked by at least two aunts, a cousin, and someone I don't know, all in various stages of baking garlic bread, straining noodles, clattering pots, smashing the oven door closed, and rooting around in the fridge.

"Hey," I say, plopping down on the big brown sofa beside Rosemarie. Peter crawls over my lap and Rosemarie's legs to get to the good corner seat of the sectional.

"Can I braid your hair?" Peter asks his sister.

"You know how to braid? I'm impressed," I say.

Peter nods. "I can French braid," he says seriously.

"No kidding? Show me."

Rosemarie scoots around on the couch, turning the back of her head to Peter, who stands up on the cushion and starts finger combing her hair. His face scrunches up as he carefully sections off pieces to braid.

Across the room, I notice Rosemarie's grandfather scowling at Peter. Rosemarie doesn't move her head—she doesn't want to mess up Peter's braiding—but she glares until he turns his attention back to his beer. She shoots me a look; she's often complained about how her grandfather pressures Peter to be more manly. I'm glad he doesn't start a fight. If his biggest worry about his grandson is something as stupid as that, he doesn't know how good he has it.

When Peter gets to the end of the braid, he realizes he

doesn't have a hair tie, so I pull the elastic out of my ponytail and pass it over.

"Gorgeous," I say, as Rosemarie turns her head left and right, framing her face Vogue-style. She checks her hair by patting the top of her head, and then she punches her brother in the arm. He falls over laughing for no apparent reason.

Dinner's a casual affair. Everyone gets bowls until the bowls run out, then they get Tupperware or plates loaded down with spaghetti and garlic bread dripping with butter, and we all sit wherever we can. Rosemarie and I reclaim the couch along with some of her aunts, Peter sits on the floor, the older relatives take the tables, and Rosemarie's mom eats standing up by the kitchen counter. It's both awkward and fun trying to balance a full glass of soda between my knees as I sit on the couch, everyone still moving around me. One of Rosemarie's aunts, who married "a fifth-generation Italian" from New Jersey, complains bitterly and loudly about the inauthentic garlic bread while licking butter off her fingers and grabbing a third piece. Peter spills his milk on the floor, then Rosemarie's homophobic grandpa spills his spaghetti down his shirt, and despite all that—or maybe because of it— everyone's still in good spirits and filling the entire tiny house with talking and laughter. It sounds like family.

After eating, the adults flood the living room, so Rosemarie, Peter, and I escape to Rosemarie's bedroom. Peter lets us paint his toenails black, but when he smears the polish on Rosemarie's polyester comforter, we kick him out of the room. We then spend an hour or so Facebook-stalking Joey Albertus, doing an online quiz to see which character on Rosemarie's show we are most like, and making plans to go to a concert in Boston that neither of us will ever really be able to go to.

An hour after dinner, my phone buzzes. "I've gotta go," I say, reading the text from Mom.

Rosie grabs the phone out of my hand. "She's just asking if you're okay and when you're coming home. Tell her that you're fine and will be home later . . . like a normal person."

I grab my phone back. "Nah," I say. "I gotta go." I know what Mom really means.

When I get back to the house, Mom's in the kitchen doing the dishes. She always rinses them with hot water and soap before putting them in the dishwasher, a move everyone in the family tries to convince her is unnecessary. Dad's already back in his office, and Bo has hung a sheet where his door used to be. I pause by his room, wondering if I should see if he's up, ask how he's been, just talk or something. I think about the easy way Peter and Rosemarie live together. Rosemarie would have no problem going into Peter's room. She'd just walk right in. He'd smile at her and say, "What's up?" and she'd suggest they do something together, maybe get some ice cream and watch a movie. She'd say . . . No. That doesn't matter. There's no point pretending Bo and I could be like Peter and Rosemarie. But if it were me, if it were Bo, *I'd* say, "Hey, how's that school? Do you like Dr. Franklin? He seemed nice." And then I'd say, "I heard a girl in your class died. Are you okay?" And maybe he'd tell me and maybe he wouldn't, but it'd be something.

My toe stubs against the new gouge in the hardwood floor where Dad dropped or threw down the drill.

I walk past Bo's bedroom and into my own, putting my earbuds in, cranking up the music, and staring at the ceiling until I fall asleep.

CHAPTER 21

When I wake up in the morning, it takes me a second to remember where I am. That I'm in the bedroom where I spent most of my life.

That's the weird thing about being at home. Because this is still, technically, my home. If someone asks where I live, I give this address, not Berkshire's—even though I spend more time at the Berk. The toothbrush I like best is at the academy. I have another one here, but it's stiff and tastes gross. I have the same shampoo brand in this bathroom as the one in Berkshire, but it's fuller here, and older, and there's a crusty rim around the opening where the shampoo comes out.

And I actually have a door at the Berk.

How can this be my home when I'm treated like some sort of criminal here?

I pick the pants I wore yesterday up off the floor and pull them on. Something hard and sharp in the pocket pokes my leg, and I withdraw the smashed USB drive. I start to toss it into the trash can, but I hesitate.

Only the plastic casing was destroyed; the actual drive looks intact, which means I could watch the videos if I wanted to.

It's just footage of our sessions with the Doctor. No big deal. Except . . .

It's footage of Sofía too.

Seeing her on-screen won't be the same as seeing her in person, but it's better than nothing. I open my laptop and jam the rectangular end of the drive into the port. Just as I'd hoped, it still works. Folders, each labeled by month, pop up on my screen. All our sessions with the Doc. All those days sitting beside Sofía.

I select one of the early ones at random, and the video starts playing immediately. At first, there's nothing but an empty room on the screen. No—not empty. The Doctor's at his desk, so still that for a moment I don't notice him at all. His brow is furrowed and his eyes downcast. His hands are clasped in front of his face, his knuckles ashy. He looks as if he's contemplating something . . . dark. He seems almost . . . afraid.

The door opens, and the students stream in—Ryan and Gwen first, then Harold, his eyes darting. I watch myself stroll into the room, cocky.

Then she walks in.

Her footsteps are graceful, like a dancer's, toe first and fluidity up her legs. But there's a bashful nature to her movements as well, a hesitating grace, as if she doesn't believe anyone would ever look at her even when she's visible. The me on the video screen looks back and smiles at her, and she almost fades away, barely holding on to her opaqueness.

Dr. Franklin has, as usual, set up the chairs in a semicircle around his desk. Harold sits between Ryan and me, and Gwen and Sofía sit next to each other, Gwen pulling her seat closer to Sofía and away from the Doctor. The arrangement has Sofía and me together, as I had hoped we would be.

The session I'm watching wasn't long before our first date. We were still trying to figure out what we meant to one another. I knew exactly how I felt about Sofía, but I also knew that she was . . . scared.

Not that I understood it then. I was so busy looking at her that I never really *saw* her. At the time, I had just thought Sofía was shy. But now, through my laptop screen, I can see something else, something beyond the surface, something *wrong*.

"I'm sorry," I whisper to the Sofía on-screen.

I watch the past version of myself shift in my seat, angling my body closer to Sofía's. I let my hand drop, making a point to brush my fingers against the back of her hand. Sofía jumps and snatches her hand away.

I close my eyes, remembering that moment, the way she faded into invisibility, a transparent blush creeping across her skin.

When I open my eyes, though, Sofía's still on the screen, her long hair hiding her still very visible face.

That's not right.

This was the day the Doctor started talking about the history of powered people. I pause the video, forcing myself to recall the exact discussion. Dr. Franklin told us all about famous people in history who had powers. Van Gogh could see auras around people and knew when they were lying or telling the truth. Tesla could control electricity with his hands. Abraham Lincoln was something the Doctor called an "audiopath"—if you could hear his voice, he could alter your mindset and make you agree with whatever he was saying, sort of like hypnotism.

This had been one of the first times the Doctor talked about powers directly, explaining that we could be among the greats. It was the first time I started to truly accept myself and what I could do. It was the first time I started to believe that my powers mattered.

It was also the class that gave me the confidence to experiment more, to show off my powers for Sofía, to take her with me . . . and then leave her in the past.

After the Doctor's lecture, Ryan had asked if it was possible to learn powers if you weren't born with them. He was fascinated by Lincoln and wanted to be an audiopath too—I guess telekinesis and telepathy weren't enough for him. Ryan had tried to convince Harold he was a girl, not a guy, and when it didn't work, he instead made his chair float around the room, just out of reach of the Doctor, causing all of us to laugh ourselves silly. Dr. Franklin had to end the group session early.

I unpause the video. Everything I see on-screen—where we're sitting, what we're wearing, our facial expressions—it's all just as I remember it. But as the video plays, it's all slightly . . . different. The Doc *is* talking about Van Gogh and the others, but he's not talking about their powers. I hear the word *depressed*, I hear *bipolar*.

And Ryan doesn't use his powers to make the chair dance. Instead, he calls Harold a little girl and mocks him when he starts crying. When Dr. Franklin reprimands Ryan, he turns violent, picking up a chair and throwing it at the Doctor. One of the chair legs hits the Doctor's temple, and blood spurts from his head as he collapses on the floor. The girls get up, screaming, and Harold cries harder. The me on the video just sits there, staring, a smile playing on my face.

"This didn't happen," I mutter, staring at the screen. None of this happened.

Dr. Franklin doesn't move. Blood leaks down his face like tears, and it takes him several moments before his eyes open again. He touches the wound and winces.

None of this happened. None of it. Ryan made the chair float, he didn't throw it. It was something fun and funny, not violent and mean. I don't recognize the Ryan on the screen, his face scrunched in rage, his eyes flashing, his chest heaving. The Ryan I know is always in control—of himself and usually of others. This person is volatile and evil and totally, entirely chaotic.

I clutch my head, my fingers yanking at my hair. This *didn't* happen. I was there. I know what happened, and it wasn't . . . it wasn't any of *this*.

Static crackles across the screen.

I lean closer, looking intently at each figure. At Ryan's unrecognizably furious face. At Harold, rocking back and forth in his seat. At me and my hollow gaze.

At Sofía.

And as I watch, Sofía's back stiffens. She turns in her seat, and it looks as if she is staring through the screen, directly at me. I have the sound turned low so my parents can't hear Ryan cursing and shouting, but when Sofía opens her mouth to speak, her words ring out, filling my room.

"Bo," she says. "None of this is real."

CHAPTER 22

I stare at the screen.

It had looked like—no, that's impossible. Had the Sofía on the screen looked through the camera and given me a message?

I rewind the video and start it again at the moment Ryan flips out and throws the chair. I keep my eyes on Sofía the whole time.

She doesn't turn around. She doesn't speak to me.

But I know what I saw.

What's going on? The video just keeps playing.

I watch the next video, my eyes on Sofía, waiting for her to speak to me again. This recording is of the day Gwen opened up about her fire power. Discovering the power was traumatic for her—she was young, and her dad reached over to grab her hand, and a fireball in Gwen's palm burned his skin. He still has a scar.

But in the video, Gwen's story is different. "I got the lighter from Dad's dresser," she says. "I was fascinated with flicking it on and off, on and off . . . I didn't mean to set the mail on fire. I didn't mean for Dad to touch it and get burned."

The Doc leans forward, meeting her eyes. "Gwen, you knew the paper would burn. You intended to set that fire."

Gwen's voice is small. "Yes, but I didn't mean to hurt him."

"That didn't happen!" I yell at my computer. "That's not how any of it happened."

But the computer doesn't answer me. Sofía doesn't answer me. The video just keeps playing, showing me a weird parallel version of reality.

The next video plays. The Doctor's talking to me about control, just like he always does. On that day, he asked me to go back in time, to show everyone what it was like. Ryan was making fun of me, calling me worthless, so I went to Times Square on New Year's Eve of the year he and I were born, and I brought back a pair of those stupid glasses that have the year where the eyeholes are, and I tossed them to him.

The snide tone of Ryan's voice. The bitter cold of New York, so freezing that my skin burned. The trashy, shiny confetti that fell from the sky when the ball dropped. The cheap glasses. I remember it. I can see it, smell it, taste it.

But on the video, the Doctor doesn't tell me to go back in time, and it's me, not Ryan, who says I'm worthless. On-screen, I grow very still in my seat. My eyes look dead, and I stare straight ahead. "The spaz is doing it again," Ryan says.

"Shut up," Sofía responds, but no one hears her. The Doctor snaps his fingers in front of my eyes, and I don't even blink.

And then I shake my head, and I look at Ryan. "See? I told you I could do it!"

And then the video cuts into static.

None of this happened, I think to myself. *Not like this.*

But my hands are shaking, and I taste bile in the back of my throat. My head is fuzzy, and there's a ringing in my ears, and I can't think.

There's nothing to think about. You saw it. The proof is right here, in front of you. It's you who's crazy—

No, I'm not! I'm *not*. The words echo inside my skull, over and over and over. *I'm not, I'm not, I'm not.*

I'm. Not.

Everything's suddenly still and silent.

I look at the video screen. It had been showing static, black and white lines blurring in and out of each other, but now it's *completely* frozen in time.

I look around me. Everything's still. I jump up from the bed and sweep aside the curtain blocking my door. The big clock at the end of the hall isn't ticking. My sister's bedroom door is cracked open, and I press my face against it. She's sitting in the middle of the bed, her cell phone screen illuminating her utterly motionless face.

Time has stopped.

I walk slowly back to my room, to my bed, and pull my laptop closer, staring at the frozen static.

I stopped time.

But . . .

"Is this real?" I whisper.

And all around me, time snaps back into place. The static

fizzles on the screen, fading to black. I can hear the ticking of the hallway clock. My sister giggles, the sound carrying across the hall and into my room.

Time still weaves around me, bending to my will, no matter what those videos show now.

The next video starts playing automatically. Sofía's face fills the screen as she walks by the camera.

I slam my laptop shut. I don't know what's real or not anymore.

But Sofía does. And I know just how to reach her.

CHAPTER 23

I toss my computer to the foot of my bed and bring up the timestream again. I wish I had my calendar with all my coded markings on it, but it's at the Berk. I don't feel safe picking a day to see her when Sofía would be at the school. Berkshire doesn't feel safe.

Christmas break, then. I was home, and Sofía was with her father in Austin. There will be no chance of a paradox, no chance of me running into my past self. And I'm not going back to warn her or stop her or do anything to change the past. I just want to confirm that my present is real.

My hands tremble as I sort through the timestream. The threads of time weave in and out of each other, each of them flowing back to me. I find the red thread, Sofía's thread. I let my fingers glide over it, relishing in the way it rubs against my skin, reminding myself that this—this is what's real. Time is real. Sofía is real.

I follow the string to Austin and see that there are tangles and knots in the patterns there, all mixed in with the loose ends of other colored strings. I touch them, twisting the ends with my fingers, and my mind shoots further back in time and bursts with images of other people—an older woman and three younger girls—and I realize that one of the younger girls is Sofía. This was her family before the car accident. I drop the threads as if they were on fire.

It feels wrong, peeking this far into Sofía's past.

Here is something I've learned: You never know all of a person; you only know them in a specific moment of time.

The Sofía I knew was kind and quiet, but she carried her grief around, hidden by a cloak of invisibility. When she told me about her past, it was nothing more than a story to me. I didn't live it with her; I didn't know her during that moment of her life. The Sofía from the past was an entirely different person.

But then I knew Sofía in a way her mother and sisters never did. They never could. They would never know a Sofía without them. Just like I can never know a Sofía with them.

This is the most important thing I learned from being a time traveler. You are not one person. You are a different person in each moment of time. Your name means nothing. Go see a person with the same name in a different time, and it's someone else entirely. I don't know Sofía. I know Sofía-at-Berkshire. Sofía-before-her-family-died is a stranger, someone I'm not sure I should ever meet.

I pull back, carefully arranging the timestream so I touch just the strings from after Sofía came to Berkshire. They feel like guitar strings under my fingers, pressing into my skin and rolling under my fingertips with a twang as I try to find the correct one, the one of Sofía on Christmas break. When I do touch it, I feel the rightness of it. I wrap my index finger around the thread, crooking my finger and drawing my hand closer to me. Traveling in the timestream is often like this, a give-and-take as I draw the threads closer to me and they pull me further into time. The thread connecting me to Christmas break bites into the skin on my finger, pulling taut and turning the tip purple as my blood flow stops, but I don't let go. I relish the pain. I revel in the thought that it's real.

The thread evaporates, leaving behind the sensation of it having been there, but no visual evidence. I blink in the bright sunlight. It's December, but Austin is warm, far warmer than a Massachusetts winter. The sky is a cloudless blue, almost matching the bright blue paint of the tiny house before me. All the buildings on the street are made of varying shades of beige stucco, but Sofía's house is made of wide, flat wooden panels painted a vivid cobalt, with bright yellow shutters by the window and a blood-red door welcoming me from the front porch.

"My mother liked color," I remember Sofía telling me. "She said it made her feel alive." Ironic, I guess, that the colors are all of her that remains.

There's no car in the driveway, but I'm confident that Sofía's in the house. The threads of time led me here. I bound up the steps to Sofía's front door and knock a few times before I notice the doorbell. Still, I'm not prepared when she answers the door.

"Bo?" Sofía asks, looking shocked.

"Hey," I say. But there's so much more I try to put behind that one word.

"What are you . . . ?" She peers past me, out into the street. "What are you doing here? How did you even get here?"

I cock an eyebrow at her.

"Oh. Yeah." She sort of half giggles. "Powers."

"I needed to see you," I say. "So . . ." I hold my hands out flat. "Here I am."

Sofía steps inside, motioning for me to follow her. The scent of bleach fills the air. As soon as the front door closes, Sofía grabs me, pulling me closer, and her arms are around me, her fingers weaving through my hair, my name a whispered promise from her lips. She stands up on her tiptoes and kisses me, hesitantly at first, and then deeper, as if she wasn't sure I was real before but now claims me as her own.

When she pulls back, she buries her face in my chest. "I needed you too," she says in a soft voice.

I tuck her head under my chin, wrapping my arms tightly around her, and we just stand there for several long moments. Sofía's house is bigger than I thought it would be from the outside, but the inside has none of the bright colors. The walls here are all white, and the slick glossiness of the paint makes me think it's fresh. There are hardly any pictures or decorations on the walls, no rugs on the tile floor, very little sign of life at all.

"Come this way," Sofía says, pulling me deeper into her house. We pass the living room—nothing but a television on a metal stand in front of a nondescript sofa—and the kitchen. There aren't even magnets on the fridge. Nothing decorates the hallway, and every door is firmly shut.

Sofía's bedroom certainly has more personality than the rest of the house, but it still doesn't have as much color as her room at the Berk. The pink here is softer, more childish, not the bright hot pink of her fuzzy lampshades or the neon of her picture frames in her room at school.

On her wooden dresser by the door, Sofía's propped up a Christmas tree made of green construction paper. Once I see that, I realize that the house is missing far more than pictures and color—it's missing Christmas decorations. Sofía used to tell me about the way her mom and sisters would go all out for the holidays, throwing tinsel all over their living room until their carpet looked silver, stringing lights around not just the tree but the curtain rods and picture frames and over the tops of tables. They'd bake cookies and empanadas and fruit tarts and churros until every dish on the big dining room table overflowed with sugary goodness.

And now there's nothing but a green triangular piece of construction paper.

At the bottom of the handmade tree is a card written in Gwen's handwriting and a small box. I gave that to Sofía before we left for the holidays—I was too shy to let her open it in front of me—but I hadn't even bothered to wrap it. I didn't know that the little silver dolphin necklace was the only gift she'd get that year. I should have wrapped it.

"So why are you here?" Sofía asks, closing the door. We're the only ones in the house, but I guess her father could come home at any minute.

"I—I just wanted to see you," I say.

"You saw me yesterday," she replies, grinning.

Right. For her, yesterday was the last day of the semester. My dad had picked me up, and the school's van drove Sofía to the airport. That was her yesterday.

"I wanted to see you again. Can you blame me?" I say, and before she can ask any more questions, I lean down and kiss her.

And it is everything I have longed for, and everything that breaks my heart.

When we pull away, she has a love-drunk look in her eyes, and I almost kiss her again. But I'm not sure how long this will last.

"When you see me again after break?" I say. "Don't mention this."

If Sofía talks about seeing me when we're both back at school, then past-me will know that future-me came back, which didn't happen in *my* past, and . . . time travel is confusing.

"I won't," she says. "But why did you come back here, then, if we're going to pretend like it didn't happen?"

"Because I need to know it did," I say before I can stop myself. I feel a lurch in my stomach. Time is warning me. I can't get too close to the truth.

Sofía frames my face with her hands. "What's wrong?"

"I just . . ." I run my fingers through my hair and step back. I can't think when she touches me; I can't think of anything at all but the way she feels.

"Yes?" she asks. She sits down on her bed, bouncing softly, and I'm distracted again.

"This is . . . this is real, isn't it?" I say. I reach her bed in two strides and grab her hand, squeezing it. "This is real. *You* are real. You're really here, and I'm really here. I can travel through time, and you . . ."

Sofía smiles, letting her face disappear. "This is real," she says while still invisible. Her lips appear in a Cheshire cat grin, and then the rest of her, and she stands up again and kisses me. "And so is this."

CHAPTER 24

I want to tell her everything. But "everything" is too close to the truth I can't tell her—that I've left her in the past, that I think Dr. Franklin's given up on helping me save her, that the school is under investigation, and it's all my fault.

Instead, I tell her that I've seen some videos that make it look as if we don't have powers. That the Doctor has said and done things that make me question whether or not he's really our friend.

"The Doctor's good," Sofía says immediately.

"I used to think so," I say, my voice trailing off.

She shakes her head. "We can't start doubting everyone. The Doctor's good."

"But—"

"It sounds as if someone is altering your perception of reality," Sofía continues. "Someone's making you question what's real and what's not. They're putting false images in your head. If that's the case, the first thing whoever's doing this is going to want is for people to turn away from the Doctor. Create chaos. Create doubt. Make us question not only reality, but each other."

I think of the videos I watched. I *know* none of that happened. I nod slowly, agreeing with her. But if the Doctor's not the one altering the videos, then who—

The officials. When they came, everything started falling apart. One of them—Dr. Rivers or Mr. Minh, or maybe both— they can alter the way we see things. The way we think, what we believe.

My mind churns with possibilities. Ryan was right to be suspicious. Dr. Rivers and Mr. Minh are trying to confirm our powers so they can use them. In my glimpses of the future in the timestream, I saw experiments and abuse: Gwen chained to a wall and Harold locked in a cell as men in lab coats tried to take them apart and see how they ticked. In those scenarios, I'd thought that the government officials were merely the spies who informed on us, but if they have powers too, like the ability to alter our perception of reality . . . then it'd be much easier to break down our resolve, to get us to turn on the Doctor and join them, to get us to do things for them.

"But Bo," Sofía says, her voice small. "That's not the only reason why you're here, is it?"

I look up at her, and all my questions fall away.

There's fear in her eyes. "You've never tried to visit me before, on your own. You could have just called me today, but instead, you're here."

"I'm here," I repeat, as much for my sake as hers.

"Is something wrong?"

I *want* to answer her. But I can feel time tugging at my

navel, pulling me back, forcing me into silence. "I'm sorry," I get out, just before time snaps me back to the present.

I grip the cloth of my duvet cover. She was right there. I can still smell her shampoo.

And now she's gone. Or, rather, I am. I left her in the past, not the other way around.

My phone buzzes, and I flip it over, reading the text message on the screen.

You throw that thing away? Ryan asks.

I look at my computer. The drive is still sticking out of the port.

Yeah, I text back.

I wonder how far his powers reach, if he can tell that I'm lying all the way from where he is.

I ask Dad to take me back to Berkshire early, and he agrees to drive up with me instead of going to church. After our fight yesterday, I think he's glad to get rid of me. Mom doesn't like it, but she doesn't protest that much.

"But Phoebe didn't get a chance to have a family dinner with you this weekend," she says in a petulant tone. "Let's wait until brunch."

"I have a lot of work to do," I say. "And we have next weekend."

What neither of us says is that Phoebe doesn't really care whether or not she has a meal with me. I mean, she's nice enough for a sister or whatever, but it's not like we're close. We just happen to live together and share the same blood type.

So Dad takes me up past Ipswich and back to school. As soon as the car stops in front of the brick facade of the academy,

I rush past the Doctor, who's waiting to greet me. I hesitate at the door when I notice that the Doc's continued down to the car to talk with Dad, but I don't have time to worry about their conversation.

The first thing I have to do is figure out a way to get rid of the government officials. For good. The problems began with them. At this point, I'm starting to wonder if *they're* the reason I haven't been able to control my powers well enough to save Sofía. I have to get rid of them. And to do that, I'll need help.

I go straight up to the dorm rooms on my unit's level and bang on Ryan's door.

"Told you it'd work," Ryan says, grinning. He steps back so I can enter his room.

"Yeah," I lie. The drive's perfectly safe, stuffed between my mattress and box spring back at home. "Listen," I add, "I watched the first video."

Ryan's usually good about keeping his cool, but something flashes across his face in the brief instant between when my words fall silent and he first registers their meaning. Something hard and angry. It's quickly replaced with a mask of calm, but he can't control the emotion in his eyes.

"You what?" he asks in a level voice that nevertheless sends chills up my spine. "I told you to get rid of it."

"It's safe. At my house. Hidden. No one will find it."

"No one would find it in a landfill near your house either."

I shrug. "I watched them. Or the first few, anyway. And we have big problems."

"We wouldn't have any problems if you'd destroyed the damn thing."

I shake my head. He's not listening. "Those government officials . . . they're powered too."

Ryan freezes. "What?"

"They have powers too, like we do. Or at least one of them does. I noticed it with Gwen, before. She thinks Sofía is dead. I had thought it was just that she'd lost faith in me, but now . . . And the Doctor's been acting strange. At first I thought he was in on it, but now I think the officials . . . they're altering reality. Or at least our perception of reality. They're making us think we don't have powers. I'm immune because I can just go back in time and see reality before they altered it."

Ryan narrows his eyes in thought. "And I'm immune because . . ." His voice trails off.

"It must be the nature of your power. Telekinesis and telepathy. You have superior control of your mind, so they can't reach you."

A grin smears across Ryan's face. "Yeah," he says, "that must be it."

"So just . . . be careful, yeah?" I say. "And start thinking of ways we can really get rid of them. Everyone believes they're from the government, and I don't know, maybe they are, but they're dangerous. They're trying to destroy us."

"Yeah," Ryan says. "I'm on it. And, dude, next weekend? Destroy that drive."

"Yeah, okay," I say, reaching for the door.

"Thanks," Ryan says. This is the nicest he's ever been to me. The most he's ever paid attention to me, honestly. We're not friends; we barely speak. But he's making such an effort now.

He really wants that drive gone.

Ryan shuts the door behind me after I leave, pushing against it so it clicks firmly closed. There are no locks on our doors—well, there are none that we can control. Dr. Franklin warned us that there are lockdown procedures in case one of the students' powers goes completely haywire, and we're safer locked in our rooms than anywhere else, but the lockdown has never happened while I've been here. Still, I have a feeling that Ryan wishes he could have locked me out as soon as I left. I hesitate, about to knock on his door again and demand some more answers, but I'm not even sure what to ask. There's just something . . . off about Ryan lately. He's not acting like himself.

Maybe the officials are starting to get to him too.

"Bo." Gwen's voice is quiet, like she doesn't want anyone else to hear, but she strides down the hallway toward me with purpose. "You're back."

I nod.

"And you're talking to Ryan."

I shrug. "Yeah?"

Gwen frowns. Before Sofía was gone, they were best friends, always together. I was never close with Ryan, and no one is really friends with Harold, so I sort of drifted around. Being with Sofía put me in Gwen's group, but I don't think she ever really considered me a friend.

"Listen," Gwen says, lowering her voice and walking with me back toward my room. "Don't put too much trust in Ryan, okay?"

"Why?" I ask. Ryan's not my favorite person in the world, but he's a part of our unit. Unlike the officials.

Gwen glances back at his room. "I don't like him," she says bluntly. "He's an asshole."

I snort. "Well, yeah, everyone knows that. But he's *our* asshole."

Gwen shakes her head. We're at my door now, but neither of us makes a move to leave. "It's not like that. He's not like us. You look at me and him and Harold as part of this unit. This team. But it's not like that, is it?"

"And Sofía too," I say, searching Gwen's eyes. "She's part of our unit as well."

"And Sofía too," Gwen says, her voice cracking over her name. "Before she *died*." She places gentle emphasis on that last word, clearly worried about my reaction to it. But after we talked in the foyer before the weekend started, I knew there was something wrong with her. And her words now confirm it. Whatever reality the officials are trying to weave around us, she's caught in the web.

"But Bo . . . it's not like that," Gwen continues. "We're *not* a team. At least Ryan's not. He only ever looks out for himself. He doesn't care about you or me or anyone here at Berkshire. He only cares about himself."

"You don't understand," I say. "He's trying to *save* the academy."

"Save it? From what?"

"The officials and whatever it is they're planning."

Gwen's frown deepens. "I don't know how to get this through to you," she says, "other than this: Sofía didn't like Ryan either."

I shrug. "Well, no one really likes Ryan."

"No," Gwen says in a very serious voice. "She *really* didn't like him."

I narrow my eyes, trying to understand what she's not say-ing. "Why not?"

"She had her reasons, and I'm not going to betray them even though she's not here now. But she didn't like him. She didn't trust him. And you shouldn't either."

CHAPTER 25

I go back to my room and shut the door.

Can't trust the Doctor. He's being manipulated by the government officials.

Can't trust my parents. They believe the Doc.

Can't trust Ryan. He may want to help me get rid of the officials, but Gwen's right: He's helping me because what I want lines up with what he wants. If that ever changes, Ryan wouldn't hesitate to drop me.

Can't trust anyone.

I call up the timestream, focusing on the swirling black hole where 1692 is. I can't go there and I can't pull Sofía out, but I'll get as close in time as I can, maybe reach Sofía that way.

I rub the back of my neck. These futile attempts to save my girlfriend are wearing me down, mentally and physically. I'm *exhausted*. But I can't give up.

I reach out, grabbing for the red string swirling into the vortex. It slides through my fingers like water, but I grab some other threads woven into the timestream that lead to a time close to where I left Sofía in the past. I hold on with all my might, gritting my teeth against the pain of their pull, refusing to let go. I steel myself for the fight, holding on to the threads of time with the same desperation as I'd hold on to a rope if I fell off a cliff, but then I feel it, the familiar tug in my body, the sweet release as time lets me slip through its cracks.

I am standing in a field.

No, not a field. There's grass, but the soil is sandy. I'm definitely still on the island. I whirl around. No academy. No remains of the camp for sick kids.

The house, however—the one built in Salem—is in front of me. The paint is bright white and new on the wooden siding, and the bricks of the chimney are not yet soot-stained.

I head toward it. The air is warm and the sun high in the sky, but even so, there's smoke rising from the chimney. Behind the dark glass windows, the house looks abandoned: no people and few pieces of furniture—a table and two chairs, one of which is knocked over, as if the residents had left quickly. But someone has to be here, or nearby. The fire in the hearth blazes like it was set just moments ago.

I whisper-shout for Sofía. No reply. Still, she could be close but invisible, hiding. Not from me, but from something or someone else.

The door to the house is slightly ajar, and I step inside, still calling her name.

Nothing.

She *has* to be here, somewhere. The threads of the timestream brought me to this moment and this time for a reason, and the threads connect me to her.

I step back out onto the porch. At the Berk, in my time, the boardwalk cuts through the marshy parts of the island, creating a nature preserve for birds and the old dudes who watch them.

In this time, there's nothing but dark water and shadows. The perfect place to hide.

I leave the house, aiming for the swampy wilderness. The island is vast, so I could search all day and not cover it all. Which is weird, since in my time, the island feels tiny. Nothing to do. Nowhere to go, really. But when you add it all up, it *is* actually large.

Large enough to hide a girl with powers from the future.

The ground grows mushy as I approach the swampy water. It isn't deep—only knee-high in most places, to my waist at worst—but there's something truly icky about the way the cold, silty water squishes between my toes. No point in shoes here.

She has to be here.

Maybe she went to the lighthouse? Was it even built by this point? Or maybe it's just an empty beach, like the southern part of the island where one day Berkshire will be. Either way, I don't have many options. I have to pick a direction, so I start heading northeast, toward the lighthouse . . . or where the lighthouse will one day be.

The silence of the marsh is weird and unsettling. I can see little fish swimming in the water around my legs, darting away as I slosh forward. In my time, the marsh is murky. But here, the water is clearer, the sky is wider. A bluebird cuts through the air, a bright flash of color that reminds me of Sofía's house.

I hear people.

I drop down, squatting behind a clump of reeds, crouching so low that the water's up to my neck. The people I heard were on horseback, and they stop not too far from me. The horses flick greenhead flies away with their tails and snort so loud that I'm sure the men can't hear me breathing.

"Nineteen," one of them says.

"For truth?"

"In Salem." The first man sounds a little older. "Nineteen."

"Madness."

I strain to hear more. The men's voices are loud and deep but heavily accented, their words almost indiscernible.

"How many in the prisons?" the younger man says.

My mouth drops open as it finally dawns on me what the first man means. Nineteen. Nineteen witches. Nineteen *people*. Hanged. Crushed. Dead.

They move again, heading away from where I'm hiding.

I stand up. The men could turn around and see me, but I rise anyway. They know what's going on. They might know if Sofía is among those taken.

"Fifty or more," the old man says.

I start running toward the men, not caring about the noise I'm making.

"The dark one will be next to hang, surely," the first man adds.

"Of the devil, no doubt."

I shout for the men to stop, and they do pull their horses up short. Water sprays all around me as I surge forward. But as hard as I'm running—and I'm straining every muscle, my body aching to move forward—I barely shift an inch. The water droplets hang impossibly in the air around me.

Time snaps me back to Berkshire.

CHAPTER 26

Damn it.

I ended up right back here.

Not in my nice warm bedroom.

Nope, in the marsh. Without my shoes.

At least I'm close to the boardwalk. I pull myself up and begin the soaking wet walk of shame back to Berkshire, praying that no one will see me when I return.

Nope again.

Dr. Franklin's there, waiting for me. He has a flashlight and a radio in his hand, and there are a few other staff members in the main entryway. They were about to go look for me.

Great.

"What were you doing?!" Dr. Franklin shouts as the other staff members scurry back to their own units. "Where are your shoes?" His face sort of crumbles as I try to think of an answer. "This is about Sofía, isn't it?" he asks in a softer tone.

I nod, hoping that he can understand what I really

mean—that this was about saving her. How much of her and the reality of her situation have the officials erased from his mind? How much control of his own memories—of his own reality—has the Doc already lost?

"Go get changed," he says, "and meet me back in my office."

I need a shower, but the Doc didn't seem in the mood to be kept waiting, so I pull on some dirty clothes and head over to his office. The door is already open. Inside, I can hear low-pitched angry voices.

First I hear Dr. Rivers, but I can't make out what she's saying.

Then Mr. Minh starts talking. "I must say, we're very disappointed here, Dr. Franklin. Very disappointed. Your school may be private, but it still must follow Massachusetts law—"

"We're not breaking any laws!" the Doctor protests, his voice drowning out Mr. Minh's. "Sofía's accident was never supposed to happen, and I've been fully cooperative with law enforcement since then!"

I cringe. So the government officials have the Doctor so turned around that he's brought in law enforcement?

"Well, of course something like that isn't *planned*," Mr. Minh's voice is harsh, cruel. "But regardless, it *happened*, and we're trying to ensure it doesn't happen again. Which, frankly, I'm not sure this school is capable of guaranteeing. I was shocked to see one of *your* students coming into the school late tonight. How tight of a rein do you have on your students if one can wander off into the *marsh* at night?"

Well, crap. I didn't realize they'd seen me too.

The Doctor splutters, but Dr. Rivers cuts him off. "It's just extraordinarily disappointing that not only were the master files of the video observations you compiled destroyed, but the additional files are missing, and there is apparently no way to replace them."

"What are you trying so hard to hide, Dr. Franklin?" Mr. Minh shouts. "This level of encumbrance from you makes me question just how much you want to reveal to us at all."

"My practices have been transparent from the start!" the Doctor shouts back. "And my students are the most important people to me—not you and your damn paperwork!"

"That's what we want to see," Dr. Rivers says in a clear, high voice, silencing the men's argument. "We want you to put your students first. But clearly something here at Berkshire Academy is wrong. That boy came back soaking wet and stinking of the marsh. Why was he allowed outside, alone, at this hour? He could have been a danger to himself or others."

Is this an allusion to my powers? If so, the Doctor misses it.

Mr. Minh says something indecipherable in a low voice, but whatever it is, it's obvious from Dr. Franklin's flustered tone that he's offended.

I push the door open further. The hinges squeak, cutting through the conversation.

"Bo," the Doctor says, relieved to see me.

"You told me to come back for a late-night, uh . . ." I start.

"Therapy session," the Doctor supplies. "I didn't want to wait until tomorrow morning to discuss this situation."

Dr. Rivers nods her head, clearly approving of this, but Mr. Minh still scowls. I stare him down as he sidesteps me and they both leave the office.

"That sounded rough," I say.

Dr. Franklin collapses behind his desk, completely ignoring

my comment. "I'm concerned that you're not progressing," he says bluntly.

"I—I'm trying, sir," I say. I stare into his eyes.

I'm trying to save us all, I want to say.

Sofía told me to trust the Doctor. I don't understand why he's been cooperating with the officials, but . . .

"You have a Band-Aid," I say, staring at the Doc's hand.

He blinks in surprise, then glances down, staring at the Band-Aid wrapped around his left index finger. "I cut myself when I was changing my razor blade," he says. "Bo, we need to talk about Sofía, about how you've stagnated since her death."

That word—*death*—guts me. First it came from Gwen, and now the Doc's acting like Sofía is really gone. But his words sound like buzzing in my head, and all my eyes can focus on is that Band-Aid.

The Doctor can *heal*. His power is *healing*. There is *nothing* in the world that should hurt him enough for him to need a Band-Aid. A razor cut? That should be gone in two seconds. I've *seen* him recover from injuries far more serious than that.

"Bo?" the Doctor says. "Are you listening?"

A test. I'll test him.

I tell him a joke he told me a month or two ago. He laughs politely, like he's never heard that joke before in his life.

"Remember when I told you about my pet turtle, Shelly?" I ask. "How my dad accidentally killed him but lied to me about it?" I never told him I had a pet turtle because I never did; I got that from an old sitcom I used to watch at home. But Dr. Franklin nods along as if he knows exactly what I'm talking about.

"But let's talk about Sofía now," the Doctor says. "I worry that you blame yourself, and you shouldn't . . ."

He keeps going on, blah, blah, blah, but it's pointless. This isn't the Doctor we all know. This Doctor can't heal—doesn't know he can heal. This Doctor is treating me like he's a school counselor, not like an advisor in a school of superpowered kids.

This Doctor has forgotten the way things really are.

Ryan and I really are the only ones left who know the truth.

"I know you don't fully understand what I'm saying now," I tell Dr. Franklin, looking him dead in the eye. "But I want you to know that I haven't given up. Not yet. Not ever."

The Doctor sighs and sinks into the chair behind his desk. "Is this about Sofía?"

"I can save her," I say, praying that my words penetrate the fog of illusion that's clouding the Doctor's mind. "I can save us all."

"Bo," Dr. Franklin says, leaning forward, tears making his eyes watery. "Bo, she's dead. Sofía is dead. You can't save her. It's over."

All around me, the world stills. The Doctor becomes a motionless statue. The clouds moving in front of the moon freeze. The clock on the Doctor's desk stops ticking. His words cut me so deeply that I have accidentally stopped time.

I blink, and the clock starts ticking again. But my heart is calm. Even though Dr. Franklin's not aware of what I've just done, *I* am, and I know that my powers are still real.

I still have a chance.

"I *can* save her," I say again.

"No," he says in a gentle voice. "You can't."

CHAPTER 27

I leave Dr. Franklin's office and walk slowly back to my room. The Doc watches me go, as if he suspects I'll get lost along the way.

I pause by my door, looking back at him. All up and down the hallway, doors are closed. On the left side of the hall, the heavy wooden doors to the library are locked for the night, as are those to the common room and our classrooms. On the right side of the hall are the dormitory rooms. Harold's, then mine, then Ryan's, Gwen's, and Sofía's.

And by each of their doors, there's a keypad.

There's one by mine too.

They've never been there before. I look closer. The keypad is made of metal, but there are dings and nicks in it, and it's slightly worn from use.

"Is there a problem?" Dr. Franklin asks.

I jump; he'd moved silently down the hall, and he's waiting for me to go into my room. "How long has that been there?" I ask.

"It's always been there," the Doctor says. "Bo, it's well past lights-out."

"But—"

"Bo."

I step inside my room, and Dr. Franklin closes the door behind me. I listen as the Doctor punches in a code, and I can hear the heavy metallic thud of a lock clicking in place.

Lights-out is literal—our overhead lights don't work from midnight to seven in the morning. But I don't go to bed. Instead, I cross the room to the window, where moonlight filters through my thin curtains. I sweep them aside, hoping to catch a glimpse of the ruins by the marsh, hoping that will give me some inspiration for what to do to next to save Sofía.

But my gaze outside is marred by iron bars on the window.

I try to get a closer look at the bars, but the window is sealed shut. I strain against it, but it's utterly immovable. I grab my cell phone and use its flashlight to illuminate the bars. They're painted black, but there are cracks of rust in them, tiny slivers of red leaking through the edges.

These bars have been here for a while.

But at the same time, they've never been here before. The locks on the doors, the bars over the windows . . . none of this was here before I went home this weekend.

I turn my cell phone off, letting the darkness wash over the room. For just a moment, I see a glint of something—fire, maybe, or just sparks—in the distance, near the edge of the marsh, near the ruins where I lost Sofía.

But I blink, and it's gone.

I move to the bed and sit cross-legged in the center.

The video from the USB drive plays through my mind. It wasn't real, I *know* that, but it seemed real.

And this does too. The iron bars and the locked doors. It's ironic; I just came back from a house where I wasn't even allowed to *have* a door, and now I'm in a room trapped behind one.

I jump up from the bed and test the door now. It doesn't budge.

We never used to have locks . . . I think, but then another thought: *Yes, we did. We always did.*

There have always been locks on the doors, iron bars on the windows.

No, there haven't.

I don't know what's real anymore.

Except . . . Sofía. She's real. I may only ever be able to see her in the past, but I still know that she's real. I can still taste her kiss on my lips, reminding me of truth.

I grab my calendar from the desk and use my cell phone to illuminate its pages, picking a weekend when Sofía was at Berkshire and I was home. I blindly reach into the timestream, grabbing the strings of that date and practically throwing myself into the past, before everything went pear-shaped. When I open my eyes, I'm in my bedroom, but my calendar confirms that it's March 15.

I burst out of my room. It's not yet time for lights-out, so I head straight to the common room. But first I check my door behind me.

No keypad. No locks. No iron bars on the window.

Ryan and Harold are still around here somewhere, and

there's a chance I could run into the Doctor or someone else on staff, but I'm too excited to be careful.

I throw open the door of the common room.

"Bo?" Sofía asks when she turns around.

I almost lose it right there.

"Sofía." I breathe her name.

"I thought you left already."

"I decided to stay here instead," I say. "I'd rather be here." *With you.*

She smiles. "I was about to watch a movie, but would you rather—"

I stop her. "A movie would be great." I want a normal date. I just want to remember that she's real. I don't need more than that.

The movies in the common room aren't that great—about a dozen crappy DVDs and Blu-rays that are a decade or more old, most of them for little kids. Ryan has a few newer movies that he brought with him from home, but he doesn't share. We can only watch them when he feels like it.

"How about this one?" Sofía asks, holding up *Titanic*.

I laugh. "That was my sister's favorite movie when she was a kid."

"Too girly?" Sofía starts to put the DVD back on the console.

"It's fine," I say.

I drag two beanbag chairs in front of the television while Sofía loads up the ancient player with the disc. She plops down on the red beanbag beside me, leaning into my shoulder. Her head finds that perfect place on my chest, where my arm and body meet, and she snuggles in, and I'm in absolute heaven.

I watch her more than I watch the movie.

I guess when someone's gone from your life for a while, all you think about are the big things. The big regrets, the could-have, should-haves. Or the big moments, the memories that are going to be with you forever, those life-changing moments, like first kisses and first confessions and first trusts. And you think about the lasts too: the last kiss, the last words, the last moments.

But the firsts and lasts and the big highlights between aren't a life. They aren't a person. They aren't what you love. When you fall in love, you don't fall in love with the first kiss, you fall in love with every kiss after that. The big moments are great, and it's obvious why you remember them, but it's the little things that make a person real: the smell of her hair, the warmth of her head resting on my shoulder, the way her ear curves, how her legs curl under her when she's relaxed, the little gasps and mutterings she makes when she's so focused on a movie she forgets that she's making sounds. The big moments are just photographs in your head; the little things *are* the memories.

Tomorrow, when this moment is gone, I'm still going to try to hold on to this feeling for as long as I can. I'm going to try to feel her head resting on my shoulder. I breathe deeply, memorizing her scent. This is what I want to remember.

But I know that these will be the first memories to fade, the way they always do. The little things fade, leaving me only with broad sketches that aren't real at all. I'll be left with the idea of Sofía, not the reality.

And that will never be enough.

CHAPTER 28

Even though I last saw this movie when I was ten and Phoebe forced me to watch it with her on her birthday, I still remember most of the story: guy, girl, forbidden love, ship sinks. It's all more than a little predictable, but I still pull Sofía closer to me as Rose tells Jack she'll never let him go.

"It just sucks so much for her," Sofía says, and I keep myself from laughing at her glistening eyes.

"For *her*? He's the one who dies."

Sofía shakes her head. "I think death is easier than guilt sometimes." The movie's not over, but she leans up on the beanbag, away from me. "You're not really here, are you?"

I cock my head. "What do you mean?"

"I saw you leave with your dad earlier. You were wearing different clothes. Your hair is a little longer now than it was just a few hours ago." She grins lopsidedly. "You're out of time, aren't you?"

I kiss her nose. "Yeah. I'm from the fuuuuture." I waggle my fingers at her, and she giggles.

But then her face sobers. "That's twice now," she says. "At least twice." When I don't answer her, she adds, "Christmas too. You came to see me then. And now you're here. There's no reason for you to come back in time just to watch a stupid movie with me. Something's wrong."

You're stuck in the past, and I'm starting to lose track of what's real and what's not because there are some shady government officials at the Berk who may be playing with my perception of reality, and I don't know how to save you, much less the rest of the school.

"Everything's fine," I say.

Sofía frowns. "It's not. Just tell me. Maybe I can help."

Time doesn't work that way. My intent matters. If I tell Sofía too much, I'll get snapped back to the present.

"I just came back to see you." As soon as I say the words, I know they are the wrong ones.

"Me? What happened to me?"

"Nothing, nothing," I say, throwing up my hands. "I just . . . I'm still trying to figure out my powers, and I ended up here, and I thought, why not chill for a little?"

Sofía cocks an eyebrow, but she drops the subject. "So how are things going with your powers?" she asks.

I shrug. "Still learning."

"You can stay put longer," she says. "It's been more than two hours, and you're still here."

I wish I could stay here forever, but I know I can't. Lights-out is only a couple of hours away, and every second with Sofía is stolen from a past I don't really have a right to claim.

"Have you ever jumped to another point in the past from the past?" Sofía asks as the credits begin to roll. She turns the volume down.

"What do you mean?"

"Like, could you take me from here to the Titanic? The ship, I mean."

"I . . . I don't see why I couldn't," I say. Usually when I'm in another time, I start to feel the pull of my own timeline, like a rubber band tugging to bring me back home. But I don't feel that here. Sofía's more my home than any point in time. With her, I could go anywhere.

A wicked grin smears across her face. "Let's do it, then," she says. "Let's go to the ship. Just for a second. Let's see what it's like."

"I think we'd stick out a bit," I say, looking down at my T-shirt and jeans.

"I'll make us invisible," Sofía responds. "I don't care if they can see us, I just want to see the ship."

I nod. "Give me a second," I say, closing my eyes and focusing on the timestream.

I've tried to go to the Titanic before. Phoebe used to make me play with her while I pushed her on the tire swing and she screamed out that she was king of the world. I didn't get my powers until high school, but I remembered playing pretend with her so vividly that it felt real. So of course one of the first places I tried to go after I got my powers was to the ship. I had gone with the intention of warning people about the icebergs, though, so time pulled me back. I was blocked from there, never able to return.

But my intentions are different now. I just want to see the

ship, to stand on the deck and see the stars over the frigid sea and maybe spot the iceberg but say nothing. I know now that this is a moment in time that cannot be changed.

I scan the timestream, looking for the moment in April 1912 when the vast ship disappeared in a sea that was far vaster than it.

"Ready?" I say, reaching blindly for Sofía's hand.

Sofía's fingers slip through mine, and she grips me tightly. "Ready," she whispers.

I glance at her and watch the timestream wrap around her the way it does me. The strings move like ripples in water, easily gliding over her body. It's clear she can't see what I can, but I wonder if she feels the threads of her own present and future and past wrapping around her, if she can feel the red thread that connects us together, or the way it cuts off abruptly in 1692.

She turns and smiles at me.

I squeeze her hand and reach out with my other one for the dark spot in the timestream indicating the night the Titanic sank. The strings are so cold they burn my skin, but I don't let go, feeling the familiar tug at my navel as I'm pulled into the past.

At first I see only darkness and pinpricks of lights—*stars*, I think, but no, it's more than that, it's the lights of the ship, glittering in the lonely sea. Sofía's grip on my hand tightens as the sound of the hull slicing through the waves fills our ears and the wooden boards of the ship's deck solidify under our feet.

As soon as the cold air hits our skin, Sofía turns us both invisible. I hadn't realized that her powers had grown so much stronger—it's not like we talked about our powers on dates— but it gives me some comfort to know that she probably has the strength to stay hidden and safe in Salem.

I feel her body scoot closer to mine. I want to let go of her hand so that I can wrap my arm around her shoulders, but I settle with dropping my chin on the top of her head.

"It's freezing out here!" she whispers.

"That's the only thing you can think of?" I ask, smiling. I pull her across the smooth wooden deck of the ship, turning her around so that, rather than the dark waves of the ocean, Sofía can see the lit-up, glorious ship we're on. She gasps, and I can feel her head tilting back, leaning as far as she can to drink in the exterior of the ship.

"It's gorgeous," she breathes.

"Come on," I say, pulling her to the railing.

With the bright lights behind us, we can see the endless sky and stars. There are few people out here this late at night, just some well-dressed men talking in low voices and a few workers. I reach out for the timestream and feel that it's close to midnight.

Close to the moment we'll hit the iceberg.

Sofía's twisted around, holding my hand awkwardly to keep us invisible, her back to the railing and her eyes still on the enormous ship. But I face the other way, squinting into the dark, trying to find the iceberg. The sky is moonless, and I can see nothing but the sparkle of stars and reflected lights from the ship on the waves immediately in front of us. A bell rings, and the ship changes course, enough to make us lose our footing. Sofía's hand clutches mine in a death grip.

The men who'd been talking stand up, shake each other's hands, and then walk together away from the deck, toward the cabins. As soon as they're out of sight, Sofía lets go of my hand.

"Someone could see," I say as we both become visible again.

"Anyone who sees us now won't be able to tell," Sofía replies.

It takes a moment for her words to sink in. Anyone who sees us now would be a worker, someone low on the totem pole, someone who wouldn't merit a spot in the lifeboats.

In the distance, we can still hear signs of life—voices carrying over the still night air, children laughing and running on the promenade—but we're alone on the deck, entirely alone with the stars and the smell of wood oil and the cold, crisp air.

Sofía rubs her hands up and down her arms. "I knew it would be cold," she says, "but this is ridiculous."

"Want to go inside?" I ask. Invisible, we could slip into the beautiful rooms, stare at the opulence that's about to sink into oblivion.

She shakes her head. "I thought I wanted to see it all, but those men . . . I don't want to see any people," she says.

I pull her close and wrap my arms around her. "Want to go?" I ask, already bringing up the timestream.

The sound of children playing and running grows louder, and Sofía's distracted, turning out of my embrace. "Why are there children out here this late at night?" she asks.

"They're coming this way," I say, grabbing her arm. "Quick—"

Without another word, she washes us both in invisibility. I can hear the children's voices better now—a girl and a boy—and they're coming closer. There are other sounds—shouting from adults, a bell ringing—

And then the ship slams into the iceberg.

CHAPTER 29

The impact is near the side of the ship, violent enough to make Sofía lose her footing, but I still have a hold on her and keep her from crashing to the deck. Ice skitters across the smooth deck, and Sofía bends down to touch it, her fingers glazing over the cold surface. The nearby children scream, and I can feel a surge of power like static electricity pulse from Sofía's hand into mine, maintaining our invisibility.

"This is it," she says.

A chunk of ice slams across the deck where we are, almost hitting us, and I jerk Sofía back. The kids we'd been hearing race forward, using the ice as a soccer ball. "Look!" the little girl says. "Look at me!" She rears back to kick the ice again but slips, slamming first into the metal rail and then onto the hard wooden deck.

"Pheebs!" the boy shouts, running over to her.

No. No. No. That's impossible.

"They look . . . modern," Sofía whispers to me.

The girl is crying, clutching her arm. The boy drops to his knees in front of her, grabs her good hand—

And they disappear.

The shock of it snaps inside me like the timestream pulling me back. It's violent and harsh and painful, and I'm so glad I already have Sofía wrapped up in my arms. When we open our eyes, we're on the floor of the common room, breathing deeply, the world spinning around us.

"What just happened?" Sofía says, still wheezing and trying to catch her breath.

"That was me."

"What?" she gasps. Her eyes are wild, and I wonder if she feels the pain of being snapped back into the normal time as much as I do. I'm just glad time brought me back here, with her in the past, rather than throwing me all the way back to my own present.

"That was me," I repeat. "That kid. The girl is—was—is my sister, Phoebe."

"What? How?"

I stand up. I want to pace, but the world is still spinning too much for me to try that. "That was me," I say once more. "Phoebe was really into the *Titanic*. We'd play outside and pretend to be on the ship, but I didn't realize I *actually* took her there. But I did. I must have had my powers when I was younger and just . . . didn't realize it? I must have blocked it out? I thought we were pretending . . ."

"That's some good imagination."

"Did that ever happen to you?" I ask. "Did you have your powers when you were little too?"

"I was always *very* good at hide-and-seek."

I run my fingers through my hair. I don't remember this happening, but at the same time, I *do*.

The lights in the common room flicker.

"It's time to go," Sofía says, and the way she looks at me makes me realize she isn't just talking about lights-out. It's time for me to leave, to go back to my own time. The time without her.

She stands up and walks over to me, wrapping her arms around my waist and burying her face in my chest.

"Something bad happened, didn't it?" she whispers.

I nod, unable to speak.

She leans up on her tiptoes and kisses me on the lips. Not anything passionate, but a sort of sad, slight pressure on my lips that's gone too quickly.

"If I could control reality, this would be my life all the time. One magical moment with you after another," she says, leaning into me.

"Me too," I say, my voice cracking.

"Whatever happened, this was worth it," Sofía says. "And remember what I said before."

The lights flicker again. Last warning.

"What you said before?" I ask.

She kisses me again, quicker this time, already twirling away from me, toward the door. I blink, and I see the threads of time weaving in and out, and I can feel the tether pulling me back to my own timeline, away from here, now, her.

She doesn't look back as she leaves me behind, alone, as time swallows me up and deposits me where I started.

CHAPTER 30

Phoebe

I try not to look too hard at myself in the mirror. I never really figured out makeup, and I feel most at home in T-shirts and jeans, but I like to look nice. *Put together*, my grandmother would call it, although she wouldn't say it about me now. Put together to Grandma was a button-down blouse and a skirt, not a navy blue T-shirt with an elephant on the front and jeans that are ragged at the bottom because my short legs have walked the hem off.

There was always something wrong with me, at least in Grandma's eyes. It's not like she hated me. But I would sit with my legs too sprawled, or I talked too much, or my hair was too short. Always something little, some point of contention that proved I wasn't good enough.

Bo, on the other hand, was her golden child. "He needs more love," she'd say, as if an extra hug and piles of compliments would make him better. Maybe they did. He was always happy around her.

I turn away from the mirror and open my jewelry box. It's ancient, something I've had forever, made of heavy, paper-covered cardboard in shades of pink and purple. And even though it's worthless, this box contains all my greatest treasures. When I open it, a little plastic ballerina spins halfheartedly. It's supposed to play music too, but it's long since lost its song.

At the bottom of the box, underneath the little silver ring my first boyfriend gave me and the monogrammed necklace I got for my sweet sixteen, is a blue velvet box. The hinges creak when I open it. I remove the folded-up paper that's on the top without reading it. I know what it says. *Given to me by Joseph on our wedding day*. Grandma started doing that a year or two before she died, writing down the reason why the things she still had were significant. When she passed away, Mom and I went through her house, and we kept finding little notes like this. Some of them referenced people we didn't know—*Bought this when I went with Lauren to Connecticut*—and some of them told us of a past we hadn't known she'd lived—*Mother gave me this when I broke my wrist, 1962*. I loved discovering the hidden secrets behind the objects I had thought were junk. A paper fan was a souvenir from her brother when he went to Hawaii; a cheap plastic beaded necklace was the first thing I had ever given her, curled up beside her gold and diamonds. Mom, however, quickly grew tired of the little notes and eventually started throwing away things without reading them.

"They make you hang on to a past that isn't yours," she said, pointing to the pile of Grandma's things that I'd squirreled away.

Grandma had given me the little blue box before she died, even though she'd already labeled it for after her death. I was in middle school, staying overnight at her house, and I was furious. My parents were taking Bo to a special concert in the city as a reward for passing all his classes at the end of eighth grade. Not acing—passing. Here I was with near-perfect scores, and I didn't get a concert.

"Your brother worked harder than you," Grandma told me as we watched old episodes of *Law & Order* on her crappy TV.

"I still did better than him," I said sullenly.

"It's not about that," Grandma said, shaking her head. "I'm going to give you something." She left the living room, and I could hear her rooting around in her dresser all the way through the commercial break before she came back, the blue velvet box in her hand. She placed it in my palm, then sat down on the couch beside me, watching as I lifted the lid.

The diamond earrings inside sparkled.

"I want you to have these," Grandma said.

"For my report card?" I lifted the box closer to my face, imagining the diamonds glittering in my ears.

"No," Grandma said. I looked up at her. "I want you to have these because everyone should have something that makes them feel special."

The memory makes me smile, and on a whim, I pluck the earrings from the satiny card that holds them and put them on. They're large, and they sparkle like ice crystals when I turn my head. I sweep my hair up into a ponytail to make sure their glitter isn't hidden.

Sometimes, growing up with Bo, I feel like I'm invisible. How can my family notice me when they have to spend all their time watching him? These earrings remind me that I'm more than a shadow.

When I get downstairs, Mom already has a bowl and a box of cereal waiting for me.

"What're you wearing?" she asks.

I look down at the white elephant printed on my shirt, not understanding her meaning.

"Are those your grandmother's earrings?" There's a hint of accusation in her voice.

I nod.

"Phoebe," she says, leveling me with a look, "those are for special occasions only."

"They don't have to be," I say.

She purses her lips at me.

"They're *mine*," I say.

"Go." She points up the stairs.

There's no point arguing. I trudge upstairs, taking the earrings out and leaving them in the blue velvet box in my room.

Mom has been strict about the "special occasion" rule since Grandma gave the earrings to me. The only time I've ever worn them was at her funeral.

CHAPTER 31

The government officials are sitting in Dr. Franklin's office, waiting for us during our morning session. Dr. Rivers has a notepad and pen in her hands; Mr. Minh has an audio recorder.

My eyes shoot to Ryan, who's already sitting on one of the blue plastic chairs arranged in a semicircle around Dr. Franklin's desk. He scowls straight ahead, ignoring me.

"I'm sorry, kids," the Doctor says, "but the officials from the state are going to be listening in on today's session. Please try to pretend they're not here."

That won't be hard. It's as if everyone's forgotten they have powers anyway, except for Ryan, and he won't slip up in front of *them*.

I sit down next to Ryan, and Gwen takes the seat beside me. She's more reserved than usual, and I think it's because the officials' presence has reminded us all that they're here because Sofía's not.

"Today," the Doctor says, "I want to talk about family."

"Great," Ryan mutters.

Dr. Rivers starts writing.

I think of the videos Ryan stole. They've all been altered, but they showed something very similar to what's happening here.

"It's not real," I mutter, closing my eyes and remembering Sofía.

"Our families influence us," the Doctor continues. "They are a part of who we are, whether we like it or not. In what ways have your families influenced you?"

Harold says something none of the rest of us can hear.

"Yes, Harold?" Dr. Franklin asks, moving closer to him. I really hope that whatever Harold said was relevant and not his regular stuff. The officials look like vultures, lurking behind the desk, waiting for us to screw up.

"I'm adopted," Harold says, a little louder.

"Family doesn't require blood, right?" the Doctor asks. "Your dads love you. And I'm sure your biological parents have some influence on you, even if you don't remember them."

"For example," Ryan says, "maybe they're where your crazy comes from."

The Doc glares at Ryan.

"I remember them," Harold says, his voice softer now.

"What do you remember about them?" the Doctor asks.

Harold shrugs.

"This is a safe place," Dr. Franklin adds.

Harold's eyes slide over to the officials, and he says nothing.

"What about someone else? In what ways have your

families influenced you?" The Doctor scans the room. "It's not just about parents. What about siblings?" His eyes rest on me. "What about your sister, Bo? Siblings are often reflections of each other. Maybe you're so quiet because she's boisterous at home?" He says this in a jovial tone, as if we have some sort of inside joke together. But he couldn't be more wrong. Phoebe, *boisterous*? Hardly. Phoebe's emotions are measured out carefully, like Mom when she's measuring flour for a recipe, scraping off the top of the fluffy white powder to have exactly the right amount in the cup.

The Doctor tries again. "Or has she influenced your life in some way?"

"She hasn't," I say.

"Oh, I find that hard to believe." The Doctor moves across the circle toward me. "Growing up, I had a younger brother. I think in a lot of ways, siblings help define each other. My brother was good at sports, so I focused on academics. I may not have become a doctor if it hadn't been for him."

Sure, there are differences between Phoebe and me. That's about all there is between us.

"Do you think there's some aspect of your sister that is a reflection of you? Maybe something she does helps you define yourself, maybe the way she sees the world has helped define reality for you."

I sit up straighter at that. Whether he meant to or not, Dr. Franklin actually gave me an idea. Last night, I saw her there. I saw her on the Titanic with me, as kids. She was there. She's my proof.

"Yeah, I guess," I say so that the Doctor looks away from me and focuses on Gwen instead. I watch the government officials as I lean back and surreptitiously pull out my cell phone, scrolling through my contacts until I find Pheebs's number.

Hey, I text her.

The little waiting icon flashes, and it feels like forever until she texts me back. **Bo?**

Yeah. I glance around me. The Doctor frowns at my cell phone and shakes his head slightly, reprimanding me. I pretend to put it away, but thankfully Harold starts rambling about how he misses his little sister, and the Doc's attention shifts.

Gotta ask u smthg, I text quickly.

What?

I do another quick scan of the room; all eyes are on Harold.

Remember when we were kids? I text. **Remember the Titanic?**

I watch the waiting icon on my screen, not daring to breathe. If Phoebe remembers going back to the Titanic with me, she'll confirm everything: my powers, the true purpose of Berkshire, the altered videos.

Yeah, she texts back, **ofc.**

Of course. Of course she remembers.

That's how I broke my arm, she adds, the words popping up on the screen. **But it was cool.**

I breathe a sigh of relief. *It was real.* Whatever—whoever— is altering everyone's perception of reality . . . it's centered here, at the academy.

When I look up from my phone, the room is silent. Harold's rambling had stopped without my noticing, and the government officials' eyes are glued on me. Dr. Rivers glares at me, and I shudder under her intense look.

"Bo, put away your phone," the Doctor says. "You know better."

I start to click the screen off, but I can't get over the weird way Dr. Rivers is staring at me. Just before my phone darkens, I glance down at the message. Phoebe's words, *But it was cool*, fade. I blink. Before my eyes, they change: *But it was just a game*.

"No," I gasp, staring down at the altered text.

"Bo," Dr. Franklin says again, a note of warning in his voice. "Your phone."

Dr. Rivers is still staring at me, her eyes dark and unfocused. When I shove my phone in my pocket, I can't help but notice the way she smirks at me.

I yank out my cell phone the second the Doctor dismisses us. I stare at that last word from Phoebe, *game*. Is it my cell phone that's showing me a false message, or did Phoebe change somehow? If I were to go to her right now, would she remember the Titanic, or would she think we were playing pretend?

"I'm glad to see you've recovered after your late-night wanderings," Dr. Rivers says, stepping beside me.

I cram my phone back in my pocket. "What are you doing?" I growl.

"Mr. Minh and I will be observing your classes today," she says sweetly, holding the classroom door open for the rest of the unit and me. Her eyes mock me; she knows very well what I meant.

The officials sit in the back of the classroom as Ms. Okafor teaches us math. They watch silently as Mr. Ingle passes out copies of *The Catcher in the Rye* for us to read. My eyes skim across the page.

I glance over at Gwen. She's already on chapter two of the book. I turn the page, even though I have no idea what's written on it.

My phone weighs heavily in my pocket. I hate the idea of the officials doing something to mess with Phoebe's head. I hope it was just the text that changed and not her. I never wanted to drag my family into this.

CHAPTER 32

The next morning, the officials are in Dr. Franklin's office with the door closed. Even though it's time for our session to start, we're stuck in the hallway, waiting.

"How much longer are they going to be here?" Ryan asks.

"Why don't they just go?" My voice holds more anger than I'd intended, but I don't really care.

Ryan shrugs. "They have no evidence, no videos, and no one's said anything. Sofía's dead, mystery solved, go home."

My stomach aches at how easily Ryan mentions Sofía's death, even though I know he knows it's not real. But he's right. There's no reason why the officials should still be here, not if their only purpose is to investigate the death of a student.

But if they have ulterior motives . . .

Harold steps closer, so silently that Ryan jumps when he starts talking.

"I don't like them," Harold whispers, his eyes flicking to the door where the officials entered Dr. Franklin's office.

"No one does," I say.

"They sneak, and they pry, and they're trying to drive us apart."

I think Harold's on to something, actually. There's coldness in the air now that has nothing to do with the weather. This unit used to be a family, and now no one talks. The Doctor is distant. We all just shuffle from room to room, waiting for the officials to leave so that life can return to normal.

"I don't like them at all," Harold continues. "They're trying to take you away from me."

And that's when I realize that Harold isn't talking to us at all. He's talking to his ghosts.

"Still no Sofía in the ghost world?" I ask in a low voice, my heart skipping a beat.

Harold turns to me, his clear, pale eyes eerily wide. "There is no Sofía. Nothing. Just a blank space where she once was."

I breathe again. Harold can see the dead, but not the past.

Ryan rolls his eyes at Harold. "*Anyway*," he says, turning back to me, "they need to go, like, yesterday. They've been here almost a month."

"Dude, it's only been a little over a week."

Ryan gives me a weird look. "Okay, whatever, time-man."

"No, but seriously. A week and some days. Not a month."

"You may want to check your math on that."

I turn on my heels.

"Dr. Franklin's going to start our session soon!" Gwen calls as I stride back toward my room.

I don't care. Ryan's a jerk, but I don't think he'd play me like that. By my count, the officials have been here just thirteen days. But Ryan looked at me like I was clueless.

I travel *through* time. I don't lose it.

I slam open my bedroom door and head straight to my calendar. I stare at the date.

It's been a month.

How the hell did I lose a month?

Did the officials do this? Dr. Rivers could tell that her regular mind games weren't working on me. Did she find a way to make me lose time?

I shake my head. Ryan's just being a jerk. He's playing a joke. He must have snuck in my room and altered my calendar. I flip through the pages, but each is marked with my special code.

Gwen shows up at my door. "Dr. Franklin told me to get you. Session's starting."

I follow her, but my mind's focused on my lost time. This has to be a joke. Ryan's messing with me.

"Hey," Gwen says as she leads me down the hall. "Maybe try not to be too crazy. In front of the officials, I mean. I think they're going to go soon. I don't want to give them an excuse to stick around."

I nod my head tightly. So don't blow up at Ryan for messing with me. Got it.

We all sit around Dr. Franklin's desk, and Ryan pulls his cell phone out of his pocket. The date flashes on the screen—the same date that's on my calendar, the one that's several weeks off. How did he do that? I didn't even know you could change the date on a cell phone.

"Ryan, put that away. You're only allowed to use your phone after class."

Ryan crams the phone back in his pocket, but there's a smirk on his face. If he wanted to rattle me, it worked. I just don't get why he's doing this *now*.

I can't even pay attention to what the Doctor's talking about, and within fifteen minutes, he dismisses us. I stand up to leave.

"Bo," he says, "I just asked you to stay." He gives me a weird look. I sit back down. The officials are busy recording everything that's happening.

Once Gwen, Harold, and Ryan leave, the Doctor pulls up a chair and sits across from me. "I want to say again," he says, "Dr. Rivers and Mr. Minh are observers, but it's your right to ask them to leave if you're uncomfortable with them sitting in."

He's nervous, that much is clear. His eyes widen slightly, glancing to his left, where the officials are sitting. Maybe he knows, subconsciously, that they're doing something to mess with his head.

"It's okay," I mutter. They'll just find another way to spy on me if I kick them out, and I'd rather have them where I can see them.

"Before we go on, I want to know: Do you have any questions for me?"

I sit up straighter. "Uh, yeah," I say. "What— uh, what day is it?"

The Doctor shoots me a strange look but tells me the date. The same as the date on my calendar, on Ryan's phone.

It wasn't a joke.

I've lost several weeks of time. The last thing I remember is going to bed the day I texted Phoebe. I stayed up until lights-out reading that book assigned to us in English. And then I woke up, just like normal, but somehow time has zoomed past me. What the hell happened? The officials are still here, everyone's acting like everything's normal . . . but I've lost *weeks*.

Weeks when I could have been saving Sofía.

Is that it? Is this time's way of punishing me for finding a loophole to see her again? I stole time with her, so time stole some back.

Or maybe the officials did.

"I'm holding you back to discuss your medication," Dr. Franklin says.

"Medication?"

"I'd like to add a few different scripts," the Doctor continues. "First, something for your insomnia."

"I don't have a sleeping problem."

The Doctor smiles sadly and writes something in his notebook. I lean forward, trying to see it, but I can't.

"It's a neuroleptic," Dr. Franklin continues, as if I hadn't spoken. "And it's stronger than your previous medication, but still a bit mild compared to others on the market. I need you to keep track of how you feel when you take it, okay? And I want you to continue taking it when you go home for the weekends. Family Day is coming up, and then spring break, and I need you to be responsible and keep up with your medication even when you're at home."

I nod dumbly. This isn't the first time the Doctor has prescribed pills. Everyone in the group was put on mild antidepressants when they first arrived at the Berk. "To temper your powers until you can control them a little more," the Doctor had said. And there was other medication: a fever reducer for Gwen, some little green pills for Ryan, an entire handful of stuff for Harold—though Harold gobbled up the pills eagerly, as if they were candy.

Dr. Rivers stands up and moves behind the Doctor, reading the notes he's written in his book. "I agree, Dr. Franklin," she says. "These should help Bo considerably."

I grit my teeth. So. That's what's happened. The officials know that I'm not duped by their illusions, so they're going to drug me.

CHAPTER 33

I stare at the pages of my calendar.

I lost so much time.

Time that I could have spent working to save Sofía.

But I was selfish. I stole my night with her, and somehow time's been stealing itself back.

My mind feels like it's splintering. Save Sofía. Stop the officials. Can Dr. Franklin be trusted? What is happening?

I clutch my head, bending over my bed and pressing my face against my cool pillow. Too much time has passed. The officials aren't just going away. Sofía isn't just coming back.

It's all falling apart.

An abrupt, violent feeling cracks inside me, at my core, the way cold glass shatters when boiling water is thrown on it. The timestream flashes in front of me, stuttering in and out of existence, the threads ripped up like grass being whirled around in a hurricane. I reach for it—hoping to calm it, maybe, or just find a way to calm myself in it—and a noise like radio static vibrates all the way into my bones. Reality feels jagged in my hand. I stumble off my bed, staggering to find steady ground, and–

I fall into a different time.

I haven't gone somewhere I had zero control over in ages, and this is the first time the timestream has ever acted like this, like it was made of sound and fury and little else. It felt like a television turned on to a scrambled channel inside my head.

I blink in the bright daylight, trying to figure out where I am. *When* I am. It's definitely not Berkshire, and it's sometime in the afternoon, I think . . . and I know this place. It's not somewhere I'd *elect* to go, but at least it's familiar. I'm on the grassy lawn just in front of my parents' house. Judging from the temperature, I'd guess it's springtime—although I can't tell the year. The sweet scent of Mom's cherry tree fills the air, and a few pale petals float by.

The front door opens. I drop immediately to the ground, crouching between the bushes and the bricks of the front porch. Girls' voices fill the space, one of them definitely my sister's. I'm not sure where in time I am. Is this the past or the future? The house doesn't look much different, and Phoebe sounds like herself, so it's possible that this is today. Or a month ago. Or next year. It's impossible to tell.

As the girls—two of them, plus Phoebe—settle onto the porch, I move carefully under the steps, out of sight. I can hear them walking across the wooden planks, the squeak of the front porch swing, and I pray they stay where they are. If they come down to the yard and look directly at the steps, they'll definitely see me.

If I'm seen, it might cause trouble, so it's best if I figure out what's going on first. The timestream won't let me create a paradox or conflict with my own timeline—that's been made abundantly clear—but the static-filled stutter that brought me here was *not* normal.

Maybe something's wrong with time. I can't afford to screw things up until I know what's going on.

The dirt under the porch is cool and damp, and spiders creep along the undersides of the wooden boards, but I ignore them, my heart racing. Whatever's happening now, I shouldn't be here. But time has put me here for a reason.

The girls start chatting, and I finally recognize them. Jenny and Rosemarie, two of Phoebe's best friends, are occupying the big porch swing that my father brought home from our grandmother's house after she died. They're barely skimming their toes along the wooden planks of the porch, just moving the bench seat of the swing enough for the chain to squeal in protest.

Phoebe sits down at the top step, her bright pink socks parallel with my eyes.

"I think I'm going to try to do a foreign-exchange program," Phoebe says suddenly.

"You mean, like, some kid from Africa or China or some other country is going to share a room with you?" Rosemarie asks.

"You do realize that Africa is not a country, right?" Jenny tells her, leaning over the swing so that Rosemarie can see her arched brow.

"Yeah, it is."

"It's a continent."

"No," Phoebe says. "I mean I think I'm going to be the one to go to Africa or China or something."

Rosemarie and Jenny both stop swinging. "What?!" Jenny says at the same time Rosemarie exclaims, "Why?"

"I just . . . I want to get away." Phoebe says in a distant voice, as if she can already envision herself in Africa or China or something.

I feel like I'm spying, and I hate it. But why does Pheebs want to leave? Is something wrong? I scoot around under the porch, trying to see her better, but her face is hidden from me.

Phoebe leans back over the porch, looking toward her friends. "I mean, I want to explore. See the world. All that stuff."

"There's the class trip to Europe," Jenny points out.

"Yeah, I know," Phoebe says. "That's a backup plan. I don't care where I go, really—I just want to go."

"I don't." Rosemarie kicks her feet, making the swing go higher. Jenny wasn't ready and nearly falls off.

"I might one day. In college, maybe." Jenny grabs the chain, stilling the swing. Rosemarie glares at her.

Phoebe wraps her arms around her knees. She looks very small from my vantage point, like a wounded animal or a forgotten child.

"What did your parents say?" Jenny asks quietly. Rosemarie puts her feet down, making the swing stop completely.

After a moment, Phoebe says, "I haven't told them."

"With your brother already gone—"

"He's not dead." Phoebe cuts Jenny off. "And besides, they probably wouldn't even notice I was gone."

"Well, I think it's brave," Rosemarie says when Jenny opens

her mouth again. "You're really brave, Pheebs. You're not scared of anything."

"Everyone's scared of spiders," Jenny says, trying to make a joke.

But Phoebe's not. I remember when we first moved into this house, when I was seven and Phoebe was five. It's a really old house, and our parents had to practically gut it to remodel it, but they were too poor to do it all at the same time, so they went room by room. Phoebe and I had to take turns sharing a room while each of our bedrooms was remodeled. One day, just as we were going to bed, a giant spider—a huge furry thing that made my heart race and my stomach churn—landed directly on Phoebe's head, its legs dancing across the fine strands of her hair.

I had grinned, expecting my sister to freak out when I told her there was a spider on her, but instead she just dipped her head, shook her hair out, and looked at the thing when it fell from her to her pillow. She reached out and poked it with one stubby finger, and the spider scurried away.

"I'm not scared of spiders," Phoebe says, but there is no triumph in her voice.

"It's not spiders for me; it's snakes," Rosemarie says with a shudder. "My daddy ran over one when he was taking me to band practice today, and ohmahgah, it was so gross. Its body was still—" Rosemarie twists up her arms, her face scrunched in disgust.

"I'm not scared of snakes either."

Rosemarie leans over, the porch swing squeaking. "Then what are you scared of, show-off?"

I lean forward too, curious as to what my little sister is

frightened of. Probably something stupid—if she's not scared of spiders or snakes, maybe she hates butterflies.

Or maybe it's me. I'm the freak of the family, I'm the one who's not in control. I'd forgotten all about taking her to see the Titanic and getting her injured. Maybe I've done that before. Maybe she's scared of me showing up in her life, dragging her off to a different time and place and leaving her there.

Like I did with Sofía.

"I'm scared of Capgras delusion," Phoebe says.

"What?" Jenny asks.

Phoebe turns around, leaning her back against one of the wooden columns of the porch. "Capgras delusion. It's when you wake up one day and you think someone you love isn't real. Like, maybe you think that person is actually a robot, not a human. Or a doppelgänger. Or whatever. But you look at this person that you love, that you have always loved, and instead of seeing him, you see someone else. Something snaps inside of you, and what you thought was real doesn't feel real anymore. So you look at this person you love and you feel like he's just . . . gone, replaced by this weak imitation."

"That's crazy," Rosemarie says.

"That's the point," Phoebe says, her voice rising. "And it can just happen one day, to anyone. No one knows the cause. There's no cure. One day everything's fine, and the next day everything you thought was true feels fake. You spend the rest of your life believing—*really believing*—that the person you were in love with is gone and you're stuck with this replacement."

"I'd leave him," Jenny says. "Maybe he *was* a doppelgänger. Maybe I fell into a horror movie or something."

"Some people do. Some people just walk away from their

families and never go back. And some people live with it, basically faking their love for the rest of their lives. And then some people start to think that the only way to get back the person they loved is to kill the fake person."

All three girls are silent for a moment.

Phoebe stands suddenly, her footsteps clattering down the stairs to the front yard. I scurry into the shadows, but it will do no good—there isn't enough darkness here to hide me. Pheebs turns, her eyes scanning high, looking for her friends still on the porch, but then she hesitates, her gaze drifting toward me—

And then the timestream violently yanks me back to my own world, my own bedroom, my own time.

CHAPTER 34

More time has passed. I checked the calendar. Each sheet marked in my own special code.

I've lost three days.

Three days gone, replaced by just a moment of time at my parents' house, spying on my little sister.

Three more days gone, and Sofía's not back. I'm getting worse. I'm way, *way* out of control.

But if I can't control the timestream, I can't control anything. I can't save Sofía. I can't even save myself. Is this what a supernova feels like? Melting down from the core, destroying everything close to it.

I have never felt so helpless in my life. It feels like the entire world is crumbling around me, and no one even notices me trying to save it.

This all reminds me of something Sofía once told me. About the first time she saw someone die. She was at a pool party for a friend's quinceañera. Everything was loud: the music, the conversations, the kids splashing in the water.

Everything was loud, except for Carlos Estrada.

No one noticed. There was a large group there, playing and shouting, and the soccer team was on one side of the pool having a water fight. And Carlos—he just sort of bobbed there in the deep end for a bit, and then he went under the water. And he didn't come back up. Not until his mother dove into the water with all her clothes on and dragged his body from the pool.

"That's the thing that stayed with me," Sofía said quietly, after she described his blue lips and his skin that was cold to the touch. "You always think that drowning is loud. In the movies, if someone drowns they scream, they churn the water. Everyone notices a drowning person in the movies."

Sofía looked down, and I thought she was crying, but when she looked up at me again, I realized her eyes were dry.

"Real drowning is quiet. It doesn't announce itself. It just . . . it just happens. And then you're gone."

I didn't understand what she was saying before, but now I think I do. We're all drowning here, and no one's noticing a damn thing.

CHAPTER 35

There's a fire in the fireplace.

That shouldn't be odd. But it is.

How did I get here?

I tilt my head, watching the red flames lick at the soot-stained stones.

Not soot. Rain. Rain-drenched stones.

Because the fireplace isn't in a house.

Blink. Yes, it is.

Blink. No. It's not. This fireplace is a ruin, crumbling and unusable, the last place I saw Sofía. It's not filled with fire, it's filled with dirt and rainwater, and I am standing outside, staring at the place where a house was hundreds of years ago.

But when I blink again, the house is there.

Time is stuttering. The timestream is breaking. With just a blink of my eyes, I'm thrown into the past, then back into the present.

Or maybe it's not the timestream that's breaking. Maybe it's just me.

"Bo?" a voice calls.

I'm not sure if the voice is coming from across the field or across time. But then I see Harold walking up the path toward me.

"What brings you out here?" he asks, as if it's perfectly natural for me to be standing in front of the ruins in the pissing rain.

"Something's wrong," I say.

"Yes," Harold replies.

Just yes. Like, obviously, something's wrong.

He twirls an old iron key in his hand.

"Where'd you get that?" I ask, staring at it.

Harold's eyebrows raise, one of the few times he's actually let emotion show on his face. "You gave it to me," he says. "Just now."

Time is stuttering all around me. I'm not even in control of myself.

"Do you see it too?" I whisper, almost hoping. "The way everything's out of sync?" Out of the corner of my eye, I see the sun rise and set and rise and set in quick succession, but when I close my eyes and force myself to breathe, time slows to normal again.

"I never see," Harold says calmly. "I only hear."

Time isn't stuttering for him—just me. Only me.

"I hate the voices, and I love them, and sometimes I think they're killing me," Harold says. He turns toward Berkshire and starts walking away, not looking back once to see if I'm following or not. I am following him, though. I don't remember how I got to the ruins or what I was doing, but I should get back to the academy. I don't want to get Dr. Franklin in more trouble, even if he's forgotten who I really am . . . who he really is.

"My dads," Harold says, still walking, still not caring if I'm listening or not, "they say that everyone has a jar of darkness inside of them. Everyone. When we're born, the lid is tight on the jar. That's why babies are happy. But as time goes on, sometimes the jar opens a little, and darkness gets inside of us. We can close the jar sometimes, and sometimes we can't."

He stops now and finally looks at me.

"I think my jar is broken. Or I think I don't have a jar, just the darkness."

I have no clue what to say to that.

"Sofía had the darkness in her too."

"No she didn't," I say, the words coming out angry and loud. The rain is falling harder now, and my feet are sinking in the mud.

Harold cocks his head. He doesn't seem defensive, just curious about my response. "She did," he said. "We talked about it. She was my friend. My only friend here."

"I'm your friend," I say, but I know it's not really true. I've been nice to him, at least nicer than Ryan has, but that doesn't mean we're friends.

"I feel the darkness inside me like a creature curled up in my chest, breathing smoke and fire. It is always there. It weighs on me. It's not contained by anything but my own skin. Sometimes it sleeps. Sometimes it doesn't."

"Maybe we shouldn't talk about these things in front of the officials," I say warily. "Let's keep this between us, buddy."

"Only Sofía was willing to talk about the darkness," Harold says. "That's why she was my friend. You have it too, you know."

I don't know what he's talking about.

"The darkness, I mean. You have it. But yours is in a jar, and sometimes the lid is on, and sometimes it isn't." Harold turns and starts strolling back to the Berk as the rain beats down harder on us. "Gwen hates her jar. She keeps the lid on as tight as she can. Ryan's the opposite. I think he smashed his jar on purpose. He loves the darkness."

"You know," I say, "you're really weird."

"Yes," Harold replies. "That's what they all say." There is quiet defeat in his voice, and acceptance.

"Even the voices you talk to?" I cringe. That was a low blow and a jerk thing to say.

"Yes," Harold says, completely serious.

As we start up the steps to Berkshire, I grab Harold's arm. "I'm sorry, dude," I say. "I could have been more of a friend to you. I've been so wrapped up in my own life that I just ignore you, and that's not cool."

Harold doesn't really show any emotion. He just looks at me. "The voices I hear—they're not all bad. You're not all bad either."

"Thanks, man." We start back up. "So where do those voices come from, anyway?"

"The darkness."

"Even the good ones?"

"Even those."

Ryan is waiting for us inside the foyer. "God, you idiots look awful," he says.

Harold ignores him, walking up the stairs and straight back to his room. Ryan grabs my arm. "Listen, man. The officials are packing up. They're leaving in a few days, before break, at least.

Don't screw this up, okay? Try to keep the crazy to a minimum. Harold's bad enough."

"I can't wait until spring break," I say.

"I can." Ryan looks angry at the thought of going back home. He might not be looking forward to the break, but I need it. I need to get away from here. Everything's cracking up. *I'm* cracking up. I need to get away from the officials. They're pulling at reality like it's clay they can shape in their hands, and I can't keep up with their version of truth.

"How are you holding up?" I ask Ryan.

"Eh."

"I mean, with your powers. Are you having trouble holding on to them here too?"

Ryan tosses a pen into the air, and it falls back down into his hand, gravity working perfectly. "You tell me," he says. So, yes. His telekinesis, at least, is off.

He stares at me curiously, his eyes losing focus as he considers the implications of what I've said. There's a flicker of movement behind him, and my attention shifts over Ryan's left shoulder to the second-floor landing.

Someone is standing in the middle of the landing, dripping water all over the plush red carpet. This boy isn't wet like Harold and I are—our clothes sticking to us, puddles on the floor. No, this boy is *soaking*, water streaming off him, making rivulets in the carpet. His hair hangs in clumps, and water pours from his arms as if he has two hoses hidden under his shirtsleeves.

"Who . . . ?" I start to ask.

Ryan notices the look on my face and turns, trying to find out what I'm seeing.

The boy on the landing looks right at me, and I can see the red lines in his eyes, as if he's been crying. His skin is brown, his hair is black, his eyes a golden hazel color. He looks . . . familiar, and yet I know I've never seen him before in my life, past or present.

"What are you . . . ?" Ryan starts to ask. "Oh shit." He grabs me and pulls me under the stairs, out of sight.

A moment later, I hear voices—the officials.

"I'm not saying Dr. Franklin is incompetent," Dr. Rivers says. "I just think he's in over his head with these students."

"The idea is nice," Mr. Minh replies. "Help these kids out in an isolated area, focus them on their issues while maintaining an environment of education. It's worked before."

"But it's not working *here*." Dr. Rivers sighs. "The case of Sofía Muniz aside, there are issues that Berkshire Academy must address to pass board approval . . ."

Mr. Minh laughs. "Oh, I think it's clear the board won't be approving Berkshire. This whole place will be shut down."

Dr. Rivers says something Ryan and I can't hear, and soon they walk away.

"Did you hear that?" Ryan asks.

"Did you see that?" I snap back. How could the officials be standing *right there* and not notice the boy and the water? I run up the stairs, but the boy isn't there. There's no sign of him, not even a drop of water on the red carpet. Just Harold's muddy footprints, and now my own.

"Bo, focus," Ryan demands. "They're trying to shut down the Berk."

But who was the boy? He seemed so familiar.

"Where will we go?" Ryan continues. "I can't go back home.

This is what I knew would happen from the start. This is why I've been trying to keep them out of here."

He reminded me of . . . of Sofía. He looked a little like her.

Ryan starts pacing. "There are other schools, I suppose. But I like *this one*. I don't want to leave. My parents have had their eye on military school for far too long."

And then it hits me. I know who the wet boy was, why he appeared to me.

"I'll call my father. He's an asshole, but he probably has connections to whatever board the officials were talking about. He can probably put in a good word . . . make a donation . . . something . . ."

It was little drowned Carlos Estrada.

CHAPTER 36

I don't know if I'm seeing ghosts like Harold does, or maybe time just jumped around enough to show me Sofía's dead friend, but I'd like to never have that happen again, please.

Ryan's pissed that I'm not focused on the problem at hand: the very real possibility that Berkshire may close. He doesn't understand that I *do* care. We're like a family. A tiny, broken family twisted with weird powers, but a family. I don't want to see what would happen if we're broken up. I can't imagine trying to figure out my powers with anyone other than these guys.

But time is falling apart around me, and Sofía is still gone.

At night, rather than waste time in the common room, I creep across the carpeted floor toward the last dorm room at the end of the hall. I've been to that room many times, but I haven't been there since I left Sofía in the past. At first, I avoided her bedroom subconsciously, but as time kept moving forward without her, I started to avoid it on purpose, going so far as to take a different route to get to classes just to skip passing her room. That shut door used to be open all the time, spilling out little snippets of her music and the scent of her shampoo and her bright pink lamp that cast an eerie glow in the room. The fact that the door is always shut now just serves as another reminder that Sofía isn't inside.

But now, I just want to feel close to her again. Maybe just being in a space that is hers will be enough.

My hand trembles as I twist the knob to Sofía's bedroom door. The door creaks open. But before I can even flick the light on, I can tell that something's wrong.

Sofía's room is empty.

Of course she's not there, but that's not what I mean. It's empty of everything that made it her room. There's a stripped-down bed against the wall, an unadorned desk, a closet with ten bare hangers. It's empty of *her*. Someone has come in and taken away everything that made this room Sofía's.

"The hell is going on?" I mutter, turning slowly around the room.

I cross her room in three quick strides, pressing my hand against a patched coat of paint that doesn't quite match the rest of the walls. This was where Sofía and Gwen had their first fight. The two girls were very different, but they had bonded over the first few weeks of class. And then they fought about something stupid, I can't remember what, and Gwen had flashed too hot and accidentally burned a streak in the wall. Sofía had covered the dark spot with a poster so that Gwen wouldn't get in trouble.

But the poster's gone, and the dark spot is covered up. It's as if Berkshire is trying to make it look like Sofía was never here in the first place.

There's a flash of movement near the door, and I spin around. A short, teenaged girl with soot streaked down her body pauses, a look of confusion and shock on her face when she peers inside the room and sees me. I'm equally shocked and confused—not only have I never seen this girl before, but she's dressed in a full-length black skirt with a black top and a huge white collar. She has a thin white cap on, covering most of her pale brown hair.

She's from Salem.

I lunge for her. "Are you from the past?" I demand. "Have you seen Sofía? A girl—she's got brown skin and talks differently, like me, and she may have been accused of being a witch."

The girl opens her mouth to speak; her face is twisted with fear and revulsion, as if she thinks I'm of the devil.

I blink.

And she's gone.

Cracks in time. Everywhere I go, the timestream follows, leaking moments and people that pop up in the shadows as reminders that I am not in control.

I try to get my heart to stop racing from the shock of seeing—and then *not* seeing—the girl from Salem, when suddenly the door bangs open and Gwen bounces in.

"What are you doing here?" I ask at the same moment Gwen squeaks in surprise at seeing me.

"I come here all the time," Gwen says defensively. "What are *you* doing here?"

"I miss Sofía."

Gwen's lips twist up, and for once, she doesn't have a snarky quip to fire back. Her shoulders slump and her hair sweeps into her face as she looks down, a defeated expression in her eyes.

"I miss her too," Gwen says. Her guard is still up, as if she expects that I'll demand she leave. But this place isn't Sofía's, not anymore, and even if it were, I wouldn't keep Gwen from whatever remained of her.

"Why do you come here?" I ask.

Gwen shrugs. "Privacy."

"There's no privacy in your own room?"

"I like it, okay?" Gwen says, moving past me and plopping down on the empty, bare bed. "I like the big room with no stuff in it."

She likes the very thing I hate about this place: the echoing emptiness.

"Are you going to stay or what?" Gwen asks.

I shrug.

"Whatever."

Gwen hasn't really liked me since Sofía and I started dating. I can't blame her. I took away her best and only friend—or, I didn't take her away, but I took away time with her. And then I took her to the wrong time. Guilt clangs around inside me like a bell.

Gwen stands up and flips the mattress over. This is the bed where Sofía slept, although when she slept here, the bed was covered with pale pink-and-green sheets and a quilt her grand-mother made.

And, I'm fairly certain, the underside of her mattress wasn't covered in long burn marks.

"People think fire is uncontrollable," Gwen mutters,

kneeling in front of the bed as if in prayer. She flicks her fingers, and sparks shoot up. At first I think she's remembered her powers, but then I see the Zippo in her hand. "But it's not. It's *powerful*, and power doesn't like to be contained."

She runs the flame in a smooth, even line on the silky mattress material, and it blackens and burns. An acrid stench rises up from the scorching cloth. Even though Gwen's forgotten her powers of pyrokinesis, she's remembered her grief. And her love of fire. There are dozens of similar black lines, burn marks, all in a row. Careful, even marks monitored and cultivated. They look like scars.

I count the marks on the bed.

One for every night Sofía has been gone.

CHAPTER 37

Family Day takes me by surprise.

I knew it was coming, obviously, but time's been messing with me lately. During mealtimes, the servers are tailed by a small brown-skinned girl with braids, dressed in clothes from at least ten years ago, who speaks Spanish. When I stare out the window during math, a group of Native Americans stalks through the sea grass. During free time outside, the camp for sick kids is fully occupied in one moment, then an abandoned ruin again in the blink of my eye.

All around me, time is leaking flashes of history.

Or—and this is what I fear far, far more—I'm seeing death. They're ghosts in front of me. Spirits reaching out, accusing me of messing with their pasts.

Sometimes, all I hope is to see Sofía. But other times, I'm terrified that if I see her, that means she's already beyond my help, she's already dead.

So I am somewhat distracted by the time Family Day rolls

around. I skipped breakfast and went to the morning session with Dr. Franklin, and no one was there. It wasn't until my science teacher, Mr. Glover, walked by and saw me waiting outside the Doc's door that I finally figured out what day it was.

I rush outside, where the Doctor has only just noticed I was missing. He kind of fusses over all of us, like in the old movies where the orphans are paraded in front of prospective adoptive parents. Except here it isn't about being selected to go to a new home, it's about hoping our own parents are happy enough with us to take us back.

The parents arrive individually. It seems like forever before anyone shows up, and then, suddenly, everyone's here. Gwen's mom is one of the first to arrive, then Harold's whole family. My parents arrive next, dragging along Phoebe. Only Ryan's family doesn't bother to show, but the Doctor makes him stand outside with everyone else, which is actually kind of a mean thing to do.

It's still a little too cold to be outside today, even though the season is starting to change. Everyone's wearing coats, and Gwen's hopping around from foot to foot, trying to keep warm. Despite this, the whole place smells like a cookout. The staff associates "family" with "cheap food." Last Family Day was a build-your-own-sandwich bar.

"Hey," I say in the general direction of my family. Harold's all excited to see his family, but I see mine every weekend. I don't know why they bother to come, honestly. Phoebe never has before.

Dr. Franklin greets everyone as they enter the big open foyer at the base of the ornate stairs of Berkshire. A laminated banner hangs over the first-floor landing—WELCOME,

FAMILIES—and the staff has added festive paper table covers to the buffet, where they're piling up mounds of grilled hot dogs, ruffled potato chips, and dip, but it all feels . . . forced. Everyone's smile is plastered on, but hardly anyone looks happy to be here, especially after Dr. Franklin introduces the officials, saying that they're here as consultants "during our tragedy." Nothing like reminding everyone about a missing student to bring up the cheer factor.

"Well, let me go get my thirteen-hundred-dollar hot dog," my father says. He smiles like it's a joke, but I can tell he doesn't think it's funny at all. Mom squeezes my arm, like she's trying to say everything's okay.

"Dr. Franklin," she says, turning to him. He greets her with a too-broad smile, all his teeth showing. "May I speak with you?"

She draws him aside, and they start speaking quietly. I glance at my sister, who's just standing there, texting on her phone, ignoring us all.

Ryan sidles up beside me, four hot dogs on his plate. "This blows. Let's leave."

I shake my head.

"Come on," Ryan whines.

I watch as Mom nods emphatically at whatever Dr. Franklin is saying. I wait for them to look at me—obviously they're talking about me—but instead, Mom looks past where I'm standing.

To Phoebe.

"Would you look at them?" Ryan says, pointing to Harold's family—two dads, a younger sister, and an older brother. They're so loud it feels like they're taking up the whole foyer. Except Harold, of course. He's always quiet, even around his family. But he's smiling, at least—that's something. His little sister came from Haiti, and his older brother is from Cambodia. They're among the few living people Harold ever bothers to talk about.

"They're like a window display for diversity," Ryan says, not caring if anyone overhears him. The little sister is wearing a neon yellow sundress and has her hair up in two twisted pigtails. She's bouncing around like she's eaten nothing in her life but pure sugar.

"They look like a nice family," I say. I watch Harold's whole face come alive with happiness in a way I've never really seen before.

"They look like a bunch of freaks."

I'd really like to tell Ryan to shove off, but my mother's coming toward us. No . . . she's heading toward my sister. She steers Phoebe over to the Doctor, saying something to her in a low voice. Phoebe shakes her head no, but then they're in front of the Doctor, and Mom pokes Pheebs in the back until she smiles politely at him.

Ryan stuffs a hot dog in his mouth. "Come on, I'm leaving," he says. He reaches for me, but I sidestep away. I want to know what the Doctor is saying to Phoebe. She glares at him, resentment in her eyes, and I can tell she wants to say something to him but can't because Mom is right there. What are they talking about that's making her so angry?

And then Phoebe's eyes shoot to mine. So. They're talking about me. But Phoebe's whole demeanor changes as she looks quickly away, focusing again on what the Doctor is telling her. She shifts visibly from angry to . . . afraid?

I'm just out of earshot; I can't make anything out. My focus zeroes in on the Doctor with such intensity that the rest of the world fades away. Phoebe's a smart girl, but I don't want her believing whatever lies Dr. Franklin is telling her.

A sound like a roaring ocean wave washes over me, and I stagger from the impact of it. I look around quickly—Ryan's still beside me, chewing in slow motion. Everyone in the foyer is milling around but barely moving. I see Harold's little sister's neon yellow dress fluttering; she's paused mid-jump, her feet above the ground, but it's like gravity quit working for her and she's almost floating, sinking by millimeters.

"Hello?" I say, but all the sound around me is low, almost subsonic.

I haven't stopped time—I've just slowed it to a crawl.

This is my chance. The timestream is working for me for once, helping me to get closer to Dr. Franklin and Phoebe without them noticing. I must be moving like a hummingbird from their perspective, barely visible as I scoot around the slow-motion bodies of the people between my sister and me. Even so, I try to avoid their direct line of sight, moving quickly to the shadows at the edge of the room and creeping forward in bursts.

When I'm close enough, I close my eyes and release my grip on time. A sound like all the air in the room being sucked away fills my ears, but everyone around me acts and moves and talks normally again. Ryan looks around, surprised at my disappearance, but he shrugs and makes his way to the stairs on his own.

"I know I'm here at Berkshire Academy, and I work with your brother, but in situations like these . . ." Dr. Franklin's voice trails off. "I don't just help Bo. I'm here for you too."

Phoebe sort of shrugs, flipping her phone over and over in her hand. "I don't need help," she says.

"It's not easy living with someone who has special needs, like your brother. Sometimes it can feel as if you're overshadowed," Dr. Franklin says.

Well, that's entirely untrue. I may have powers, but Phoebe's the special one to my parents. A total daddy's girl, with straight As and a mile-long list of extracurriculars. Phoebe has designed her whole life to make people love her, from our parents to college admissions officers. Nothing I ever do comes close to competing with the perfection of Phoebe.

"I've been speaking with your mother on the phone, and she wanted us to have a moment to sit down and talk," the Doctor continues.

She puts her phone in her pocket. "I don't really know what to talk about."

"Let's go to my office," Dr. Franklin says. He turns a little, just enough to make eye contact with me, to let me know that he knows I'm there. "Where it's more private."

He touches her elbow and leads her up the stairs, beyond my reach.

CHAPTER 38

Phoebe

Dr. Franklin sits behind his desk, his dark face slightly illuminated by the glow of the computer screen in front of him.

"So, Phoebe, your mom wanted me to talk to you for a bit." He leans forward, holding his palms together and pressing his lips against his index fingers.

"About Bo?" Even I'm surprised by the antagonism in my voice. Of course he wants to talk about Bo.

"About whatever you feel like talking about."

I try not to roll my eyes. I don't know how Bo can stand it here. I hate the mere concept of therapy. What's with people who think you can talk your way out of any problem? Some problems are bigger than words. And some problems don't need to be discussed at all.

"Why don't you tell me about school?" Dr. Franklin suggests.

I shrug. "It's school."

"What are your best subjects? You're a junior, right? Do you have your eye on any colleges?"

I force a smile on my face. I hate that everyone asks me this. "I don't care where I go, as long as they have a good study-abroad program."

"So you want to travel?"

"I want to escape." I cringe as soon as the words leave my mouth.

Thankfully, Dr. Franklin doesn't say anything more about it. Instead, he moves on to a new subject. "How is school different for you now than when Bo was at James Jefferson High?"

I shrug again. "It's not, really. We had different classes. We were in different grades. Most people didn't even know we were related." The most time we spent together was when he'd drive me to school when I was a freshman—a condition of his having his own car. After he wrecked the car and I got my own driver's license, we didn't even have that connection.

"You two are very different," Dr. Franklin concedes. "But I think, in some ways, you're pretty similar. You're both very guarded, for example."

I keep my face from scowling. I hate that Mom set me up for this awkward conversation, and I wish Dr. Franklin would just get to the point, whatever that may be.

"How about at home?" Dr. Franklin presses. "Are things good there?"

"They're quieter," I concede. Except when they're not. Like when Dad takes away Bo's door.

"Quieter?"

"Since Bo's been gone."

Dr. Franklin, sensing potential, leans in. "In what ways?"

I let my eyes drift from Dr. Franklin. It's easier to talk when I look above him, at the burgundy-and-cream valances draped over the windows that overlook the ocean.

"Bo was a lot angrier before he came here," I say. "I don't know if even he realized it. He always seems like two people to me; most of the time he's really chill, but if one little thing goes wrong, it's like he loses control."

"Control is something we talk a lot about here at Berkshire," Dr. Franklin adds gently, trying not to break the flow of my words.

"Yeah, well, he definitely didn't have it before. When we were kids, he broke my arm." I don't know why I've been thinking about that moment so much. Probably because of Bo's texts.

When we were little, we used to pretend that we were on the Titanic. It was a silly game, born of my obsession with the movie after I dug it out of Mom's collection, but Bo never minded playing with me because he liked the inevitable fate of the ship. We used the tire swing out in the front yard. I'd climb on top of it, and Bo would push me around, pretending the swing was the ship. When I fell off, the ship "sank." It was fun, until the time I broke my arm after landing funny. I laid there on the ground, crying and screaming for help, but Bo just stood over me with a dead look in his eyes as the tire swing rocked back and forth, empty. He didn't show any emotion at all. It was like he wasn't even there.

That was the first time I knew something was wrong with him.

Dr. Franklin sits up straighter, and the movement forces my gaze from the window back to him. "I wasn't aware he hurt you," he says.

"It was an accident. We were playing on the tire swing, and he spun me too hard, and I fell funny."

"I don't think Bo ever means to hurt anyone."

I don't answer.

Dr. Franklin notices. "Phoebe?" he says. "Do you think Bo would intentionally hurt someone?"

I don't meet his eyes. "I don't think so, not now."

"But before he came to the academy?"

I twist my fingers together. "Maybe." When Dr. Franklin doesn't speak, I find my words filling the silence, almost unwillingly. "Like, okay, I don't think he'd be, like, a serial killer or anything. Nothing like that. But . . . I remember when he was a freshman, and he had so much trouble fitting in. There were these jerks in school, right, because there are always jerks in school, the kind who pick on you if you're even a tiny bit different. And Bo was more than a tiny bit different, you know?"

Dr. Franklin nods his head.

"I was just . . ." I struggle to find the right words. "I was really glad that my dad didn't have any guns in the house, that my mom always insisted on that. But I wondered when he would go to his friend Lee's house, and if Lee's dad had a gun, if maybe that's all it would take for Bo to . . . you know."

"You think Bo might have shot someone at school?" Dr. Franklin asks, his voice lowering a notch.

"No! No," I say, shaking my head vigorously. "That would take a lot of planning and, you know, rage, and . . . Bo isn't really *violent*," I say. "I don't think he'd *actually* do something. But if the opportunity was there . . ." I swallow, hard. "I don't know. I mean, he didn't. I just think . . . maybe he could have. Maybe. And if he ever did, he probably wouldn't have even meant to do it. There are just times when he's not himself." I take a deep breath. "How horrible am I, to think that my own brother might do something like that?"

"How horrible for you to have lived with that fear," Dr. Franklin says.

He doesn't understand. It's not like that. Bo isn't a bad person. "It's just that he would . . . flip, so easily, between calm and angry, and there were moments when those two feelings would collide."

"What do you mean?"

"When the calm and the rage became one thing for him," I say. "That was when it was scary. When he was both really calm and cold but also full of rage."

"Did you see that often?"

The doctor's pen scratches across his notepad. I wish I hadn't said anything. Bo's different now; Berkshire Academy has helped him to be different. He had only been so full of anger because he saw the world in such a different way. Most people look at the world in black and white, even if they say they don't. You like someone or you don't; you agree with an opinion or you don't. Bo was never like that, never. He always saw things from a different angle. Like an artist who sees the shapes and colors and shading of an object, but who doesn't always see the object itself. That's how Bo looked at the world. He looked at it as a chance, not a done deal. He would get angry when things couldn't change, when people *wouldn't* change, even if they could.

That's why he butted heads with Dad so much. Dad is an immovable force. He goes in one direction, straight ahead. He can't handle a kid who doesn't do that, who sees so many different paths, some of them going sideways or backward. Who doesn't accept that things are the way they are.

Bo never really liked school—at least not until Berkshire Academy—and that was usually what he and Dad fought about. Bo would stay in bed as long as possible, until Dad started waking him up by dumping ice water on him, something that always ended with shouting.

"I don't see the point," Bo would yell at him, sweeping ice cubes from his bed.

"The point," Dad snarled, "is to get a diploma. And then go to college. And then get a job." He said this like it was the most obvious thing in the world, just like two and two equals four.

"But I don't want any of that!" Bo protested.

And Dad never, ever believed him. Because not wanting diploma-college-job was like not wanting to eat, not wanting to breathe, not wanting to *live*.

"My grandmother understood him," I say without meaning to actually speak the words aloud. But now that they hang in the air between us, I keep talking. "My grandmother understood Bo better than anyone. She could always calm him." I'm careful with my words now, careful not to say how jealous that made me.

Adults lie. They lie about how they love children equally. They never do. They love children *differently*, and the difference is so broad that equality is not even in the picture. My parents, for example, love me for my obedience. They love me for my academics and my ambition and the possibilities of what I could do and be in the future. They love Bo for who he is now, for the quiet, calm moments, and they hold on to that, not sure if it will continue.

Grandma loved Bo in an absolute and whole way. She accepted him entirely, but I grew to distrust her unconditional love. Because my grandmother never loved me that way. She loved me because I never gave her a reason not to. I had been the behaved, well-mannered child who was respectful and kind, but I was very aware that my grandmother's attitude toward me was based on those actions. Bo, on the other hand, could do or be anything, and Grandma loved him just the same.

Maybe more.

"When she died, that's when Bo's problems got worse," I say now. "That's how he ended up here."

"Bo has talked about his grandmother a few times. He considers her home his 'safe place.'"

He would. I never liked going to that house. It was old and dark and smelled of stale cigarette smoke. But Bo loved it.

"Thank you," Dr. Franklin says. "You've been really helpful. Bo has had some troubles here lately, and I've struggled to connect with him. I thought I'd established trust with him, but he seems to be closing himself off from me more and more."

I raise an eyebrow. It doesn't seem like using me to rat on him would make Bo trust the doctor more, but I'm not the professional.

"But I also want you to know that I'm here for you too," Dr. Franklin adds. He slides his card across the desk toward me. "I want you to feel free to talk to me at any time."

"I'm not like Bo," I say immediately. "I don't have his same problem."

Dr. Franklin hesitates.

"Do I?" I ask. "Is it genetic or something? Is there a chance that I'll—"

"No, no, I didn't mean to imply that," Dr. Franklin says quickly. "I mean, there *is* a prevalence for this sort of thing to happen in families, but not necessarily. I've worked with your mother, and we can't confirm that any of your relatives have had similar issues to Bo's."

"But it's possible."

"It's . . . possible," he concedes.

I shift in my seat. I've never had any of the same symptoms as Bo, so maybe I'm safe. Or maybe his same set of gifts and curses lies inside me, even now, curled like a snake in winter, ready to rise. If not me, perhaps my children will be like Bo, slinking from mood to mood, time to time, leaving me behind just as Bo has done.

I have built a safe haven for myself in normalcy, but it's terribly lonely here.

CHAPTER 39

"We need to talk," Ryan whispers to me. His breath smells like mustard. "I just overheard some of the staff talking about 'official letters' that are being sent out to families during spring break."

Family Day butts up against spring break—in fact, most parents take their kids home after the luncheon. Even though Ryan's shuttle to the airport won't pick him up until tomorrow morning, I saw his bags were already packed and waiting by his bedroom door.

"So?" I ask, my eyes still on the staircase that leads to the Doctor's office, where Phoebe is.

"So, official letters mean official shit. The government goons are getting ready to go; the letters probably include their verdict on all this bull." When I don't answer, Ryan adds, "I'm worried they're going to shut the school down. Haven't you noticed the way the teachers have been acting?"

I watch as the weather outside the window swirls rapidly,

from hurricane winds to a bright sunny day to flurries of snow. I clench my eyes shut, and when I look again, there's nothing but the gray overcast sky.

"Berkshire can't close," I say under my breath. "I need it now more than ever."

"*Exactly*, you idiot. If it closes, I'm off to military school, and who knows what they'll do with you. I actually *like* this place. I'm not going to let them mess it all up just because of what happened to Sofía."

"I know," I say, turning my full attention to him. "If I could just save her, they would have to go."

"Well, that's not going to happen." Ryan's distracted, his voice dismissing my words.

"What"—I take a deep breath—"are you saying?"

Something in my voice causes Ryan to pause, and when he turns toward me again, there's something unrecognizable in his eyes. Is it fear? "Sorry, dude, I mean, I'm sure you can save her, it's just . . ." He struggles for words.

I release my breath. "Nah, man, I get it. My powers are out of whack. I just thought . . . I thought maybe the officials were somehow getting to you too. Everyone's been so *different* since they arrived . . ."

Ryan smirks. "They're not getting to me," he says. "I'm in full control." He turns again, eyeing a huddle of teachers clustered near the door, their heads bent close together, whispering.

"Full control of what?" Gwen's voice is pitched lower than normal as she approaches us. She shoves herself beside me, using her body to force me to take a step away from Ryan. "What are you talking about?" she says aggressively.

"Nothing. Move along." Ryan waves his hand, dismissing her.

Gwen turns to me. "Bo," she says, her voice much softer. "Are you okay?"

"Of course I am," I say.

"What's Ryan been telling you?"

"Nothing," I say.

Her frown deepens. Past her shoulder, I can see Ryan's face is turning angry. He's never really liked Gwen, and the way she interrupted him . . . he's not a very patient guy.

"Look, Gwen," I say, pulling her aside. "Everything's going to be okay. I know Ryan's not your favorite, but I have to work with him right now—"

"Why?" Her voice slices through my words like a knife. "Why do you have to work with that asshole? You know he's just using you, right? I don't know how or why, but that's all Ryan does—he uses people."

"Now that's not very nice," Ryan says. His voice is idle, almost bored, but it doesn't mask the fury building behind his eyes.

"Well, it's true," Gwen snaps, not bothering to turn around and look at him. "Bo, whatever he's trying to drag you into—"

"Gwen, it's okay," I say, trying to placate her. Some of the teachers near the door are looking our way. "Look, I know you don't understand what's going on. It's not your fault. The officials—"

"God, there's not some weird conspiracy against you!" Gwen's voice is growing desperate. "The officials aren't doing anything but investigating Sofía's death."

"And trying to shut down this school," Ryan growls.

"Well, maybe it *should* be shut down!"

The teachers by the door shoot Gwen a look. It's Family

Day. There are people watching. Gwen nods at them so they don't try to separate us, and she continues in a lower voice, "Maybe if the Doctor had a better idea of what's going on, maybe if he was more willing to drug us up or whatever, maybe Sofía wouldn't have died."

Gwen can't help that she doesn't understand. She's too deep in the officials' illusion.

"Don't worry," I tell her. "I know you don't understand, but we're going to make it all okay."

"You're not," Gwen says bluntly. "And the school will shut down anyway."

"I will *not* let that happen," Ryan says in a fierce, low voice. Behind him, a painting of Berkshire Academy when it first opened trembles on the wall. He can't control his telepathy when he's emotional.

"Whatever." Gwen glares at him, and when she turns to face me, the sympathy in her eyes from before is gone, replaced by anger and impatience. "I tried. There's no getting through to you."

She storms off, heading in the direction of her mom. And even though Gwen's forgotten about her powers, I see sparks trickling from her balled-up fists.

"So the first thing we have to do," Ryan says, "is confirm that all records are destroyed. *If* Gwen's right and the school is definitely doomed, at least we can make sure that we're not sent somewhere worse."

I see movement at the top of the stairs. I jerk my head around, expecting to see Phoebe, but instead, at the top of the landing is a soaking wet boy staring at me through clumps of dripping hair. "Be right back," I tell Ryan. Ignoring his protests,

I creep up the stairs toward the drowned Carlos Estrada. I move slowly, as if I were approaching a deer in the wild.

"Hey," I say in a low voice.

Carlos Estrada doesn't move, but his red-rimmed eyes flick to me.

"Why . . . why are you here? Why am I seeing you?"

Carlos opens his mouth. Water pours from it, and he makes a gurgling sound.

"Do you know . . . can you speak to Sofía?" I ask.

And then he's gone.

"Who are you talking to?" a small voice says from the top step.

I turn. Ryan, who followed me, is staring at me like I'm nuts, but Harold is with him, and he just looks curious.

I go to Harold immediately. Everyone always ignores Harold. But there's no one that I want to talk to more right now.

"So you didn't see . . . ?" I jerk my head toward the empty space in the hallway where Carlos Estrada had been dripping water all over the carpet.

Harold shakes his head. He hadn't seen him.

That means I'm not seeing ghosts—although Carlos Estrada was certainly dead. No, I'm seeing people from the past. I'm seeing Carlos Estrada in the moment just before he died, pulling him from the pool as his lungs filled with water. If he had been saved, if someone had noticed in time and dragged him from the water and given him CPR and saved his life, would Carlos Estrada have sputtered out an impossible tale about swallowing water and then ending up in the lush hallway of a beautiful academy, with a boy talking to him, quizzing him about Sofía?

If I grab hold of Carlos next time I see him, will I be pulled into his present, at the quinceañera where Sofía was, underwater but in the same time as her? Would I bob up to the surface and surprise a fifteen-year-old version of my girlfriend? I'm going to try that. Next time I see him, I'm going to try that.

A giggle of relief escapes my lips. It hardly matters. What matters is that I'm *not* seeing ghosts, not like Harold does.

Sure, that means rather than going crazy or being haunted, I'm in a world where the timestream is cracking around me, and it's possible that the entire space-time continuum is shattering at my feet like broken glass, but it also means that as I crash through time, I will see Sofía, and that's enough for me.

"Thanks," I say to Harold. I turn on my heel, heading toward the dorms. I want to try the timestream again. The Doctor always says that it's our emotions that lead to a lack of control, and I am hoping that it's been my doubts that have affected my ability to travel in time. The more I questioned whether I *could* save Sofía, the more erratic the timestream became. Intent matters. Maybe confidence does too.

Dr. Franklin's office door swings open as I pass, and Phoebe practically collides into me. "Bo!" the Doctor says, surprised. "I didn't know you were there!"

I glare at him, at Phoebe as she leaves, walking hurriedly to the stairs and back to our parents without meeting my eyes. What was that about? What did he tell her? What did *she* tell him?

"Come into my office," Dr. Franklin says, holding the door open.

CHAPTER 40

He asks how I'm doing.

I lie and say everything is fine. I don't mention the cracks in the timestream. I don't mention seeing Carlos Estrada or any of the other people from the past.

I don't even mention Sofía.

But I do bring up Phoebe. "What were you talking to her about?"

"Just how she's doing. She thinks you're happier here than at home. Is that true?"

It *was*. Before all this shit happened.

"She mentioned that she broke her arm when she was a kid. Do you remember that?"

That seems like an odd thing for her to bring up.

"What'd she tell you?" I ask.

"Just that it was an accident."

So she didn't spill that I was traveling to the past when I was that young. Phoebe at least can keep my secrets, if nothing else.

"What else were you talking about?"

"Your mom just wanted me to reach out to her."

"Why?" I shoot back aggressively. "What's wrong with her?" My heart clenches, and I wonder: Am I more concerned that something's wrong, or am I worried that she's going to outshine me in this too—that she also has a power, a better one than mine?

"No, no," the Doctor says. "Nothing like that. I just wanted to make sure she's okay. She's under a lot of stress."

"Stress? *Phoebe?*"

"There are different kinds of stress, Bo," the Doctor says, his voice placating and annoying. "You're dealing with your problems, but that doesn't mean Phoebe doesn't have her own."

Choosing a college and wondering whether or not she's going to get an *A*, that's her stress. She doesn't have to worry about whether or not her power is driving her crazy, or if she can save her girlfriend from dying in the past while also saving everyone else and the school in the present.

Stress. Okay.

Dr. Franklin tells me how proud he is of me, how much more in control of my emotions I've been lately. If he knew that the timestream was leaking everywhere, I doubt he'd say that.

But I have to remind myself that this isn't the Doctor I know. This is a Doctor under the influence of the officials.

He tells me about the medication he wants me to take during spring break. "Of course, I've spoken with your parents about all this as well."

That could prove to be a problem. Whatever the Doc's been telling Dad has already made him distrustful of me. If he piles a bunch of pills in Mom's hands, I'm sure she's going to try to make me take them.

I know this is the officials' doing. They can't alter my perception, so they're trying a different tactic—they want to drug me into submission. I should warn Ryan that they might try to drug him too.

"When you get back," the Doctor continues, "Dr. Rivers and Mr. Minh will be gone. They've concluded their investigation into Sofía's death and the school's practices."

"Gone?" I repeat.

Dr. Franklin nods.

"They're just . . . going to go away?" I ask, still not believing it. They have total control of the school. Why just . . . leave?

"Their work is done. They're issuing a report to the board, and the school may change based on that, but it's all pretty much over." His voice is a little sad.

Outside Dr. Franklin's window, an old-timey ship bobs on the waves in the ocean. When I blink, it's gone.

And so am I.

I've been pulled back into a different time. Snow and frost crust the windows, and the radiator rattles in the corner. No one else is in the Doc's office. I stand up from the blue plastic chair, slowly turning around, looking for a clue. The door starts to open, and I dive behind Dr. Franklin's filing cabinets.

Dr. Franklin walks into his office, but it's the Doctor from sometime in the past. I'm not sure when. Not too long ago.

He goes immediately to his desk and sits down. I stand motionless. How did he not see me? I'm not that well hidden.

A knock at the door, a quiet, hesitant tap.

"Come in," the Doctor says, and the door to his office widens a little more.

Sofía walks in.

She looks right at me.

But it's clear she doesn't see me. Neither of them do. I may as well be invisible.

This doesn't make sense, I think. I can travel through time, but it's still me. My body. They should be able to see me.

"Let's talk," the Doctor says kindly.

Sofía fiddles with her necklace—a silver chain with a dolphin charm.

"What's wrong?" Dr. Franklin says when Sofía doesn't speak. "Can you tell me about it?"

Sofía doesn't say anything. She doesn't shrug or dismiss the Doctor; she's just still and silent.

I creep closer, looking at her, really looking at her. Sofía was very good at going unnoticed even when she wasn't invisible. But I look now, and I see the dark marks under her eyes. I see the way her lips are chapped and dry. I see the way her skin lacks its usual glow.

I see the way she sits on the edge of her seat, her eyes pleading with the Doctor's, begging him to see that something is wrong with her. Hoping he can understand. That he can help.

"You have to talk to me," Dr. Franklin says, and I notice desperation in his voice. "I want to help, but I can't do it without you."

I sit down beside Sofía, in the same seat that I was occupying before I slipped back in time. Neither of them acknowledges my existence.

The Doctor waits a long time for Sofía to talk, but she remains silent.

"I'm sorry," I whisper, even though I know she can't see me. "I didn't realize." I still don't realize. I just know that something is wrong, something important, and I didn't see it before. She needed me, and I didn't see it.

"Everything's okay now," Sofía tells the Doctor in a soft voice that still holds a note of steely determination. She sounds as if she's made a decision.

And then she turns to look at me. Her irises are invisible. They always were the first things to go.

"You need to wake up," she says, staring at me.

"Can you see me?" I say. "What's going on? Why can't Dr. Franklin see me? And what do you mean?"

"*Wake up!*" she shouts, the last word drowning into a scream.

I jerk back, stumbling out of my chair.

"Bo?" the Doctor asks.

I'm back in the present.

"Is something wrong?"

I stare at the empty chair beside me. "No," I say slowly. "No, everything's okay now."

CHAPTER 41

I sit cross-legged on the cool sandy soil in front of the ruined remains of the chimney at the edge of the marsh. I'm so still that an observer might think I'm meditating.

But I'm not. I'm waiting.

I stare at the timestream, concentrating on the areas that are leaking around me. Not all of the times and places breaking through are connected to the island, but most are. The Native American tribes I catch glimpses of look like the ones that lived here before the first European settlers, and the Pilgrims I see could be from any of the colonies, but it seems likely that they live nearby. The kids from the sick camp are obviously from around here.

It takes me a while to realize that the people who are showing up from different *places*—people like Carlos Estrada, or a Mexican family speaking Spanish rapidly, or a group of giggling girls around fifteen years old dressed in fluffy dresses—they're all coming from different places, but they all link back to her.

All the leaks in time are centered on either the island or Sofía. Somehow, they're connected. And if I can figure out that connection, maybe I can figure out how to stop the leaks, control the timestream, and save Sofía.

So I'm waiting, watching, trying to piece together all the different bits of time swirling in and around this place.

Trying to forget the way Sofía's eyes turned invisible as she screamed at me.

I am perfectly still as the timestream creaks and groans like the deck of a wooden ship. I turn my head slightly to see a group of kids rushing by, running and laughing, one of them waving a long, colorfully decorated stick. Something from Sofía's past—some childhood birthday party or similar. I consider jumping up and chasing them back into their time, where I could see Sofía when she was eight or nine years old. Maybe I could warn her to stay away from the boy who can control time.

But she'd be too young. And I'd be too out of place.

A fire crackles in the ruins' hearth. The fire spreads, both creating and destroying the house as it burns. I can feel the heat of it on my skin, and its smoke blinds me. I start coughing and stumble back, moving away from the flames. This is how the house was destroyed in the 1700s. It wasn't people who slipped through the timestream this time, it was the whole damn house.

And then I hear a scream.

"Sofía?" I gasp, choking on the smoke.

No. That's impossible. Sofía was sent back a hundred years before the fire started. There's no way—

And then I see her. In the second story of the burning building. She's screaming, beating her arms on the glass panes. She's trapped. She's burning alive.

"SOFÍA!" I roar, rushing toward the flaming house.

It disappears.

The sound and the smoke disappear too, leaving me gasping, my head spinning.

She was there.

But . . . how?

Maybe . . . maybe the cracks in time are all linked to Sofía and this island not because she's trapped in the 1600s, during the Salem Witch Trials, but because Sofía's trapped in the cracks, falling through time, and the only thing linking her to reality is this island.

As I stand there, trying to figure out what's going on, the house reappears. It doesn't smell of acrid burning; it smells of freshly sawn wood and new paint. The stone steps leading to the front door grow up under my feet, and I turn, slowly, my back to the house.

I see Sofía again.

This time, she's crying. Silently but violently, her shoulders shake and her teeth chatter in fear.

There's a rope around her neck.

Four men—two of whom I had seen before on horseback in the marsh—stand over Sofía's body. She's gotten her hands on some time-appropriate clothes; she looks like a Pilgrim. Except for her too-dark skin.

Another woman is there, a teenaged girl with blonde hair and dark eyes. She points at Sofía and yells, "Witch!"

The girl starts moving as if she's having a seizure, but her motions are too planned, too repetitive. The men standing over Sofía take action. One leaves the group to comfort the girl. The others throw the end of the rope over a heavy branch of

a nearby oak tree, and they use a horse to drag Sofía's protest-
ing body up and up and up. She claws at the noose around her
neck, her eyes wide and popping.

"Stop!" I shout, striding forward.

But before I can do anything, they all disappear.

I spin around wildly, looking for whatever break in the
timestream is going to happen next. The chimney is a ruin; the
tree they were stringing Sofía up on is nothing but a stump. I
sink to my knees. Is this Sofía's hell? To be found and killed
throughout time?

I hear laughing.

I stand back up, my legs weak, but I force myself to walk
toward the sound, toward the abandoned camp for sick kids.

When I get there, it's . . . strange. The buildings are old and
empty, abandoned as always. But there are more than a dozen
kids in shirts that look like they come from the '70s. Some of
the kids are obviously sick, in wheelchairs or braces or helmets,
but some are not. Two are in the pool, splashing around. Or . . .
I stare, my mouth dropping open. The pool is dry and dirty with
weeds growing in the bottom. But the two kids are standing in
the shallow end, laughing and flailing their arms around as if
the pool is full of water. One of the kids dives backward, and I
almost cry out, expecting him to smash his head into the cracked
cement, but he floats in water he can feel but I cannot see.

Two other kids nearby are throwing a ball. I can see the ball
when it touches one of the kids' hands, but as soon as it flies in
the air toward the other kid, it's invisible again.

"Where's Sofía?" I mutter, looking around. In my past two
visions, she was there. She needed me. She must need me now.
She must be at this camp.

I run up to the buildings, throwing open the doors and peering inside. They are empty, abandoned, decrepit. Sunlight leaks through the spaces between the warped boards of the walls, exposing rat droppings and a dead cockroach in the corner. But outside I can still hear the sounds of people laughing and talking, moving and shuffling through the buildings, including the ones I just left.

It's *creepy*.

But no Sofía.

I return to the center of the camp. The only people I see are the kids playing. No adults, no counselors, or whoever else is supposed to be here. I grab the nearest kid, a little girl with Down syndrome. "Do you know Sofía?" I shout at her.

She starts crying. All around me, the camp becomes more and more present. Water fills the pool, the grass is greener, the buildings are brighter. More people appear in the background, including some adults who are starting my way. By touching the little girl, I've pulled myself into her time.

I shake her shoulders urgently. "Can you see me? Do you know Sofía?"

Her sobs turn louder.

"Bo?"

I turn just in time for my eyes to connect with Sofía's. But before I can say anything, she points at something behind me and screams, *"Run!"*

I turn—

And then I'm ripped away. Not by a person, but by a force. By time.

I'm thrown back into a place I don't recognize. There is no sick kids' camp. There is no Berkshire. There's not a chimney from the 1600s . . . or even a house. There's only the island, bare, swampy, and loud with the sounds of waves crashing on the shore. A greenhead fly buzzes past me.

There's a rustling in the tall grass. I stand completely still as a young deer creeps forward, her nose in the air, sniffing for danger. She turns and sees me. We stare at each other for a moment, then she darts around, her tail high and white, bounding away from me.

I feel the pull of time in my navel first, and before I even have a chance to call for Sofía, I'm dragged back and back again.

I'm at the camp again, but back when it first opened, when it was just for kids with polio. Then I'm at the Berk just as it was being built, before I'm thrown again to a time that may be the far future, the academy nothing but a crumbling foundation of brick, and the camp completely hidden by weeds and trees. I'm whipped around, backward and forward through time, spun across the island, a witness to its every incarnation.

And hidden in every moment of time . . . Sofía.

I see glimpses of dark hair, whispers of her pleading voice, or screams ripped from her mouth. Sometimes she's invisible. Sometimes I can see her in the distance: running from something unknown, being held down by men from other times, walking silently into the ocean on her own, weighed down with stones. At one point I see nothing but a freshly dug, unmarked grave, but I know it's hers. Every time I see, *every time*, she's just out of my reach, just far enough away that I cannot save her.

I try to call up the timestream. I try to find the strings that will pull me to my own time or just anchor me to *any* time. I whirl faster and faster, coming apart at the seams. The island and its contents meld together, trees and grass and dirt and buildings nothing more than a green-and-brown blur. But the occasional faces I see in each time are sharp and unique, standing out against the whirl, but each one is unrecognizable. No Sofía. No Dr. Franklin or Ryan or Gwen or Harold. Not even one of the officials.

And then, out of the corner of my eye, I see a ponytail that's familiar. I reach for it blindly, my fingers barely able to entwine into the girl's hair.

Into my sister Phoebe's hair.

When I open my eyes next, I'm in my old bedroom at my parents' house. It looks exactly the same as when I was last at home, a sheet over the door, my notebook and the USB drive on my desk, but I search for some indication of how much time has passed . . . or has yet to pass.

The curtain blocking my door is swept to the side. Phoebe stands in the doorway, illuminated by the hallway light.

"About time you're awake," she says.

CHAPTER 42

How did I get here?

My parents and sister are acting like it's perfectly normal for me to be here, now. My mom cooks dinner every night, beaming at me as she puts down a plate of pork tenderloin or beef kebobs or whatever other recipe she found online. My dad reads the newspaper. Phoebe watches TV, bringing me a bowl of popcorn like there's nothing weird about the fact that I'm here.

But sometimes . . . sometimes they forget I'm here. When they look directly at me, they see and accept my presence. But if I stick to the walls and shadows, if I avoid their gaze, it's like I'm as invisible as Sofía can be.

I don't think I'm really here. I'm only half here, only made real when they remember I exist.

Or maybe I am here, and they can tell that something is wrong. My family is extraordinarily good at ignoring problems, especially when I'm the problem.

Or maybe I've fallen into a reality where this—me, forgotten and powerless—is normal.

Dad came into my room one day—remarkably easy to do when you only have to sweep aside a curtain—and took my laptop. He just took it. I was in the middle of using it, and he just lifted it out of my grasp and walked away. I'm not sure if that was during one of the moments when he could see me or not.

But before he took my laptop, I did as much reading on time travel as I could. I latched onto the idea of string theory, maybe because the timestream looks like strings to me. Each string of time leads me to a different place, a different time. But in string theory, the idea is that each string leads you to a different reality.

I've tried to call up the timestream.

I can't.

Maybe that's where I am now, in a reality where my powers don't work. Or maybe my last experience, when I cycled through different times so fast I could barely breathe, has put my powers on a temporary hold.

Time, as always, will tell.

I don't really know what to do here. This house—this family—doesn't fit me anymore. It's not even like a pair of jeans that are a few inches too short; it's like someone gave me a baby's onesie and told me to try to wear it.

My parents keep finding excuses to look in my room. Dad lingers in the hallway behind my curtained door, his feet pointed toward me, sometimes shuffling forward as if he wants to come in. Mom comes up with reasons to enter, laundry, a snack, something. At least she knocks on the wall before pushing aside my curtain, but if they're not going to trust me with a doorknob, I don't see how knocking makes much of a difference.

I keep trying to go back to the island and Berkshire. Or just back in time. I'm trying to go anywhere, really. I can feel the timestream like an itch underneath my skin, but I can't reach it, no matter how often I try to call it.

What if I've lost my power for good?

No. I refuse to believe that. Losing my power means losing Sofía.

Forever.

And I cannot live in a world without her.

I'll find a way back to the timestream.

To her.

Phoebe's been acting weird. She pretty much goes out with friends or stays locked up in her room all the time, but there's something off about her.

I don't know why my parents can't see it, but when I look at Pheebs, it's obvious that something's not right. There's some worry eating her away, something that she won't put into words, and maybe she can't. She hides it, she's always hiding it behind a bright pink lip-glossed smile, but there's something . . .

It reminds me of the way there was something wrong with Sofía. I didn't notice with her, but I do with Phoebe.

I tried to talk to Phoebe, but the words all came out wrong, and she laughed at me and went back to her room. That's all this damn house is, a bunch of shut doors. Except mine.

Maybe that's why time threw me back here. Maybe in addition to everything else that's wrong in my life, my home is crumbling, but all my family does is smile and shut their eyes.

CHAPTER 43

Phoebe

Bo moves like a wild animal, scratching at the walls of the house.

I hear him creeping down the hallway moments before Mom shouts at us that dinner's ready. I pass him on the stairs—he's pressed against the railing as if my touch would poison him, but he watches me as I descend, not moving again until I'm off the final step.

Mom has poured every ounce of her homemaker instinct into setting the table. Fresh white and blue hydrangeas are clustered in the center of the table, flanked on each side by a pair of unlit candles. Just before Mom whips the flowers off the table to make room for the roast chicken, though, I realize they're fake. Expensive, realistic fakes, but still. Fake.

Doesn't she understand that the only thing that gives the candles purpose is burning them? That what makes flowers beautiful is the fact that they eventually die?

"Rosemary chicken!" Mom proclaims, as if this is a triumph.

"Looks good." Dad snaps the paper to make it lie flat.

I slump in my chair, waiting to be served. Dad carves the chicken, dropping a piece on everyone's plate. Mom passes around baked macaroni and cheese and a bowl of green beans flecked with something red.

Bo stands behind his chair. Mom looks at him, her mouth open to speak, but then she pushes away from the table abruptly, muttering that it'd be better to use the slotted spoon for the green beans rather than the one she has sticking out of the dish. Bo leans over his chair, filling up his plate unceremoniously. He doesn't pass bowls or the platter of chicken; he just reaches over the table. As soon as he has what he wants, he picks up his plate silently and returns to his room, not saying a word.

Mom comes back from the kitchen and opens her mouth to call Bo back to the table.

"Let the boy go, Martha," Dad says, turning to the sports section. He sighs. "It's more peaceful like this anyway."

Peaceful. This house is so peaceful that it's practically dead.

Mom sort of crumples into her seat and listlessly picks up her fork. She eats her food in a circle, starting with the green beans and moving to the mac and cheese before cutting the chicken into tiny pieces. Dad eats absentmindedly, reading the paper. I stab my food and swish it around the plate, but hardly anything winds up in my mouth.

"George," Mom says.

Dad looks up.

"It's dinnertime." She looks pointedly at the paper. He

scoots it to the side of the table, where Bo would normally sit, but his eyes linger on the text.

We all chew our food.

I want nothing more than to pick the chicken carcass up off the table and slam it into the ground. The white porcelain platter would shatter beautifully, sending shards across the dark hardwood floors, splattering chicken grease everywhere.

I reach for the bowl of mac and cheese even though I haven't eaten what's on my plate yet. I wonder what Dad would do if I turned the bowl upside down on his head. Just that. Just turned it upside down and let the yellow, slimy noodles drip down the side of his face, and then walked back to my room as if nothing happened.

Like Bo did.

What would it be like to be Bo? To be already broken, to have no expectations laid upon me? Because as much as I'd like to burn this whole dining room to the ground, I know I won't. I won't ever. My parents can handle one child who walks as if he's in a trance, taking what he wants and leaving without a word.

They can't handle it from me too.

The chicken tastes like dirt in my mouth. I've never seen Bo act this way before, as if he could pretend he was alone and make it so. I've never seen him this far gone, this wrapped up in his own little bubble.

I'm so messed up. I'm *so* messed up, because right now, I'm sort of jealous.

I don't have the luxury of allowing myself to break. Bo is Bo. He can do what he wants, be who he wants. But not me. I have to be the good daughter. I have to come home every night.

I have to get good grades and have a decent appearance and goals and ambitions that line up with my parents'.

Because if I break, they'll break too.

It's a responsibility I'd never really felt before, or at least I never thought about enough to name. But Bo's actions just cement my place in my family. He can walk away from the dinner table.

I can't.

After helping Mom wash the dishes before she puts them in the dishwasher, I head back to my room. Bo's curtain is to the side, so I can see the way he sits in the center of the bed, almost as if he's meditating, his legs crossed, his head bent. His arms reach out in front of him, as if he's trying to grab something, but his fingers meet nothing but air.

"Hey."

Bo opens his eyes, and he seems a little surprised that I'm there.

I pick up his dirty plate from the edge of the bed. "Mom's doing dishes," I say as an excuse for interrupting him. He gives me a dismissive jerk of his head.

I turn to go, but then he moves, and I pause, and it feels as if we're both part of an awkward play, waiting for the other to give a cue.

"Is everything okay?" he asks finally.

I stare at him. *Everything but you*, I want to say, but we both know that's not true. Not true at all.

Instead, I try to smile. "I'm glad you're back home," I say, and I don't let myself think about whether or not I'm telling the truth.

Bo's gaze slides away from mine. It's obvious he doesn't feel the same way.

"So, listen," I say, shifting the plate from one hand to the other. I want to say . . . something. Talking with that doctor a few days ago has made me think a lot about the past, like when I broke my arm. It's made me wonder when things went wrong. And that's made me think about when things were right.

"Thanks," I say.

"For what?" Bo looks confused.

"For, um, teaching me how to drive."

Bo laughs a little. "What? I didn't do that. It was Dad or . . ."

"No." My voice is quiet but certain. "It was you." When I meet his eyes, it's obvious he still doesn't understand. "We were on the road trip, remember? In Colorado. And Dad wanted to 'take us off the beaten path,' so he drove us to this really scary, winding road. It wasn't even a real road; it was for loggers or something. Mom wouldn't look out the window, and she held on to that bar on the side of the door."

"Oh yeah," Bo says, a smile playing on his face. That trip had been our last family vacation. Driving and camping had been fun when we were younger, but we were both in high school then, and it was annoying to have to share the car charger with everyone and hope my phone's signal lasted in the woods.

"And then Dad stopped the car and told me to drive."

I still remember the crisp, cold air and the scent of evergreens when Dad and I swapped places in the car. I was fifteen at the time, so it wasn't technically legal, but the road probably wasn't technically legal either, and no one was around. Just us and the mountains and the trees. Mom had been nervous, but I was excited—my first time behind the steering wheel. But as soon as I got in the driver's seat, I sort of freaked out. Not on the outside, of course, but my brain was screaming in panic.

"It was so scary," I mused. "I mean, the mountain's edge on one side and trees on the other. The whole time, I kept thinking, 'If I go just a little bit to the left or the right, I'll crash the car and kill us all. I am going to kill my whole family.'"

Bo snorts. "You were going, like, two miles an hour."

"I was not!"

"You were. I could have walked faster."

"Whatever. And Dad was yelling—"

"He was telling you to speed up—"

"And Mom was telling me to use the brake—"

"Because she's a scaredy-cat—"

"And I was swerving all over the road—"

"Again, you were barely moving at all—"

"And do you remember what you said?"

I want him to know that this moment was really important to me. I remember it so vividly. I had been leaning forward, half my body over the steering wheel, trying to look as closely at the road as I could, squinting at the little bit of gravel just in front of the car. "You have to look further out," Bo had said from the backseat. "You can't look right in front of the car." And then, I don't know, I just got it. I understood. I needed to focus on the distance; I needed to see where I was going.

But Bo just shrugs now. He doesn't remember.

"Anyway . . . thanks," I say. I step out of his room, my foot landing on the gouge in the hardwood floor.

I take Bo's plate back to the kitchen. On the stairs as I head back to my room, I get a text from Jenny. I keep my eyes on the screen as I pass Bo's room again, not willing to make eye contact and conversation a second time.

What's up? Jenny texts.

Nothing. I step into my room and close the door firmly. **Bo's here.**

I've always been jealous, Jenny types, **that you have a brother.**
LOL, not this one.

No, you don't understand. The words come fast and furious across my screen. **You just don't get how weird it is to be an only child. It would be so much better to have a brother or a sister or something. You have no idea how good you have it.**

I turn off my phone, ignoring the buzzes as more texts arrive. Jenny is the one with no idea. Because the reality is? She may want a brother, but she doesn't want Bo. She just doesn't understand. I mean, I know she's heard me complain about him, but she thinks it's like the movies when two siblings fight and then eventually bond and become besties. But that sort of thing is just as fake as the idea that taking off your glasses and putting on some eyeliner is all it takes to change from the class freak to a hottie. The truth is, sometimes siblings have nothing in common but blood. Sometimes you just know that the concept of a BFF brother is not applicable to your family.

Sometimes you stay up late at night, thinking things that make you feel like a heartless monster, wishing for something different and then feeling sick with guilt because you know what the cost of "different" would be.

Jenny doesn't want this life. There's a difference between having no siblings and having a broken one.

• • •

An hour later, my door opens without warning, and I jump from my bed, expecting to shout at Mom. That's our silent rule—I will be the daughter they need, but I get my privacy.

But it's not Mom, it's Bo. He glances at me, then quickly away, avoiding my eyes and sticking closely to the wall as he creeps around my furniture. He makes his way to my desk and unplugs my laptop, tucking it under his arm.

"You could have asked!" I shout after him.

But he walks out of the room as if he hasn't even heard me.

CHAPTER 44

Sometimes they notice me, sometimes they don't. I wonder if I'm fading in and out of existence, or if they are.

Sofía once told me that she found a red Moleskine notebook among her mother's possessions after she died. The first twenty or so pages were filled with her chicken scratch, but the rest were blank.

Sofía had sat there, in the middle of the bedroom her mother retreated to when her father drank too much, surrounded by her clothes and the smell of her perfume, and she read every single page.

Her mother had started the book the day she took a pregnancy test and realized she was going to have another child. More than half the written pages were about her hopes and her fears for Sofía while she was growing in her belly. She poured her heart into those pages, whispering in writing that was barely legible her wish that Sofía would be another girl, that she would grow up strong and courageous, far more so than her mother had ever been.

The rest of the written pages were from after Sofía was born. More and more time passes between each entry. Some of the entries were angry—at Sofía, at her father, at the life her mother struggled with. But some of them were far kinder. These entries were written in pencil, hardly leaving a mark on the page, as if her mother was so certain the good days would not last that she left herself an easy way to erase the marks should they prove untrue.

Sofía said that when she found the notebook, she cried—for the first time since the accident, she cried. And she held that book close to her heart, upset not just because of what the pages held, but because of all the pages that held nothing at all. Most of the book was blank. Although Sofía's mother started writing in the notebook before Sofía was born, somewhere between giving birth to her little sister, raising three daughters, living with Sofía's father, and everything else life threw at her, she just . . . quit. Maybe she forgot. Maybe she ran out of things to say. But either way, the blank pages would remain forever empty.

Since I can't access the timestream and I'm stuck at home, I've been writing in an old notebook. Sometimes, instead of jotting down ideas of ways to get everything back to normal, I just write about Sofía. Or *to* Sofía. And sometimes the blank pages stare at me, waiting, and I don't know if they'll stay blank forever or if they'll become something more.

My words would give them meaning, but there's a meaning behind blank pages too.

I got Pheebs's laptop. If I can't figure out the past through the timestream, maybe I can figure out more from the USB drive.

For the most part, the recorded sessions are a weird hybrid between what I know happened and what doesn't make sense. It's all talk. Talk, talk, talk. No powers.

I don't know if it was the officials who tampered with the videos, but whoever did it did a good job. Any outsider watching these would have no idea that each session with the Doctor was a group lesson about controlling our powers. Gwen's fires are either missing altogether or they're the result of matches or lighters that the Doctor jumps up quickly to confiscate. Rather than travel through time, I just stare blankly ahead. When Ryan uses his telepathy, it simply looks like he's throwing something.

And Sofía is always visible.

I watch her, mostly. Sometimes I can line up my memory with the way she appears on-screen. The moments in sessions when she'd turn invisible are altered so that she just grows very still and withdrawn, sometimes hiding behind her hair.

I like to think I've been a good student. I always paid attention during the Doctor's sessions, and I've always wanted to have control over my powers, to not be such a liability.

But now I'm watching her instead of Dr. Franklin. I'm looking at the moments that made her go invisible. There are times during the Doctor's sessions when it's like a gun blast going off; Sofía flinches visibly, and then that weird sort of stillness washes over her, indicating that she went transparent in real life.

It happens when Dr. Franklin talks about the way we react to things that make us anxious, about how our first instincts in moments of fear or pressure may not be our best ones. It happens when Harold talks to his ghosts loudly, in a way that overtakes the session and the Doctor has to escort him out. It happens when Ryan sits too close to Sofía or pays her too much attention.

It happens when the Doctor talks about family. He likes talking about family and the way it defines us, and every time, Sofía goes invisible.

CHAPTER 45

The videos cycle quickly, one into another, cutting on and off at the very beginning and end of each session. Except one.

I sit up straighter in bed. I vaguely remember this day, when Ryan had tried to strengthen his telepathy and mind-control powers. He was still developing them—he was much better at telekinesis then, but not all the mind stuff. The screen shows Ryan in full meltdown mode as he stands and screams at everyone, but in real life he just lost control of his power. We were all sitting there as he was experimenting, trying to implant an idea inside of us. The Doctor had started with something innocuous: Make us all think about wanting to eat an apple. At first it worked. In fact, the Doctor had a basket of apples, and we all stood up to get one, even though we'd just had breakfast. But as we ate the apples under Ryan's influence, they turned bitter in our mouths. He lost control not just of his own mind but of ours as well.

I gag thinking about it now. For me, the apple turned to

dust. Sofía said hers became slimy and filled with worms, so soft she could squish the rotten insides in her hand. Whatever Harold saw of his apple made him scream and throw it across the room, nearly breaking the office window.

It got worse after that. It wasn't just the apple inside our heads, twisted and gross, it was Ryan's entire mind. His whole mentality poured into our brains, taking over, erasing us, flashing us with memories we didn't want to see, things Ryan had experienced that none of us knew: his mother, an actress, who could barely remember his name; his father, a director, who hated his mother for cheating on him and took it out on his son. A parade of nannies, each increasingly incompetent, except for one when he was twelve, who hurt him in ways none of us could ever have imagined.

It was too much. To have ourselves in our bodies but also Ryan, to feel everything he felt coating our brains like black mold. By the end of the session, we were all clutching our heads and crying, and the Doctor had to use his healing power on each of us just to get us off the floor.

Except Ryan. The Doctor couldn't heal Ryan, because the memories he lived with, the thoughts inside his head—those were all his own. The Doctor couldn't take them away.

Maybe that's why Ryan worked so hard to advance his telepathy and control his own mind. Maybe with that control, he could block part of himself off, the part that poisoned us all when we touched it.

In the video, though, that whole session plays out much differently. Basically, we all just talk, and then Ryan breaks down, crying—actually crying, I'd never seen him do that before—and spends the rest of the session confessing his darkest secrets, telling us about a nanny who abused him, parents who neglected him. We're disturbed, obviously, even the Doctor, but we didn't have those feelings literally pressed into our brains, and at the end of the session, we all leave.

Except Ryan. The Doc calls his name.

"Yeah?" Ryan asks sullenly.

"Come on back in, buddy," he says. "I want to ask you some things."

Ryan plops back down in one of the blue plastic chairs, and the Doc pulls up another one so he can face him.

"What?" Ryan asks, an edge to his voice.

"I wanted to thank you for opening up to us today," Dr. Franklin says.

Ryan shrugs.

"And I also want to say that when you're ready, we could go to the police with some of this information. It's not right, the way the adults in your life have treated you. You understand that, yes? In fact, it's criminal, particularly what your nanny did. We could press charges . . ."

He stops when he notices Ryan laughing.

"Oh my God, really? *Really?*" Ryan says, his eyes lighting up with glee. "I thought I laid it on too thick, honestly, but you really bought all that, didn't you? Hook, line, and sinker."

The Doctor leans away, his eyes narrowing. "You made all that up today?" he asks. "Ryan, I'm deeply disappointed in you."

Ryan shrugs. "I just wanted to see if I could make you guys believe me. And I could. Good to know."

"Trust, once broken, is hard to establish again," Dr. Franklin says.

Ryan slumps in his chair. "I just wanted to have a little fun."

"Making up a story about being abused as a child is not 'fun,' Ryan."

"It is for me."

The Doctor glowers, but Ryan continues. "Look, I'm *bored*, okay? Bored. I don't belong here. Locked up with these crazies."

"No one here is 'crazy,'" Dr. Franklin says. "Berkshire Academy is for the emotionally and behaviorally disturbed."

"Whatever. They don't tell you everything. They're crazy. Which, to be fair, is sometimes amusing. I wonder if I can use that for my benefit. It'd be neat to make Harold believe his 'ghosts' are real. Or maybe make Gwen burn this whole place down."

"Gwen's been responding very well to her therapy," Dr. Franklin says.

Ryan snorts. "I bet I could make her do it."

"Why?" The Doctor is trying very hard to keep his face straight, to be the kind, patient listener, but I can see there's disgust in his eyes.

"It'd be fun," Ryan says. "To see what I could do. To make them all fail. If I had a lighter, I'd give it to Gwen right now, and I'd make the little pyro burn this whole school down."

"You could cause serious damage, Ryan. Your lies and manipulation aren't just words. People could get hurt, even die."

Ryan shrugs.

Dr. Franklin leans over, moving his face so that he meets Ryan's gaze. "Ryan," he says in a very serious tone, "your manipulation seriously concerns me. I need to know that you understand the difference between right and wrong."

He talks for a while more, but my eyes are glued on Ryan's face. This is not a side of him I've ever seen before. *Or have I?*

"Do you?" Dr. Franklin asks him.

"Do I what?" Ryan's eyes shift to the wall, as if the wood grain holds more entertainment than this conversation.

"Do you understand what I'm saying? Do you feel like you know the difference between right and wrong?"

"Yeah," Ryan says, pushing up from his chair and heading to the door. "Of course I do."

But there's a difference between knowing what's right and wrong and actually acting on it.

The Doctor stares at the door for a long moment, and he looks torn about whether or not to chase Ryan down. In the end, he gets up and moves toward the video recorder, about to turn it off. For a moment, I see the Doctor's face close up. This had been an evening session, just before a weekend, and Dr. Franklin carries the weight of the entire week on his face. There is so much about these videos that's fake—everything that happened in them, really—but that look on his face, that's real. His eyes are still on the door, but I can see the crinkles in the corner, the way his brow furrows down, the cracks in his usual cheerful facade. He's showing exhaustion—a moment of defeat. He reaches for the door, his mouth already opening to call Ryan back.

Before he can, though, the door opens. His face tightens with anxiety as he turns, expecting to see one of us again. Instead, it's the unit leaders for the rest of the school, as well as a few of the teachers. Ms. Grantham is carrying a plate of cupcakes, and Mr. Glover has three bottles of wine in his arms, and the rest of the unit leaders burst inside, all singing "Happy Birthday" to him.

I had no idea that day had been the Doc's birthday. From

the look on his face, it seems like the Doctor himself didn't realize it. But it's kind of nice to see all that worry melt away as he blows out a candle on the biggest cupcake.

The other unit leaders spread out in the chairs we'd been sitting in. It's so weird to see the leaders acting like . . . I don't know, like people. I'm used to them bossing us around, not laughing and joking and smushing cupcakes in their mouths and getting a little tipsy on wine.

The party doesn't last long, but Ms. Grantham is the last to leave. She lingers on purpose, finding excuses to clean up dropped napkins from the floor or help put away the chairs, until she's the last person in the room. Dr. Franklin looks at her, and there's a question and there's hope drawing them closer, wrapping around them like strings. Before they do anything, though, Dr. Franklin reaches over and cuts off the video feed.

CHAPTER 46

Phoebe

I'm half-asleep when someone knocks on my door. "Yeah?" I call.

Mom steps inside, holding two letters. "Mail!" she says brightly as she tosses one of them to me. It's from James Jefferson High; inside are details for the class trip to Europe this summer.

"What's that?" I ask, looking at the open letter still in Mom's hand. The Berkshire Academy for Children with Exceptional Needs logo is emblazoned across the top.

"Bo's school wrote us a letter," Mom starts.

"Is he in trouble?"

She shakes her head and passes the letter over to me. I get the impression that this whole "mail call" thing was just an excuse to show me the letter. I read quickly. The first page is a cut-and-paste form letter that was probably mailed out to every family. I already know most of it—that a girl from his class, Sofía Muniz, committed suicide. That government offi-cials have been observing the students, and that the board will be voting to determine the school's future in a few weeks. Parents are invited to give their opinions by phone or email.

The second page includes a personal note from Dr. Franklin, describing how the situation with the officials and the investigation affect Bo specifically. He warns us that Bo's therapy isn't working as well as he'd hoped, that he's changing his meds again, that Bo may have to be transferred to a new facility regardless of the school's fate.

"Huh," I say, handing the letter back to Mom.

"I just wanted you to know," Mom says. "We should be extra careful around Bo. It's a . . . sensitive time."

"Okay."

"Do you want to talk about it?" Mom asks.

"I'm not the one who needs to be talked to." I don't break eye contact, the challenge between us clear. But when Mom leaves my room, she doesn't go to see Bo. Instead, she heads down the hallway to consult Dad.

Typical. She has the perfect way to start a conversation with Bo, but instead, she's going to squirrel away the letter and her fears behind Dad's office door. It's like they're actively trying to keep the silence, as if silence was the best—the only—possible option for this family.

I play on my phone until well past midnight, but what I really want is a distraction. I want my laptop back, and I'm a little pissed at the way Bo took it. I mean, I don't *really* care, I wasn't using it, but he didn't even ask. He acted like I wasn't even in the room. And besides, it's mine.

I push myself off the bed and throw open my door. Bo's light is off, and I can hear him snoring on his bed, but it's easy to break into his room, considering he has no door. My laptop's battery light glows just enough for me to find it on his desk, and I creep inside his room, stepping over his dirty clothes on the floor, and snatch it back.

It's not until I'm sitting on my bed, my laptop plugged into the charger and open on my pillow, that I notice there's a small drive attached to the side. It's broken and jagged, but the actual drive seems to work. I click on the USB icon and find video files. Each file name is just a series of numbers, but it doesn't take long to figure out they're dates and times. I select one at random, and in the brief instant between when the file loads and starts to play, I worry that I've just stumbled onto Bo's private porn stash.

But the video just shows a room. Dr. Franklin's office. There he is, behind his desk, taking notes.

I crank up the volume on my laptop as Dr. Franklin pauses his work and the door opens.

Bo is the first person in the room. Other kids, ones I recognize from Bo's school, follow. They all sit in a circle as if they've done this a hundred times. It's all routine for them.

I lean in closer, the screen illuminating my face.

"Good morning," Dr. Franklin says. "I trust you all had a good Monday?"

Bo looks over at the girl he's sitting beside. She's short, with brown skin and black hair. "The best," he says with a smile.

Is that his girlfriend? I wonder. Bo's chair is scooted close to hers, but she hasn't moved closer to him. He keeps looking at her; she sweeps her hair over one side of her face, the side closest to him, like she's trying to hide. But then she tucks some of her hair behind her ear, and her hand drops beside his, her fingers brushing his open palm.

Dr. Franklin starts what looks like a group therapy session, with a theme of reading other people's emotions and caring about their comfort zones. He has one of the boys, a tiny little guy who's practically paper-white, stand in the center of the room for a demonstration about appropriate ways to treat people. Seems a bit cruel. The kid's shaking like a leaf, but most of my attention is on my brother.

I've never seen him like this. Unguarded. Real.

And more than that, I've never seen Bo as anything but my brother. Every time in my whole life that I've ever laid eyes on Bo, he's just been my brother. If I saw him in a crowd of people, like at an assembly, I would think: *There are all those people, and there's my brother.* He was separate. He was defined.

But here, in this video, at Berkshire Academy surrounded by people he knows that I don't, I'm seeing him not as my brother but just as a person. A stranger, even.

It's fascinating but also a little creepy.

I've never seen him wear such a puppy-dog look on his face, like the one right now in the video, as he stares at the girl sitting beside him. It makes me want to know her. Is she cool? Is she using Bo? Does she feel the same way toward him?

On the screen, Dr. Franklin turns toward the girl. "Sofía," he says, "do you have anything to add?"

She shakes her head mutely.

So that's Sofía, the girl who killed herself. Dr. Franklin told me that she and Bo had been close, and now I can see the way he feels about her. More than "close."

He loved her.

I can't see how she feels about him, though. She's guarded, but not obviously depressed. I guess I figured that someone who killed herself would look sad and tragic. A total emo, dressed in black, with a cutting habit. But Sofía looks . . . *normal.* There's nothing in the way she sits by my brother, in the way she listens to the others, in the way she sweeps her hair over her shoulder, to indicate that she's going to take her own life. I check the date on the file. It's like a countdown clock over her head. Three weeks after this video, this girl sitting by my brother will kill herself.

I watch the rest of the video, and maybe it's because I'm an outsider who doesn't know her personally, or maybe it's just because I know what will happen, but I can start to see the pieces of Sofía's fate fall into place. It's in the way she stands, as if just breathing is exhausting to her, as if carrying the weight of her own body around is dragging her underwater. It's in the way she watches other people, detached, curious, like a scientist observing animals in the wild. She goes through the motions. When someone else is upset or sad or happy, it takes her a second to realize that she should mirror that emotion back, and another second for her to arrange her face into a mask of whatever emotion she's hiding behind.

The little details all add up to one girl's death. Each warning sign is tiny, almost imperceptible. I watch the last few videos straight through, knowing that Sofía has only days left. Her eyes lose focus during the group therapy sessions as she gradually becomes more and more disinterested in what's happening around her. She gives the other girl in her class a silver bracelet as if it means nothing to her, but I saw the way her fingers lingered on it in earlier videos. When Bo smiles at her, it takes her longer and longer to smile back, as if she has to remind herself what that configuration of facial features means, or maybe she's just mustering up the energy to mimic him.

Sometimes she is—I don't know how to say it, and it's weird to think this way because I never knew her, but sometimes it seems like Sofía is more herself. But then sometimes she just seems . . . absent.

I wonder, if I had been in Bo's class, if I had occupied one of those blue plastic chairs, would I have noticed that Sofía was fading away? Would I have seen the signs, and would I have known what to do? Or would I have been like everyone else in the video: completely oblivious?

That's not fair. Not everyone's oblivious. The doctor tries to draw Sofía out of her shell. They have a private meeting four days before she kills herself. He changes her medication, he asks about side effects, he wants her to start keeping a "feelings journal."

"I want you to know," Dr. Franklin tells her, "that people love you. I know you feel alone in your family, but you're not. People care about you. They see you. You matter."

"I know," Sofía says in a soft voice. But she doesn't sound like she believes it.

That's the last time she speaks on the tapes.

She doesn't disappear. She's still there, in each session.

Until she isn't.

There's a jump of several days without videos, and when they resume, a lot of the sessions are what I would expect—some students cry, and Dr. Franklin helps them through it, even though he seems on the verge of breaking down too. But not Bo. I watch him. I *know* he was close to Sofía, that he cared about her as much or more than anyone else. But any time her death is brought up, Bo's face falls blank. He gets a sort of dreamy look in his eyes.

He never once seems to realize she's gone. That she's been gone for a while.

CHAPTER 47

Phoebe

I'm still thinking about the videos when I wake up the next morning and stagger downstairs for breakfast.

Bo's already sitting at the dining room table, shoveling sugar-drenched Cheerios into his mouth. I almost ask him about Sofía, but I can't think of a way to bring it up without being morbid.

"What?" Bo asks, his mouth full.

"Nothing," I say, looking away and grabbing the box of cereal.

Bo's spoon clatters on the table, and he scoots his chair back, ready to leave. The sweet dregs of his sugary milk are still on the bottom of the bowl. I will never understand how he can possibly skip the best part, but Bo never finishes the milk.

Rather than leaving as soon as he stands, though, Bo stares at me and then sits back down.

"Hey," he says.

I look up at him, instantly on edge.

"I just . . . are you like me?" he asks.

"What?"

"Are you, you know"—he pauses—"like me?"

I shake my head silently. No. I'm not like Bo. If there's one thing I've learned since Bo went to Berkshire Academy, it's that mental issues are hard to diagnose, harder to treat. There's a lot of trial and error. There's a lot of hoping that this drug balances out this chemical in the brain or that this symptom being reduced makes up for this side effect. There's not a lot of clarity when there's something wrong with your mind. But at least when there's *not* something wrong, that's pretty clear too.

Bo's shoulders sort of sag with relief when I tell him there's nothing wrong with me, and my heart clenches. I've wondered before if Bo resents me for being "normal," but now I see that beneath whatever jealousy he might experience, there's also worry.

For the first time, I feel like Bo really cares about me. He's been nice to me before, of course, but it's not like he was ever my defender at school or on the bus. He let me fight my own fights. I've seen Rosemarie tackle a kid who was calling her brother gay, but Bo never did anything like that for me. Then again, to be fair, I worked hard to make sure I was never in a position to need help. I never wanted to test whether or not I would get it.

I thought he didn't care about me.

But now it seems like he does care, at least when it matters. Maybe he's cared all along. He's just shown it in ways that I haven't seen.

Bo plays on his phone while I eat my cereal, but when I

start to stand up and leave, he drops his phone on the table. I look at him, surprised at his sudden movement.

"So, uh," he says awkwardly. "How 'bout them Patriots?"

I laugh. "I think they have a real shot at the Bowl next year, Dad," I say sarcastically.

Bo shrugs, smiling at me. "I dunno," he says. "Just—how are things?"

Even though I can tell Bo's trying to keep it light, this whole conversation feels weird. I shift my empty cereal bowl from one hand to the other. "I don't know," I say.

"What're you gonna do after college?"

I lift one shoulder up. How many different ways can I tell people, *I don't know*?

"I mean, you don't have to go to college," he adds. "You could just, you know, leave. Backpack in Europe or camp across America or sit out in the woods and paint or something."

I cock up an eyebrow at him. That's new. Everyone's asking me what I want to do in the future, but what they really mean is which college, which major, which career.

I sit back down. "It's not as simple as that, though, is it?" I say.

"Why not?"

Because I'm me and you're you, I want to say. *Because you get to have the unknown.* That's why everyone keeps asking me what I'm going to do when I graduate—because they want some level of certainty with at least one of us. No one knows what Bo's going to do, but everyone knows what my future holds, even if I keep pretending like I have a choice. A nice, respectable, in-state college; a reasonable major that will lead to a career with a salary and a 401(k) and a savings account; a retirement plan. I'm two years younger than Bo, and all I know is that whatever my future entails, there'll be a retirement plan.

"Listen," Bo says seriously. "You can do anything you want. You really can. You can start a company or get a doctorate or hitchhike to Wyoming."

"Why would I want to go to Wyoming?"

"I don't know," Bo says. "I *really* don't think you should go there. And, um, I want to talk to you if you ever decide to hitchhike. Seriously. But if you do it anyway, just know that it'll be okay."

I squint at him. He's really not making any sense.

"All I'm saying is, your future is full of possibilities." Bo looks me straight in the eyes. "Trust me, I know."

I snort. "You don't," I say, my voice full of defeat. "Because you know what I really want?"

Bo looks at me, waiting.

"I want the freedom to mess up," I say. Just once, I want to be the one who's allowed to screw up. I want the freedom to choose. Right now, I have no choice. I *have* to be this way. But one day, I'll be free. I'll be able to live my life without having to be perfect. I'll be able to do anything I want—or nothing at all. I'll wander around aimlessly. I'll make mistakes. I won't worry about being safe, being perfect.

I won't worry about disappointing my parents.

At least that's what I tell myself. Because being free? That comes at a price I don't think my parents can pay.

CHAPTER 48

I was two when Phoebe was born. I don't remember it at all, but I do remember the doctor visits.

Phoebe was born with a hole in her heart. That sounds like a huge deal, but it wasn't really. Turns out it's pretty routine. But when Phoebe turned three, the doctors decided the hole wasn't going to heal on its own, and she needed surgery. Before that, however, they did an EKG, and I got to watch.

Phoebe lay down on a hospital bed, and Mom clutched her hand like she was saying her last goodbyes even though everyone else, including Pheebs, was pretty chill about it all. Phoebe watched the cartoon the technician put on for her, but I watched the monitor. The technician rubbed a wand over Phoebe's chest, and a black-and-white picture of her heart showed up on the screen, contracting and expanding with every beat.

"What's that?" I asked, pointing.

The technician showed me the arteries and the different chambers of Phoebe's heart.

"And this is what's causing all the trouble," the technician said. "This is where the hole is."

"It looks like a bird," I said, and the technician laughed.

With every heartbeat, the wings of the bird flapped. This was blood flowing over the loose tissue, but to me it was like one of those drawings little kids make of birds in the sky, the ones that look like elongated letter *m*'s. I watched, mesmerized, as the bird's wings moved up and down, up and down.

They got her into surgery, and she was only in the hospital for a day, and then she milked my parents for ice cream for dinner until she was sick of ice cream, and that was that.

But sometimes I look at Phoebe and I think about how she had a bird inside her heart. On the outside, she's just like everyone else, but I like to think that maybe she carries within her something magical and free.

CHAPTER 49

Phoebe

I can't sleep.

Instead, I leave my room, creeping down the stairs and out of the house. The stars stretch out in front of me, glittering over the tops of the trees. Our yard is small, but it feels huge, tucked away in a clearing and surrounded by trees on three sides. A car drives past slowly, the headlights briefly illuminating the trees and casting long, creeping shadows deeper into the woods. As soon as it's gone, the night returns to its cozy darkness. Even though the grass is damp, I sit on the little hill behind our house, staring up into the sky, pretending that all that's left of the world is me and a hundred million stars and the blackness of the night.

At first it's quiet outside, but then I hear someone walking toward me from the house. I look over and see my brother's silhouette, then I turn back up to the heavens.

"Hey," Bo says as he approaches.

"Hi."

He sits down beside me, looking back at the house instead of up at the sky.

"What are you doing?" he asks.

"Just thinking."

He open his mouth to speak, but no words come out. Instead, I say, "I saw you."

He looks at me, confused.

"I saw you earlier this week, watching me with Rosemarie and Jenny on the porch. Why were you spying on me?"

"I didn't mean to spy on you," he says.

"Don't do that." But I mean more than just "Don't spy on me." I mean, "Don't give me false hope about my future over bowls of cereal." I mean, "Don't pretend that something's not wrong." I mean, "Don't treat me like you treat Mom and Dad."

I mean, *don't*.

"It's weird," I say.

"What is?"

"When you're gone." I'm still not looking at him. If it was daytime, I don't think I could say all this. But I'm so tired, and I can't spend my life pretending, like Mom and Dad do. "It's different. And now that you're back. It's all different."

I wonder what Bo thinks life is like here when he's gone. Does he think we all just hit the pause button and wait for him to return? No, we keep living—but no one hesitates outside his room, questioning whether it's worth it to reach out or better to keep the silence. No one's on edge, wondering what mood he'll be in. No one hides. I get home and Mom asks me about my day at school, listening to my stories without being preoccupied about what she could be doing to help Bo. Dad sits in the living room and watches sports because he wants to, not because he's trying to pretend there's nothing wrong. There's life-with-Bo, and there's life-without-Bo, and they're entirely different, and I'm getting whiplash trying to live them both.

"It's getting cold," Bo says, interrupting my thoughts.

"So go inside."

Bo stands and heads back to the house. I wish I knew how to connect with him. He's my brother; we should be close. We shouldn't just be going through the motions, awkwardly trying to find something—anything—that we have in common.

I jump up and run over to him. We walk back toward the house in silence.

When we reach the door, he stops, staring at the lock. It stands out in shiny gold tones against the brushed nickel trim. Dad replaced it last week, before he went to pick Bo up from Berkshire Academy.

"I wish you didn't have to go away again," I say, staring at the lock. Maybe we could find some sort of identity as a family if Bo were here for more than just a weekend.

"I have to," Bo says. "For your safety. I have to learn control."

I blink, surprised that he's so self-aware. "That was . . ." I start, not sure if it's worth bringing up. "That was the most scared I ever was," I say in a quiet voice. "The night before they took you to that school for the first time. You had a fight with Dad. Do you remember?"

Bo nods, but he looks confused.

"Mom came into my bedroom while you were arguing. I was reading in bed, and I had my music cranked up really loud. I haven't been able to listen to that song since then. 'The

Remedy,'" I add. "By Jason Mraz." I want him to say something, anything, but he doesn't. "Anyway, Mom came in, and she just locked my door from the inside and then left again."

"Why were you so scared?" Bo asks.

"I was scared because a mother shouldn't have to lock one child in a room to protect her from the other."

CHAPTER 50

My blood turns to ice water.

Phoebe looks up at me, and I see the truth in her eyes. That moment changed who she was, and it's my fault, and I didn't even know it. I've never thought of myself as someone to be afraid of. Sure, I know that learning to control my power is key, that the whole point of going to Berkshire was to be in control so I wouldn't hurt someone. And I know that, despite it all, I still have hurt people. It's my fault Phoebe broke her arm when we were young, and it's my fault Sofía's trapped in the past. But that night before I left for the academy, that fight with Dad hadn't been about me controlling my powers. It had just been us, fighting like usual: He was angry at me for being a freak, and I was angry . . . I was just angry.

The thing is, that was just a normal fight. Just words. Shouted words, yeah, but words. I had no idea that it scared Mom and Phoebe. I never once thought about Pheebs hiding behind her locked door while I yelled at Dad. I thought she was too wrapped up in her own life to notice mine, even when it was loud.

"I'm sorry," I say.

Phoebe's shoulder lifts in a half shrug.

"You're here now," she says, as if that's enough.

"I'll be going away again soon." I've felt it all day, the pull of the timestream, dragging me back to where I'm supposed to be. I think, if I let myself, I could float back to my own time and place as easily as drifting on the current of the ocean.

I consider going back inside to find my parents. To apologize or say . . . something. But I don't want to. I'm not sure how to look my mom in the eye after what Phoebe just told me.

"Yeah," Phoebe says. "Break is almost over for me too."

"Break?"

"Spring break," Phoebe says. Her eyes search my face. "That's why you're home—for spring break. Dad's driving you back up tomorrow."

"Driving . . ." My head is throbbing. Driving? Spring break? No—I'm here because I slipped through the timestream.

"Do you like it?" Phoebe asks.

"The Berk? Yeah. It's good." My mind is reeling. This is spring break? But I didn't drive here; the timestream dumped me here.

"Bo?"

"Yeah?"

"I . . . I'm glad you're getting help. I was . . . I didn't think that school would change anything, but, I'm glad you're getting help."

"Thanks."

"I know Berkshire Academy must be horrible. But it's . . . it's for your health. They're going to make you better again."

"I'm not sick!" I say, staring at my sister. "What the hell have they been telling you?"

"Sorry!" She raises both her hands and steps back, hitting the side of the house. "I didn't mean to say you were sick, just that Berkshire—it's, um . . . it's good, right? It's helping?" When I nod, she adds, "I'm glad. Of that. That's all. And you're happy? Even without that girl? Sofía?"

My hands clench into fists. "Look, Pheebs, you know my power. You know I can save her."

"Power?"

"Remember the Titanic? When we were kids?"

"I remember playing the game on the tire swing in the front yard."

I shake my head violently—*no*. We weren't playing. We were there. "You *know*," I say, grabbing Phoebe's shoulders. "You know. You know what I can do."

"You're scaring me," Phoebe says in a very, very, very small voice.

I let go of her as if she were made of fire. "Tell me you know," I demand.

"I know," she says, but I don't think she does.

"I can save Sofía," I say urgently. "Tell me you know I can save Sofía."

"But Bo," she says, her eyes wide and reflecting the starlight above us. "Sofía is . . . she's dead, Bo."

I shake my head back and forth, my brain rattling around

inside, clattering against my skull. "No, she's not!" I say, and Phoebe flinches from my raised voice, cowering against the house. "Sorry. It was an accident. But don't worry, I'll save her. That's why I'm at Berkshire. To control my powers, so that I can save her."

Phoebe's head cocks, and there's confusion in her eyes and something else. Sympathy? "Oh, Bo," she says, her voice cracking.

A curtain near the door shifts—our father has noticed us outside, a frown on his face, and the curtain swishes closed again. In moments, he'll be at the door.

I grab Phoebe by her shoulders, whirling her around to face me. Her face pales, her eyes widen. "What have they told you?" I snarl. "About Berkshire? About me?"

"You know why you're there," she says, but as her eyes drink in my face, she adds, "Right?"

"Why?" I demand. "You tell me. Why am I at Berkshire?"

"You're . . . you're sick. They haven't found a full diagnosis yet, but I've been researching on the Internet. The doctor you see, Dr. Franklin, he mentioned a dissociative disorder, but I think it's more complex than that—" She pauses, seeing the rage building on my face. "Berkshire Academy is designed specifically for teens with mental issues. They said it was a specialized environment, that they could help you better than the special ed programs at school, that they can treat you better . . ."

Already, I can feel the timestream pulling me further and further away. Phoebe is slipping through my fingers, evaporating before my eyes.

"It's all a lie!" I shout with all my might, flinging the words across time and space. "It's a lie! I'm not sick! Don't let them tell you that! You know the truth!"

Despite the fact that I'm shouting, my words are nearly whispers. Phoebe's face blanches, and she grabs at me. Our hands slide away from each other, as if we were both made of water.

"I'm not sick!" I scream, but Phoebe can't hear me anymore.

CHAPTER 51

My eyes open, but I can't see anything. My vision is blurry, and my head feels fuzzy. I'm in my room at the Berk, the painted walls covered with scraps of art I drew or posters from home, my closet an odd mirror to the one I have at home—everything that wasn't there is here. I shift in the bed. I'm not wearing my clothes; I'm wearing an odd sort of medical robe. There's a bandage around my elbow and a Band-Aid on the top of my hand.

"Wake up, asshole."

My attention focuses on the doorway. "Ryan," I mutter.

"Man, you are *really* messed up."

"Huh?" I strain against the fatigue, trying to focus on Ryan's face.

But when I look again, he's not there.

I struggle to sit up, but it's like I've been buried under sand. There's movement by the door again, but this time I see Dr. Rivers and Mr. Minh. I thought they had gone. They cluck their tongues as they walk by, almost comically, their movements long and swinging. I rub my eyes, not sure if I really even saw them. I'm left, however, with a rising sense of dread filling my stomach. Real or not, I know I can't trust those people.

Wait. What am I saying? It does matter if they're real. It matters if I'm just . . .

Hallucinating.

Had I even been home at all? My shift to my parents' world was sudden—maybe the timestream threw me back here violently, far more violently than it ever has before.

I try to call up the timestream. Maybe it has answers. But I cannot control my power—I can barely focus enough to stay awake.

And then I can't even do that anymore.

I wake up to the sensation of someone sitting at the foot of my bed. I keep my eyes shut. I'm tired. But then I smell lemons and lavender, the same scent as Sofía's shampoo, and I shoot up in bed.

She's here.

"How . . . ?" I start, shocked.

Sofía smiles. "You came here in your sleep," she says. And then she frowns. "If you're randomly showing up places while you're asleep . . . You're losing control, aren't you?"

I run my fingers through my hair. "I don't know anymore."

"You're losing control," she says firmly, "and you need to wake up."

"Bo?"

I open my eyes. The fuzziness is gone, but the grogginess remains. The Doctor sits in a stiff-backed chair by my bed.

"What happened?" I ask.

293

"You were briefly treated at a local facility, and then your parents sent you back here."

That doesn't really answer my question at all.

"Bo," Dr. Franklin says in a kind voice. "I want to be honest with you, and I want you to be honest with me."

I nod as I peel the bandage off the back of my hand. There's a puncture mark over my vein.

"Can you tell me why you're at Berkshire Academy?"

Because I can control time. And you can heal. And we have powers, powers normal people wouldn't understand.

"Because I'm not normal," I say.

"You *are* normal," Dr. Franklin says immediately. "But can you be more specific about your reason for being at Berkshire?"

I can tell him what he wants to hear. "I'm crazy."

Dr. Franklin shakes his head. "You're not. But you do have some needs that have to be addressed. We've changed your medication again. Are you feeling any negative side effects?"

"I don't know," I say. My eyes slide over to the window, to the sunlight slicing through the iron bars in front of the glass. "Where are Dr. Rivers and Mr. Minh?"

"They're gone," Dr. Franklin says, sighing. He sounds frustrated, angry, but I'm not sure if it's at me or at the situation. "Bo, we're going to increase the frequency of your therapy sessions," he continues after a moment. "Your lessons are on hold until we can get you the right balance of medication and therapy."

He reaches over and puts his hand over mine. "I'm concerned about you, Bo. And I'm concerned that you're not processing what happened to Sofía."

Sofía was just here, I think. She was here, and I saw her. I felt her. She was real.

As real as he is.

Before I can think about it, I yank my hand away from the bed and rake my fingernails over the back of his, clawing him and scraping his skin away. I watch the red welts rise up on his wrist.

"That hurt, Bo," Dr. Franklin says, jerking away and staring down at his hand. "Why would you do that?"

"To see if you can heal."

"Of course I can heal," Dr. Franklin says, exasperated. "But we've talked about this before, in group, remember? You can't just break something to see if it can be fixed. Destruction for destruction's sake is not an appropriate release of your feelings."

That's not what I meant, and he should know that, at least on some level. The welts should be gone now, not pricking red with blood. Even if his mind has forgotten his powers, his body should still be able to fix the damage done.

Unless . . .

Unless it's true. We don't have powers. We never did.

And maybe I don't need powers. I could live with that.

But I can't live without Sofía, and no powers means no Sofía.

Over Dr. Franklin's shoulder, I catch a glimpse of someone in the shadows. As I stare, the figure moves into the light, standing in the center of my doorway.

Carlos Estrada stares at me silently, water streaming down his body and soaking the carpet.

And my heart leaps with joy, even if this means that time

is still leaking around me. Because if I can see Carlos, it means that my powers are real, and if my powers are real, I can still save Sofía.

When I look up again, though, it's not Carlos in the doorway.

It's Ryan.

He's watching me with narrowed eyes and a grim smile. The Doctor, noticing where my gaze is, turns around. "Go to your own room, Ryan," he says. "Or the common room. Bo and I are having a private conversation."

"Yeah, okay," Ryan drawls. He steps backward, but he keeps his eyes on me for as long as possible.

CHAPTER 52

The Doctor gave me drugs to help me sleep but nothing to help me stay awake after. And even though it's dark and I actually want to sleep now, I can't.

Especially with that music playing.

It's haunting and melodic, and I know immediately that it's a cello; my sister practiced enough when we were growing up that I can recognize a cello anywhere. But who has a cello at the Berk?

I creep down the hallway, following the sound of the music. At first I think it's coming from the common room, but it's deserted.

There's a light in Sofía's room.

My heart thuds in my chest. I must be traveling in my sleep again. Sofía's door is cracked, and when I push it all the way open, I'm greeted by the sight of her. Her room is exactly as I remember it, covered in various shades of pink with a plushy rug over the floor and posters on the wall—a boy-band group, an art print by Frida Kahlo, and a calligraphic rendition of a Shakespearean quote: "To thine own self be true."

"Sofía?"

She's sitting on the edge of the bed, a cello between her legs. Her whole body moves as she glides the bow over the strings, the rich, deep notes filling her tiny room.

"I didn't know you could play the cello," I say. I didn't know she *had* a cello. It's kind of a big instrument to hide in here.

"This is a fugue," she says, her voice melding in and out of the music.

"A fugue," I repeat.

"A repetition of a short melody," she says. I listen for a moment, and I can pick out the strain of music repeating over and over, the sounds as intricately woven together as the strings of the timestream. "In a good fugue," Sofía continues, "there are layers. You play one melody"—a short burst of music erupts from the cello—"and that melody is not only repeated, but developed. It evolves. It changes. It's the same melody, but different." She continues playing, and I hear the subtle changes. I can still recognize the original melody, but it's bigger now, deeper.

"Sofía," I say. "How did I get here?"

"The key to a fugue is not in the way things are the same," she says, "but in how they become different."

"Why do you have a cello?" I ask. Panic is rising in my voice. Something's not right. "When did you become an expert on fugues?"

"This is a fugue," Sofía says, her voice soft. "A repetition of a short melody. In a good fugue, there are layers. You play one melody, and that melody is not only repeated, but developed. It evolves. It changes. It's the same melody, but different."

"You just said that." My hands are clammy.

"The key to a fugue is not in the way things are the same," she says, "but in how they become different."

"Sofía?"

She continues to play, her whole body bent over the cello, her eyes closed. "This is a fugue. A repetition of a short melody. In a good fugue, there are layers. You play one melody, and that melody is not only repeated, but developed. It evolves. It changes. It's the same, Bo, but different."

I back away slowly, my hand reaching for her door.

"The key to a fugue is not in the way things are the same," she says, "but in how they become different."

"Sofía, please, please, say something else." My voice betrays my fear. "Anything."

The music stops.

Sofía looks up at me, her neck twisting uncannily.

"You shouldn't be here," she says in a growl. She stands abruptly, and the cello drops to the floor. The strings make weak, broken sounds, muffled by the pink rug.

"Sofía?"

She grips the bow like it's a sword. "This is a fugue," she says in a horrible monotone. Her eyes are dead and empty as she advances toward me. My back's pressed against the wall.

She pulls her arm out, her soulless eyes locked on mine, and drives the cello bow into my chest.

Everything goes black.

I don't mean I passed out. I mean, one moment I'm there,

with a cello bow sticking out of my chest, the wood splintering but still powerful enough to pierce my skin, and the next moment I am floating in nothing. There's no more cello bow.

There's no more Sofía either.

There's no more world.

There's only . . . nothing.

"Hello?" I say into the void.

Silence.

For a long time, I exist in the nothing. And then light starts to glow around the edges. I start to feel pressure on my back; I'm lying down. My room comes into focus, and I sit up in bed.

On the nightstand beside me, my clock ticks.

CHAPTER 53

When Dr. Franklin comes to my room the next day, I keep my guard up. I pretend everything is fine. Dr. Franklin talks about banal things, like paranoia and trust, and I nod along. Soon enough, I'm allowed out of my room and back with my unit.

"Where have you been, spaz?" Ryan asks me quietly as I make my way to the library. I've been given permission to skip all my classes and do silent study, as long as I have private sessions with the Doc.

I don't answer, so Ryan follows me down the hallway.

"You're going to get in trouble for skipping class," I say.

He shrugs. "I bet they won't care. This place is all going to shit anyway."

"The Doctor will care."

"If he's even the Doctor for much longer."

I stop short in front of the library, my hand on the door. "What do you mean?"

"I overheard the officials talking to the Doc the day before spring break. They completed their investigation. They're contesting the, uh . . . the accreditation of the school. I didn't know what that meant, but I looked it up, and it's bad."

"So what does it mean?" I ask in a low voice.

"My dad said the school would lose funding, and there's no way it'll stay open if that happens." Ryan looks back at Dr. Franklin's closed office door. "Dude, it was brutal. Those officials tore Dr. Franklin a new one. They said the school wasn't safe and Sofía was proof of that—and so were you."

"Me?"

"Yeah, they brought you up. I told you not to be such a freak in front of them. They said Dr. Franklin let you get away with too much and that he wasn't 'providing you with all the resources you need.' They mentioned Harold too. That he should be put in a home or something."

Poor Harold. He'll be locked away in a padded cell if Berkshire shuts down.

The sound of hammering fills my ears, and rattling shakes my bones. I look down, and the floor is gone. I am balancing on wooden beams, high above the unfinished construction of the academy, as carpenters and electricians and plumbers work to create the building.

I blink, and the floor is back, the hardwood nicked with age and dust gathering along the baseboards.

"I'm going to be pissed if the school closes," Ryan continues, oblivious to time cracking up around him. "I think I know what I need to do, but . . ."

What will my parents do with me?

I think about how much I frightened Phoebe, on both the

night before I left for Berkshire and the other night when we sat outside, before time snapped me back here.

Maybe *I* should be locked up.

"I wish Sofía were here," I say softly.

"Me too, man," Ryan says, his voice bitter. "If she were, those officials never would have come." His fingers are curled into a fist, and he punches the wall beside the library door. Hard. "Damn it!" he says, seething. "I will *not* let those damn officials mess this place up! They're ruining all my plans!"

There's something about that last sentence, something about Ryan's *plans* that rings in the air like a struck bell. But I'm too distracted to really focus on it. All I can see is the way the wall ripples and moves like water where Ryan struck it.

I blink, and the wall is normal again.

"I've got to go," I say, pushing the library door open.

Ryan follows me inside. I wish I knew how to get rid of him.

I go to the ancient computers in the back of the room. Ryan talks at me while the hard drive boots up. He's bragging about all the stuff he has in his home in LA, how he spent all break swimming and surfing and doing all kinds of cool things he doesn't get to do here. I want to call him on his bull—Ryan doesn't look like the kind of guy to go swimming without a T-shirt on, let alone be a surf expert—but I just don't care enough to push it. He exhausts me, honestly. And I don't think he even likes me. He just wants an audience.

"Look, I've got work to do," I say. "You may not give a shit about your classes, but I do."

Ryan flips me off, but at least he leaves me alone for a bit, wandering up and down the book aisles.

I turn back to the computer and quickly type in *Sofía Muniz.*

Several links pop up—mostly social media profiles for other girls named Sofía Muniz—but when I add *Berkshire Academy* and *Pear Island* to the search, the top hits are all newspaper articles, as well as an official statement from the academy's board.

I click on the news first.

STUDENT DISAPPEARS AT LOCAL ACADEMY FOR ELITE TEENS. My breath catches at the picture of Sofía taking up a column of the article. It's an old picture, probably from her high school before she came here, but it's her. I reach out and touch the image on the screen with two fingers. The article is straight facts: Sofía went missing on this date, Berkshire Academy has issued no comment, state and federal officials are investigating. It ends with a list of numbers for people to call if they have any more information about her disappearance.

"What are you doing?" Ryan asks, looking over at me. He starts heading my way. The closer he gets, the blurrier the screen becomes. Before my eyes, the headline shifts.

STUDENT DIES AT LOCAL ACADEMY FOR TROUBLED TEENS

Sofía Muniz, 17, was found dead last night on the grounds of the Berkshire Academy for Children with Exceptional Needs, located on Pear Island. Her death has been ruled a suicide by local authorities. The academy, which serves a small group of students aged 15 to 21, specializes in treating severe cases of emotionally and behaviorally disturbed children who need greater guidance than a traditional school setting can offer.

Muniz was discovered by her psychiatrist, Dr. Demitrious Franklin, and another student. Preliminary reports indicate that Muniz overdosed on prescription medication, and an investigation is ongoing. "Her access to the medication poses a serious breach in policy," Dr. Alexander Hartford, chairman of the board of the academy, said in a press release. "We are working with local and state authorities to determine how best to redesign our practices." Hartford added that the school is willingly hosting officials from the state board of education to help determine the future of Berkshire Academy.

"Sofía was beloved to all who knew her," Dr. Franklin said prior to the private memorial service held on the grounds of the school. "She will be sorely missed." One of her fellow students, Gwendoline Benson, added, "She was my best friend. I never thought she'd just be gone one day."

Muniz is predeceased by her mother and two sisters, victims of a car accident in her hometown of Austin, TX. Her father was unavailable for comment.

The article concludes with numbers for suicide-prevention hotlines.

"Finally decided to enter reality, huh?" Ryan asks, bending over the computer and looking at the screen.

The closer he gets, the clearer the image becomes, until there's no hint of the real article I saw before Ryan came over. The picture of Sofía sharpens too, but in a twisted way, obscuring her features just enough so that she no longer looks the way she did before, when I knew her. She looks like a stranger.

"Go away, you dick," I growl, staring at the picture.

Ryan rolls his eyes. "Whatever. But listen, tonight I want your help."

"With what?" I don't bother hiding my anger; my eyes are

on the twisted picture of the girl I love and the lies surrounding her face.

"I want to look at what Dr. Franklin has in his office," Ryan says. "The video feeds of our sessions are gone, and that's good, but there are paper records too, records that might lead to me getting the shaft."

"Go away," I say. I don't care what Ryan wants.

"Fine. But Sofía's records are in there too."

My eyes flash to his. He's always trying to manipulate me. "I said, go away."

"Yours too. Don't you want to know what the Doctor is saying about you? What's going on your permanent record? What if he recommends that you go to the loony bin like Harold?"

"If I agree to help you, will you leave me alone?"

"Tonight, an hour after lights-out."

"Fine."

Ryan pushes himself off the desk he was leaning against and saunters away.

The farther he goes, the more the screen flickers and fades, the damning headline replaced by the original. I watch as the words *Sofía Muniz, 17, was found dead last night* change into *Sofía Muniz, 17, has been reported missing.*

I turn around in my seat, glaring at Ryan as he disappears into the shelves.

He did this.

CHAPTER 54

When Ryan punched the wall, it rippled. When he got close to the screen, it changed, and when he left, it changed back.

This whole time I thought it was the officials who were manipulating our reality. But that doesn't really make sense, does it? If they wanted to use us for our powers, they wouldn't have made us forget them.

But Ryan . . . he never forgot. Not because he could protect himself from the officials, but because *he* was the one creating the false reality.

Ryan is a telepath. *He* could change the videos. He's been pushing the boundaries of his powers since he got here. He knows *exactly* how to mess with someone's mind. He's messed with our heads before, and his powers have only been growing—far beyond anything we ever thought possible. Beyond anything the Doctor or anyone else could control.

It must have scared him when the officials arrived. He had to have known from the start that the academy was in danger of closing. Maybe this all started out as a way to save the school and make the officials go away, but if Ryan had good intentions at the beginning, his desperation has twisted them. The officials are gone, and he's still maintaining an illusion that no one has powers. He can't stop the school from closing—that's out of his grasp—but he can stop everyone else from remembering who they really are. He can stop the officials from sending him to another academy.

As soon as Ryan is out of the library, I waste no time in calling up the timestream. For a moment, I'm worried it won't work.

But it's there. All of time, laid out before me, strings floating atop a river, tangling and weaving together into beautiful chaos. I work hurriedly, finding a date when I can see Sofía in the past. The red string connecting me to Sofía is as slender as a hair, but it cuts my finger like a razor when I touch it. I snatch my hand back, sucking on the blood springing up.

I grab the string again, with my whole hand, not just wrapping my finger around it. It slices into me, and I grit my teeth against the pain.

I have to do this.

I feel my bones crunch, squeezed together by the red string as I wind it around my palm. Blood makes my hand slick and warm. I can't let go.

I can't let go.

The pain disappears. I look down and the string is gone, along with the blood.

Sofía stands in front of me.

"Hi," I say.

She smiles, but the happiness doesn't reach her eyes. "What are you doing here?" she asks.

"I had to see you."

"You have to go."

I shake my head, crossing the short distance between her and me. "No," I say.

"You have to."

I want to tell her everything, but time won't let me. So I just say, "Things are bad right now."

"You've been coming to me in the past," Sofía says. "I figure something is wrong with the future—I mean, the present. Your present. Am I right?"

I nod.

"And I'm not there to help you."

I nod again. I expect time to snap me back at any minute, but it doesn't. We're both still here. "I was afraid," I say tentatively, still testing the boundaries of time.

"Of what?"

"That my powers weren't real."

For a brief second, everything wavers. Colors shift and swirl in and out of one another. Everything stutters . . . except for Sofía. She is still in front of me, real and vivid and true.

She reaches up and puts the flats of her hands against the sides of my face. Her skin is cool and calming. "But Bo," she says, "what if I'm not real? What if none of this is real?"

"You're the only thing I'm certain of," I whisper.

She opens her mouth, but instead of words, water pours out. It dribbles down her chin, a waterfall over her neck, rivulets across her chest. I reach out and grab her, but my fingers puncture her arm as if her skin were a water balloon, bright blue liquid that stinks of chlorine erupting from her body. "Sofía!" I cry, reaching for her again. My hand brushes against her hair, and every dark brown strand turns invisible, then reflective, like the surface of a pool. Her body grows translucent, liquid, melting away until there's nothing left of her but a puddle at my feet.

Ryan comes to get me in my bedroom an hour after lights-out. I don't know how he gets around the door locks, but he does. Further proof that the locks—like the iron bars—are just part of his illusion.

"Ready?" Ryan asks in a low voice.

I stare at the water stain on my floor, its edges creating an odd, circular shape in the hardwood.

I nod my head.

The door to Dr. Franklin's office is locked, but Ryan somehow got his hands on a key. We creep into the darkened room.

It looks strange here without the Doctor, without people at all. The chairs are shadowed tombstones, all circled up around an empty space, signifying nothing.

Ryan turns on the lights.

"We're looking for permanent records. The Doctor's notes. Anything that could incriminate me or land me in a worse school when this one closes."

"Which notes?" I move over to Dr. Franklin's desk, where a pile of papers sits in disarray. I'm not really paying attention to Ryan. I'm here for my own reasons. I need proof. After seeing Sofía melt away, I have to know what reality is—outside of the illusion Ryan has created. I don't want to live a lie . . . but I also don't want to live in a world without her.

I just want the truth. Maybe I can find that here.

Ryan shrugs. "I'll know what I'm looking for when I see it. All schools keep records. What I need is a clean start." He grins maliciously. "So if you see something with my name on it, tell me. I can't have a bad record if I don't have a record at all."

When I look out the window, sunlight glitters for a second. I blink, and the moon replaces it. All around me, the timestream is still cracking. I need help. I just don't know who can help me.

I sit down at the Doc's desk, riffling through the papers there. They're all notes written in his nearly illegible handwriting. Words I don't know are circled or crossed through.

Water drips onto the paper.

I look up. Ryan has moved on to the second drawer of the Doc's filing cabinet, scanning its contents quickly. But Carlos Estrada stands across from me, pointing down at one of Dr. Franklin's desk drawers.

I bend down, yanking on the heavy drawer. It's full of more files, and I almost slam it shut again. But then I see my name. And Ryan's name. And Gwen's and Harold's. My hand shakes, and I notice that only one file is red, a bright swath of color hidden among the manila folders.

Sofía Muniz.

I pull out all of our files in one armful, spreading them across the desk.

I reach for Sofía's file first, but a wet hand slams across the folder. I look up. Carlos Estrada shakes his head silently.

"Why?" I demand.

"What?" Ryan asks, not turning from the filing cabinet.

"Nothing," I say.

Carlos Estrada removes his hand, leaving behind a big wet stain soaking into the red file folder. He is still shaking his head no as I shift Sofía's folder to the side. I blindly pick another one from the desk.

Gwendoline Benson.

I flip the folder open. Glued to the right side is a sheet of information about Gwen—a small picture of her, generic and square, her parents' names, her address, her dad's address, a list of pills. I had no idea that Gwen was on so much medication. I read the names of the drugs silently in my head, stumbling over the long, unpronounceable words.

On the left-hand side of the folder is a list of notes in the Doctor's scratchy handwriting. Across the top, typed in bold letters, is one word:

Diagnosis.

My brows furrow as I read the words the Doctor has scribbled underneath. *Impulse control disorder (pyromania). Trust and abandonment issues.*

I slide Gwen's folder away and open the next one. Harold's. It's structured just the same, with information on one side, including a list of medications and a series of diagnoses that don't make sense. Ryan's folder is similar, although I can recognize most of the notes on him: extreme narcissism, power complex, calculated manipulation, need to be in control, anger issues. Sociopathic tendencies. *He likes to play with emotions,* the Doctor notes, *for fun, but when there's something he wants, he'll use any means to get it. His narcissism makes him believe that normal courses of events are directed at him; if there are no apples at breakfast, it's because the staff hates him for being so clever, and he plots a revenge against them, either psychological or physical. The closer he is to a person, the more this tendency escalates.*

When the officials came, he thought they were out to get him. He always presumed that their arrival would doom him to military school. That he was the only one who had anything to lose.

I look up, expecting Ryan to turn around and catch me in the act of reading about him, but he doesn't. Carlos Estrada is gone.

I open my own folder.

There's my name. My parents' names. Phoebe. My address. A note that I had an "episode" while at school, another one during spring break at home.

A list of medications.

But . . . that's not right. I'm not on any medications. I don't take pills or shots.

The Doctor *said* he was going to put me on meds, but aside from those pills that made me sleepy when I first got back to Berkshire, I haven't taken any.

Have I?

My eyes skim over to the right-hand side of the folder to my diagnosis. *DSM-5* is written near the top and circled several times.

Bo's case is far more complex than I previously suspected. Bo has exhibited signs of having a break with reality following Sofia Muniz's death. His symptoms include prolonged delusions and, more recently, paranoia, both of which are exacerbated by insomnia. The lack of REM sleep likely feeds the symptoms, though Bo is unaware of the problem, often entering into a delusional state instead.

Blood work indicated that no additional or recreational hallucinogenic drugs have been ingested, and Bo's insulin levels are well above diabetic range. Scheduled brain scan and additional blood work within two weeks, at off-site facility in Boston, to examine the possibility of brain lesions. No neurodegenerative diseases in his immediate family history, but the prolonged delusions may indicate peduncular hallucinosis.

FURTHER NOTES: Private sessions and group therapy show that Bo is experiencing a dissociative fugue with select amnesia indicative of something far more serious than his previous diagnosis. This is supported by the mental break he had while visiting his parents April 13–20. Although Bo's paranoia has risen and he therefore is more reluctant to talk during therapy, he has alluded to hallucinations that seem to tie back to Sofia's death.

At parent conference prior to spring break, I discussed possibilities of a prolonged complex visual hallucination and grandiose delusion diagnosis and what that might mean for his parents. Sister indicated that some proclivity for violence existed prior to diagnosis and treatment. The tendency for violence has diminished with medication and therapy, replaced by more personal delusions that lead to withdrawal rather than demonstrative frustration.

The last sentence is written with a heavy hand, making it stand out on the page.

> *Regardless of the fate of the school, it is recommended that Bo be relocated to a more secure facility that can more closely monitor his health.*

I let the folder drop, and the sound makes Ryan turn.

"Find anything?" he asks.

Ripples radiate around him. The filing cabinet melts like candle wax, then I blink and it's just the same as it was before.

"Here, look at this," Ryan says. He uses his telepathy to float a folder from the filing cabinet to me, but I don't open it.

"These papers make us sound crazy," I say finally, staring at the closed folder.

Ryan snorts. "Well, obviously."

"No, but look." I hold up the folder detailing Ryan's medical history, expecting Ryan to use his telepathy to bring it closer to him, but he just slams shut the cabinet drawer and walks across the office toward me.

Ryan scans the contents of the folder. "Yeah, so?"

"It says you're a narcissist and have anger issues."

"Yeah?" Ryan shrugs and drops the folder on the desk.

"It says I'm paranoid and have delusions."

Ryan doesn't hide his sardonic laugh. "I figured you for a schizo."

I swallow down the bile rising in my throat. "We . . . we're not crazy. We're special."

"Yeah, 'special,'" Ryan repeats, mocking me. "Like on the 'special' bus."

"No, I mean . . . our powers?"

Ryan rolls his eyes. "This? Still?"

"You *floated* that folder over to me using your *telepathy*!"

Ryan picks up the folder and drops it back on the desk. "I *tossed* it to you using my *hands*," he says. "Man, you *are* crazy. Like, really crazy. Damn."

The walls in the Doctor's office ripple and twirl like oil mixing with vinegar.

I glance down at the information in my folder. All the Doctor's notes are about me after Sofía went missing. When Ryan's powers were growing stronger. When he started the illusion.

Ryan flips through his file, letting his eyes drift over the diagnosis the Doctor gave him. He casually gathers the forms and crams them into Dr. Franklin's paper shredder. He watches with a smile on his face as the Doctor's notes turn into nothing but long, thin strips.

"Let's go," Ryan says, heading to the door.

"It really is you, isn't it?" I stand up slowly, pushing back the chair and moving against the wall, positioning the desk between Ryan and myself. I hadn't wanted to believe it, even when all the evidence pointed to him.

"The hell is wrong with you?" Ryan says, turning back toward me.

"*It's you.*"

"What are you on about?"

"It's been you the whole time. It's not the Doctor or the officials. It's *you.*"

"What the fu—?"

I snatch my own folder. "You guessed I'd figure it out. '*It is recommended that Bo be relocated.*' You're trying to get rid of me. You're doing all of this."

"What the hell are you talking about?" Ryan says, his voice dangerously close to shouting.

"You. *You.* You can control minds. You're controlling all of us. You've made it look like we're all crazy, that the Berk isn't for people with powers. You even have the Doctor scammed . . ."

"You are *nuts*," Ryan says, turning back to the door. "I mean, there's crazy, and there's you. This is insane. Look around you. Where do you think you are?"

I do look around. I see the Doctor's license in psychiatry, and then I blink and see his doctorate in history. I see the diagnosis folders. And then they melt into dossiers detailing our individual powers.

It's all fake.

It's all an illusion. A brilliant, terrifying illusion.

"Look, dude, face facts," Ryan snarls. "Your little girlfriend died. Dead. Totally dead. If you would rather go to la-la land than admit that, fine. But me? I'm looking out for number one." I stare hard as Ryan heads for the door. He turns to face me, but whatever he was going to say evaporates on his lips.

He looks terrified. Of me. And the truth I now know.

CHAPTER 55

His fear makes my blood surge with power. Now that I see him for what he is, he can't control me. I sweep the remaining folders back into Dr. Franklin's desk drawer and get up, chasing Ryan into the hallway. All around me, the walls ripple as Ryan struggles to hold on to the world he has created. I see flashes of other people, other times—breaks in the timestream. An old man with fluffy white hair— Berkshire Academy's first director, I recognize him from the portrait downstairs—walks by us, muttering to himself before disappearing.

Small children wearing bright yellow camp T-shirts run by. The very last kid looks back at me and waves, and I recognize Carlos Estrada, his T-shirt darkening with water.

Ryan sneers at me. "What are you looking at?"

The other kids disappear. It's just Ryan and me in the hall.

I know what this all is now. My powers have been suppressed by Ryan, dampened by his mind control. But like a balloon that pops when it's full of air, my powers have been bursting out around me. It wasn't the timestream that was breaking; it was me.

"Stop!" I shout as Ryan opens his door.

The world blinks from reality to reality so fast that my head spins. Light streams out of Ryan's window as if it's still daytime, then turns into darkest night with the speed of a strobe.

I grab Ryan's wrist, holding on even as he tries to shake me off.

"Let go, freak," Ryan growls.

"I know what you're doing," I say in a low voice.

The world stills. The sun outside doesn't move. The walls are steady. The ghosts of the past are gone. I am in control.

"You can only shift what's real," I say. "You can't create a whole new world, but you can shift it a little. So what does that say about you?"

"What do you mean?" He tries to wrench himself free again, but I tighten my grip.

"Your 'diagnosis.' You really are a narcissist, aren't you? Can't hide that fact, even in a world you made yourself."

Ryan shoves my chest with his free hand, and I have to let go. He backs into his room and slams the door.

And with that sound, his false world shatters back into place. There's a keypad by his door, bars on his window.

I take a deep, shuddering breath. "I am in control," I tell Ryan's closed door. As the air escapes my lips, the illusion melts away again.

I am in control.

"You are," says a soft voice to my left, the last word lilting up as if the speaker was asking a question.

My heart thuds, hard, once, a pounding so violent that I actually clutch my chest. I whirl around on my heel.

Sofía stands in front of her bedroom door.

A grin cracks across my face like lightning. "I'm winning," I tell her, rushing forward. "I can see through Ryan's illusions, I know what he's doing."

"You can see through the illusions." There it is again, that slightly higher note on the last word.

I reach for Sofía, but she steps back, holding her hands behind her back. Outside my reach.

She shakes her head and backs further into her bedroom. I catch just a glimpse of her pale pink rug, her neon pink comforter on her bed, the fuzzy lamp on her nightstand—and then she closes the door in my face.

"Sofía, wait—" I start, lunging for the door and throwing it open.

The room is empty. The mattress is bare; the walls and floor unadorned. I stumble, bile rising up in my throat. No. No, I had control. I was back in power. I stagger away from her room and into the hallway.

Ryan's door is open again. He watches me with a smile as I scurry back to my room.

CHAPTER 56

Phoebe

It's Thursday. Almost time for Bo to come home for the weekend.

But it's like he never left. The house is quiet. Everyone walks around on eggshells.

Actually, we all walk around as if *we* were eggshells. We're all afraid of breaking here.

Mom cleans more and more the closer we get to the weekend. The wood floors are like mirrors, the windows are washed, and there's not a speck of dust to be found anywhere. That is, except for Bo's room. Mom walks past his bedsheet-covered doorframe as if it weren't there. And the gouge in the floor from Dad's drill—she still hasn't fixed that. It stands out even more now, a blemish against the rest of the perfect house, but it's as if her eyes dance right over it.

Dad practically lives in his office. I think he might be sleeping there, even though it's only four doors down from his and Mom's bedroom.

Everyone is tense because this is Bo's first weekend back since "the episode."

I hate that. I hate labeling what happened. When Bo flipped out at school, my parents called it "the incident." And now we have "the episode."

It was a seizure of some kind. Call it what it is. It was a seizure that preceded delusions. I don't know much else about it because no one will tell me. When Dad drove Bo to a clinic in the middle of the night, the doctors didn't want to diagnose him without consulting Dr. Franklin first. And other than saying Bo needed to return to Berkshire Academy, Dr. Franklin hasn't said much. At least not to me.

There are pieces of Bo in every diagnosis I read about online: bipolar disorder, schizophrenia, depression. The more research I do, the stranger the diseases I find: brain lesions and mind-controlling viruses, flesh-eating amoebas and bacteria and fungi. There are no cures, only temporary treatment options. Sometimes minds are just plain broken—they see the world in a fractured way. Does it really matter what we call the problem with Bo's brain if there's no way to fix it?

It's not like there is a name for the look in his eyes when he clutched at me, begging me to see the truth of a world that doesn't exist.

I have gone over that night a thousand times. In the quiet of every night since, when my mother shuts the door to her bedroom and my father shuts the door to his office and I shut the door to my room, in those long empty spaces where no one moves but everyone's awake, I have relived that last night with Bo over and over and over again. The crazed way he insisted that his girlfriend wasn't dead, that I knew more than I was letting on, that he had some sort of power over all this. I can still feel the way his fingers dug into my shoulders when he clutched me, trying to shake his reality into my brain.

And I will never forget the way his eyes lost focus, the way his muscles seized. When you see seizures on television, they're full of violent shaking, with people falling down and their bodies flopping around like a fish out of water, but that's not what happened with Bo. Instead, he just went stiff as a board. His eyes closed, but I could see through his eyelids that they were still moving, violently shifting back and forth. His jaw went super tight, and his fingers became frozen claws. When Dad came outside, he couldn't get Bo to walk; he had to pick him up by the shoulders and awkwardly shuffle him back inside while Mom called 911.

I kept backing away until I hit the dining room wall, and I stayed there, my back pressed against the beadboard the whole time. I watched as the EMTs arrived, as Bo came out of the seizure only to pass out. I stood there as Mom and Dad got into the car—Mom still in her pajamas and wearing a big overcoat—and followed the ambulance. I sank to the floor, my eyes still on the spot where Bo had been, and I fell asleep there, curled beside Mom's china cabinet. When my parents came home the next morning, after checking Bo into St. Lucy's, they didn't even notice me. They walked right past the dining room, headed to their bed, exhausted from the night. Once I heard Mom snoring, I got up, walked up the stairs, and went to my room.

Bo was at St. Lucy's for almost a week so that they could keep an eye on him and do an MRI and some other scans. Mom was there every day, but Dad stayed in his office, working. When the hospital was ready to release Bo, they sent him straight back to Berkshire Academy. Dad didn't even have to drive up; the hospital sent Bo in an ambulance.

It's been two weeks now, and he'll be home in two days, and I don't know how all of this is going to play out.

Mom cleans. Dad works. And I . . .

I just sit here.

At seven, there's a knock on my door.

"Yeah?" I call.

The door budges a crack, then Mom pushes it open. She's meek about it. "Dinner's almost ready," she says. She could have yelled for me from the base of the stairs like a normal mother, but she didn't.

In the distance, a faint beeping rises up from the kitchen. "Oh!" Mom says. "The tenderloin! Go get your father and come on down, okay?" She dashes down the hall—passing the office where Dad is—and runs down the stairs toward the kitchen.

I push up from my bed, tossing aside the book I'd been reading.

The floorboards creak under my feet, and when I reach Dad's office, I knock on the wooden door three times with the back of my knuckles. "Dad," I say loudly from the hall. "Dinner."

He grunts in response.

I start down the stairs, but something holds me back. I turn around and head back to Dad's office, the door cracked open from when I knocked.

He's standing by the window, but the curtains are closed. In his hands is a child-sized football, the kind Bo used to play with when he was in elementary school. Bo wanted to quit football in middle school, but Dad kept him in. But when Bo made the team at James Jefferson as a freshman reserve, he dropped out during the summer practice before school had even started. He made sure that Dad couldn't reenroll him either, by flipping out on the coach and nearly getting himself suspended. I guess he actually got kicked off the team. But he did it on purpose.

Dad tosses the ball up, spinning it in the air before catching it again. The motion is repetitive and hypnotic. Maybe Dad didn't really hear me when I told him about dinner. I raise my hand to knock on the door again—

And then a sliver of light from between the curtains passes over Dad's face, illuminating the tear tracks on his cheeks.

I lower my hand, pressing my face against the small opening in the door to get a better look at Dad. I've never seen him cry before, and now he's just standing there with big fat tears rolling down his face. His fingers fumble, and the ball drops to the floor, toppling end over end under his desk. Dad kneels down to pick it up, and I hear a sob escape him. I can't see him anymore, not really, just his hands and feet and the tops of his legs as he crouches under the desk to pick up the ball, but that shaking sob guts me.

It's the sound of defeat. No. That's not right. Defeat implies that there was a fight, that you stood a chance of winning but just happened to fail. No. That sound was more hopeless than that. It's the sound a man makes when he realizes that there's no way to win because there's no way to fight. Things just *are*, and nothing can change them.

I want to throw open this door and run to him, wrap my

arms around him. I don't want to tell him it'll be okay, because neither one of us would believe it, but I just . . . I want to tell him I understand.

But I don't move.

I need school as my place to pretend that everything's okay. Maybe Dad needs his office. He's just trying to survive this too.

From under the desk, I can see Dad's grip on the little football tighten. I wonder what he's thinking about. This whole situation—Bo being the way he is—it's hard on Dad. Maybe harder on him than on Mom and me. Everything's one way or the other with him: black or white, this or that, here or there.

But Bo? Bo is elsewhere.

Dad's phone rings. He lets the football go, and it rolls silently across the expensive rug in his office toward me. Dad moves to get up from under the desk, and I jerk away from the crack in the door, my back pressed against the wall. A moment later, Dad answers the phone.

His voice is clear and rich, no hint of tears or sorrow as he answers. "Hey, Tim," he says cheerfully. "How 'bout them Patriots?"

CHAPTER 57

I can't sleep. I was up at dawn, and from my window I could see the Doctor leaving the academy. I scramble for clothes and race out in the early morning light. Dew still clings to everything, and a chilly sea breeze swirls around me as I burst through the door.

Maybe if I get far enough away from Berkshire, Ryan's powers won't be so strong. Maybe if I can talk to Dr. Franklin outside of Ryan's influence, then we can break through the illusions and figure out a way to stop him once and for all.

Dr. Franklin was heading north, probably to take a walk around the grounds. I pass the camp ruins—the Doctor's not there—and then I veer toward the boardwalk.

I find Dr. Franklin sitting in front of the ruined remains of the chimney. He looks incredibly small and vulnerable, sitting cross-legged in the sand, staring into the blackened bricks as if they could still provide him warmth.

"Hello, Bo," the Doctor says, turning his head toward me as I approach.

"Hey." I sit down beside the Doctor, facing the chimney as well. What should I say? How do you tell someone that the life they're living is a lie, an illusion created by a crazy teenager with far more power than responsibility? That the world is stranger than you believe, and you have powers you cannot fathom?

I open my mouth to speak, but then, out of the corner of my eye, a flicker of movement catches my attention. I see Carlos Estrada, dripping wet and shivering. He raises a finger to his lips. I nod subtly and wait for the Doctor to speak first.

"I don't know what's going to happen next," Dr. Franklin says finally.

"No one ever does," I say. "Even me." This is the most important thing I've learned since Sofía disappeared: The future is all possibility, countless options that you can choose to take or not.

I start to speak again, but behind the Doctor, the image of Carlos stares me into silence.

"I've failed a lot here lately, Bo. I failed Berkshire. I failed Sofía. I failed you."

Ryan is doing this to you, I want to say. *Ryan is making everyone believe something that's not true. He's powerful. We all have powers, even you. But his are stronger.*

I want to say all this, but I don't. I don't.

"You were in my office last night, weren't you?" Dr. Franklin asks.

I look down at my hands. "I had to find out the truth."

"And did you?" He won't look at me.

"I think . . . I don't know, but . . . maybe?"

"Good." The Doctor works to keep the emotion out of his voice, so I don't know if he's surprised or proud or disappointed. But he smiles a little when he pats my shoulder. "I shouldn't be surprised that you came out here, to the chimney, like I did," Dr. Franklin continues. "You've fixated on this place, and little wonder. Bo," the Doctor says, touching my arm and forcing me to pull my attention directly to him, "I want you to know it's natural to feel guilt in a situation like Sofía's death. I feel guilt too. In fact, a lot of my guilt is rooted in her death. But Bo, it was suicide. Sofía's depression was not something you were equipped to deal with. There was nothing you could have done to prevent it."

Suicide. The word reverberates inside me.

"Do you remember that first day here at the academy, when we were introducing ourselves?" The Doctor doesn't wait for me to answer him. "We each talked about our biggest problems, our biggest triggers and worries. And I told you about myself. Remember?"

Vaguely. He told us that he could heal, and he showed us the scars to prove it.

"I discussed my drug addiction when I was a kid," Dr. Franklin says. "I said that was the reason I took this job, why I wanted to help kids with problems."

There's a roaring ocean in my ears, but I push it down, so my head's above the water and I can hear. My heart can drown, but I need my mind.

"I keep going back to that time now," the Doctor continues,

his voice contemplative. "I keep reminding myself that not everyone can be saved."

That's not true, I want to say.

"Sometimes people don't want to be saved," he says. "And that's frustrating."

"Yeah," I say.

"You understand, don't you?"

I nod. It's not something I could put into words, but yeah. I understand.

It's complicated.

Life is like the timestream, all knotted and twisted and convoluted. And maybe if we could all see exactly where the threads of our fate lead, we'd be able to make the right choices all the time, but we can't. Not even me. Especially not me. Because I never saw *this*. There are possibilities we can't imagine, futures we could never envision. And there are spots of darkness we cannot see past.

"I wanted to save Sofía," Dr. Franklin says. "And I truly believe she wanted to be saved."

"But you can't save everyone," I say in a low voice.

Beyond the Doctor, Carlos Estrada, dripping wet and slowly turning blue, nods.

I remember the day Sofía told me about Carlos's death. The way no one noticed. Everyone was playing and splashing in the pool, everyone but him. He sank quietly underwater. He never came back up.

Real drowning is quiet, Sofía had said. *It doesn't announce itself.*

It just happens.

And then you're gone. *She's gone.*

Carlos Estrada nods again, and then he disappears.

I understand why she told me about Carlos Estrada now.

"You wanted to change the past so much that you believed you could," Dr. Franklin says.

I stare at the empty place where Carlos Estrada was.

I'm not even sure I know what the past is anymore. The past is Sofía in 1692. The past is yesterday, and realizing how much power Ryan has. The past is my sister's bedroom door locking. The past is a deer in an empty field, a camp for sick kids, two men riding on horseback in the marsh.

I remember the way she tasted on my lips the first time I kissed her, with a rocket soaring into the stars behind us. I remember the way she held my hand, as if it were a secret. I remember the sound of her voice, the faraway look in her eyes, the sweep of her hair over the side of her face.

I remember the morning we snuck away from the Berk to watch the sun rise over the ocean, and we fell asleep in each other's arms until the waves licked at the bottoms of our feet. We'd missed the sun, but found each other.

I remember another morning. The morning that she left me.

I saw her from my window, just like I saw the Doctor this morning. I don't remember what I was thinking; I just knew I wanted to be with Sofía. I dressed quickly and ran outside. I went to the camp ruins first.

I saw her shoes. Her red shoes.

It was cold, and I picked up her shoes because I knew she'd need them.

But Sofía wasn't at the camp.

I walked to the edge of the grounds, to the ruins of the chimney, where I found Sofía, curled up inside the fireplace. Sleeping.

No, not sleeping. There was vomit on her shirt, bright red and orange like fire, some of it clinging to her lips.

No. I took her back in time. There was literal fire in the fireplace, and a house, and she got stuck in Salem.

But then the Doctor was there. He'd followed us. "Oh my God," he said.

I found her. I was there. I saw it.

NO! I scream, but the word never reaches my lips.

Ryan's influence is too strong, even here at the edge of the academy grounds. This isn't how it happened, Sofía's not dead, she's just lost, and I can bring her back. I can, I can.

The Doctor pats me on the back and uses my shoulder as leverage to help him stand. "I just want you to know, Bo, that whatever happens, you're a good kid. You couldn't prevent Sofía's suicide. I don't think anyone could. If she hadn't taken the pills, she would have found another way. When someone's depressed like that, when they don't have the will to live anymore . . . if time can't heal them, nothing can."

That's just the thing, though, isn't it? Time can heal her. It can. It can do anything. As long as I control it.

CHAPTER 58

Phoebe

I'm home alone.

It's actually somewhat rare for me to have the entire house to myself. Dad works from home, and Mom doesn't work at all, so there's almost always someone else around. But today Mom went to a women's meeting at church, and Dad had "business" at a bar in Boston, so it's just me.

This house is always quiet, but it's the uncomfortable sort of quiet, the kind where you can almost hear people trying not to make a sound. Today, there's real silence, which is kind of nice.

I half considered inviting Jenny and Rosemarie over, but it's not like the three of us would have a wild party or anything. We'd just end up watching movies, and that just feels so exhausting right now.

We got a letter from Berkshire Academy. It said that the school was being shut down.

It's been a source of much debate between my parents—what

do they do with Bo now? He'll be coming home at the end of the semester, and Mom has nowhere to take him in the fall. Dr. Franklin called our house personally to suggest that Bo move to a more secure facility in the future, and he recommended one in upstate New York.

Dad was immediately against it. The school Dr. Franklin recommended puts academics on the back burner in favor of focusing on therapy; it would take Bo an additional two years at least to graduate, and Dr. Franklin recommended a six-year program that would give Bo an associate's degree at the end. "Six years?" Dad had raged. "For just an *associate's degree*?"

"It's not about the degree, George," Mom had said quietly.

It's not about the money either.

The school in New York is even more expensive than Berkshire Academy. I added it up. Three months of Bo's current tuition would fully pay for me to go on the class trip to Europe this summer. Four thousand dollars. That's the recommended allowance for the trip and spending money. Four thousand—though I could probably swing just three, if I didn't buy anything and was careful with food. That's nothing compared to what Bo costs, between tuition and medication and travel and that last hospital visit and . . .

I threw away the pamphlet about Europe.

Rosemarie isn't going on the trip either. She has no problem telling anyone who asks that her family can't afford that much money, not for something like a trip, not with college expenses just around the corner.

Jenny is going.

The thing is, I *deserve* that trip. I study, hard, all the time. I bust my butt in every college-level course James Jefferson High

School offers, even science, which I hate. I'm in the top 2 percent of my grade. I've joined every club, I stay after school for orchestra practice, I even tried out for the tennis team just so colleges would consider me more "well-rounded." Not because I want to do any of that.

Because I know I need a scholarship to escape. Bo may get tens of thousands handed to him to go to a school with bars on the windows, but my parents aren't going to have that kind of money when it's my turn.

I deserve a trip to Europe. I deserve, just once, just once in my *whole life*, to be selfish. That's all I want. It's not even about Europe; it's about getting the chance to be selfish. Bo asked me what I want in the future, and it's this. I want to be stupid and selfish, and I want to do things without overthinking them first. I want the chance to just . . . be normal. My whole life has been a giant compromise around Bo—what Bo needs to be healthy, what bills have to be paid for Bo, what allowances in time have to be carved out, which holidays have to be shortened, which weekends sacrificed, which things *I* want that have to wait until later so Bo can get what he needs first.

It's not fair, a little voice inside me says.

And it's not. Not for me. Not for him. Not for any of us.

Rosemarie describes my house as "richy-rich." She always says it in a joking way, but I often wonder if she just laughs to hide her bitterness. Our families are the same size; our houses are not.

But I see the credit card bills that stack up at the end of our table. I see the late hours Dad works. I saw the bill for Berkshire's tuition. I added it up.

I dig the brochure for Europe out of the trash and allow

myself to look at it one last time. Then I fold it in half and very slowly, deliberately rip it apart. I relish the way the paper comes apart, and then I stack the pieces up and drop them back into the trash can.

I know I'm being childish and stupid and trite. I know Bo's health is more important than any trip.

But none of that erases the bitter jealousy in my heart.

I can't help what I want. I can't help wishing things were different, wishing *he* were different. So that I could be too.

Across the hallway, I see the sheet hanging in Bo's doorway. I stride into his room before I can tell myself it's wrong. I don't know what I'm looking for. Just . . . a peek behind the literal curtain.

It feels like going into a stranger's room, or maybe like going into the room of someone who's died, riffling through their belongings in an attempt to find closure or meaning. It's wrong. But I don't let that stop me.

The room smells slightly musty, like the body spray Bo sometimes uses, but old. Mom has already stripped the bed and replaced the sheets and duvet cover for the next time Bo comes home. He probably never notices that she does this, that every single weekend, he has fresh sheets.

I trail my hand along his dresser, leaving a faint trace of my fingerprints in the very thin layer of dust. The top is cluttered with things he's probably not used or even noticed in years: a little carving of a turtle he bought from a Native American in Four Corners during that family trip out West; a Mickey Mouse snow globe from an "adventure" to Disney World; a box that holds a mint coin collection, something Mom gives us both every year at Christmas, because what kid doesn't want money he can't spend.

These are the things our parents would say were important. But Bo wouldn't. That's why he left them behind.

In one corner of the dresser there's a huge marble made of black-and-red glass, so large that it barely fits in my palm. It's on a little clear plastic stand, and when I move it, I can see the stand's footprints in the dust on the dresser.

I gave this to Bo for his birthday last year, just before he left for Berkshire. I stare down at it in my hand. I had bought it for him because I had no idea what else to get him. He had no reason to want a huge round marble, but it looked kind of cool—at least I thought so when I saw it in that little shop at Quincy Market. He had seemed happy with it, rolling it across the table and letting the colors flash. He had thanked me, and though I never knew if it was sincere or not, I had hoped it was.

I slide the marble into my own pocket now, wondering if he'll ever notice it's missing. I leave the little plastic stand behind as a clue.

On top of Bo's desk is a notebook with a broken USB drive awkwardly sticking out of the pages—the same drive that I used to watch videos of Bo's class.

I flip the notebook open, curious to see what Bo's thoughts on the videos are, but it quickly becomes apparent that he wasn't taking notes at all. The pages are chaos: brief snippets of ideas, reflections on people he knows or little stories about history, nonsensical lists scratched through. I try to read a few pages, but I can barely make the words out, much less make sense of them. *Attempt 1* is written at the top of one page, but everything under it is scribbled out. Another page has a different list of "attempts," all crossed out with the word FAILURE written in caps.

Another entry is just the words *I'm sorry* written over and over again, each one methodically scratched through.

I touch the apology page, my fingers dancing over the bumps made from the grooves of each letter.

Each page becomes more and more chaotic, more panic-ridden. *I don't understand* and *I'm scared* jump out at me from one of the pages. I read the passage—the words are all in English, but they don't make any sense.

None of it makes sense.

It's like a visual representation of Bo's mind. It starts out organized, but descends into something unrecognizable.

None of us can understand him, I think.

Soon enough, the ink-stained pages give way to nothing—more than three-quarters of the book is empty. Still, I turn the blank pages, one by one. In a weird way, seeing them gives me some peace. They're not riotously scribbled in. They're calm. They're the quiet without the storm.

If I could choose, I think I would give him the blank pages instead of the black ones.

My hand pauses, hovering over a crisp, clean, empty page.

If the ink on the first pages represents Bo's mind, what do the blank pages mean? And what kind of person am I to prefer them?

I told Bo's psychiatrist that I was horrible for thinking that Bo might do something terrible if given the opportunity. But that's not really horrible. That's just fear. No, I'm horrible for what I'm thinking right now.

For wondering if we would all be happier with the blank pages.

I close the book and brush my fingertips across the mottled cover. My hand is shaking when I pull it back. I slam it on the book, then sweep it off the desk with a roar of frustration and bitterness and sorrow and rage. Black ink or blank pages, who am I to say one is better than the other? Who am I to want to choose for him? Who am I to wish I could?

Who am I at all?

CHAPTER 59

Harold is the only one in the library. He sits in front of a small table, a huge book spread open across the surface, but he's not reading from it. He's deep in conversation with himself.

I sit down across from him. His eyes do not flash with recognition, and I doubt he's even aware that I'm here.

After a while, Harold quits muttering. His gaze shifts down to the book, then up to me.

"Hey," he says quietly.

"Hi."

We sit there awkwardly.

"Well?" Harold finally says. "Aren't you going to make fun of me?"

I lean back. "Have I done that before?" I ask, genuinely unsure of the answer.

Harold shakes his head. "No. But you're hanging out with Ryan now."

"Not really."

"More than before."

"Before what?"

Harold shrugs. "Before Sofía."

That was because Sofía didn't like Ryan.

"Do you know what happened to Sofía?" I ask. I'm not sure what I believe. Do I get to choose what I believe?

Harold is quiet for a while, and then he stares at me with clear, eerie eyes. "She's gone," he says simply.

"Yeah, but . . . how?" My heart races. I promise myself that whatever Harold says, I'll believe. Maybe he has powers or maybe he's just crazy, but either way, he's no liar.

"Does it matter?" Harold asks. "She's gone. She's not here."

My chest caves in and my shoulders slump. Maybe the only reason I was willing to believe whatever he said was because I knew he wouldn't say anything.

The door to the library slams open. "Can you believe this bullshit?" Ryan's voice calls out, full of rage. "Bo, I saw you come in here. Where are you? Have you seen this shit? I can't believe they're going to do this to us!"

I stand up, giving away my location, and Ryan marches over to me. He slams a piece of paper on top of the open book on Harold's desk. Harold scoots his chair back and scurries to the corner.

"What's going on? Calm down, man," I say, staring at Ryan's face. He's practically purple with anger.

Ryan thrusts the paper at me. *"Read,"* he orders.

Dear Parents and Guardians,

We regret to inform you that, after a complicated and in-depth evaluation of our school, the board of directors has decided that the best course of action for our students is that we close at the end of the semester. We are happy to provide references for all students to similar schools, and, of course, we suggest that all students continue their treatments while at home over the summer. Full school and medical records as well as a more detailed report of the situation will be forwarded to you before June 10.

Sincerely,

The Board of Directors of the Berkshire Academy for Children with Exceptional Needs

"They're shutting us down!" Ryan growls.

My eyes linger on the page, dancing from letter to letter, not comprehending the words they create.

"Don't you have anything to say?" Ryan snatches the letter back. "My parents have already picked out my next hellhole."

"Hellhole," Harold repeats, quietly, from the corner.

"Shut up!" Ryan whirls around. Before I can move, before Harold can run away, Ryan grabs him by the collar and yanks him to the book supply closet. He throws Harold inside, flipping the old antique key in the lock and tossing it on the ground. He kicks it violently, the key skidding toward the shelves.

Anger issues.

"What's going to happen to me now?" Ryan says, turning on his heel toward me as if Harold didn't even exist anymore.

Narcissism.

"Let Harold out," I say, trying to make my tone placating.

"Forget that loser—he's one of the reasons why this school is closing." His eyes narrow. "And you're another one."

Sociopathic tendencies.

I bend down and pick up the iron key from the ground. It's for one of those old-fashioned locks that can be opened from either side. I think about sliding the key under the door for Harold, but I'm worried what Ryan will do. I can hear Harold in the book closet, quietly conversing with his ghosts. He's fine—and probably far safer beyond Ryan's reach. I slip the key into my own pocket instead, promising to come back for Harold after this all blows over.

"Stupid Sofía offs herself, that brings the officials. Harold's batshit crazy, and so are you, and when they see just how bad you nut jobs are, they close the school." Ryan punches the end of a shelf, knocking several books to the floor. "After everything I did to stop this from happening . . ."

He kicks a book down the aisle, the pages fluttering open as the cover skitters across the floor. "I bet it was Harold. You keep your crazy under wraps, but Harold is just nuts all over the damn place! No wonder we're being shut down. This place isn't equipped to handle such insane losers."

Ryan jerks around, heading to the door that keeps Harold locked inside the book closet, but I grab him, spinning him toward the exit. "Let's get out of here."

Fortunately, I'm able to distract Ryan. I'm not sure what would happen if he made his way back to Harold, but I definitely don't want to find out.

I'm walking ahead of Ryan while he raves like a lunatic, and without really meaning to, I lead him to Sofía's old room. All I was thinking about was the need to calm Ryan down, to quell the rage swirling inside him like a hurricane, and to me, Sofía means peace.

Gwen is already inside the room, using a Zippo to burn another mark for Sofía's absence. I count the black streaks in the flipped-over mattress, the number of days since Sofía's been gone.

Since Sofía *died*.

If Gwen had powers, she wouldn't need a Zippo. If I had powers, no one would need to count down the days since Sofía's death, because they would all know I could alter time and bring her back. If Ryan had powers, Berkshire wouldn't actually be closing.

But we are all powerless.

The truth sinks in me like a stone.

We are all powerless.

"What are you doing here?" Ryan sneers as soon as he sees Gwen. The sharp scent of the burnt mattress fills the room.

"What are *you* doing here?" Gwen throws the question right back at him, but there's fear in her voice. She glances behind her, at the wall. Ryan's in the doorway; I'm near the mattress. There's no escape for her, and she knows it. She flicks the Zippo in her hand, the flame jumping up then dying with a *click!* of the flip-top.

"Get out," I say not unkindly, moving aside so she can escape.

But Ryan doesn't move. "I said, what are you doing here?" His voice is cold.

"I have a right to be here," she says. "Go away."

But he doesn't move. Ryan just stands in the doorway, challenging Gwen to magically move through him.

I shift nervously. Ryan's all spit and rage; he wants a fight. He wants to destroy something, someone. I've never seen anyone look so dead inside. The only thing Ryan wants to do is spread the hate boiling inside him.

"Listen, man, so what if the Berk closes?" I say, trying to bring some level of logic to Ryan. "It's not that big a deal. There are other schools."

"This school is *mine*," Ryan snarls. "And I won't let them take it away from me."

"Well, this *room* isn't yours, so get out!" Gwen shouts at him, her voice cracking over the words.

"It is. This whole building. Everyone in it."

"This is *Sofía's* room!" Gwen yells at him.

"*Sofía's dead.*" Ryan says the words maliciously, violently, like he wants nothing more than to kill Gwen with the sound of his voice.

But the words don't stab at Gwen. They don't eat her alive like a monster. She has already accepted Sofía's death. She has been nothing but the silent counter of the days since Sofía's been gone.

I'm the one who hears Ryan's words like a saw through my brain. I'm the one who loses my breath, gutted at the way Ryan can say them, like there was never any question of her death.

I'm the one who snaps.

CHAPTER 60

You're scaring me. The words are Gwen's, but I don't know who she said them to.

I am standing in the middle of Sofía's room. The walls move like liquid.

No, those are just shadows. From the flames. The flames on her bed.

Sofía's mattress is on fire.

All around us is a raging inferno, climbing the walls and making the paint bubble.

The door swings, the movement from the air making the flames sway. Ryan just left.

Gwen's in the corner, crouched against the floor. There's blood on her lips and tears in her eyes. She looks utterly powerless, and then I realize: There is nothing of the flame inside of her. Whether Gwen has powers or not, she's always had fire inside. Now—nothing. My eyes scan the room. The Zippo lighter is in the center of the mattress, melting through the burning cloth.

Did Ryan do this?

I reach for Gwen. She flinches.

Did I do this?

Gwen struggles to stand on her own. "Bo?" she asks, hesitating, as if she's not sure I'm going to respond. As if she's not sure I'm me.

I nod at her.

"We have to go," she says.

I open my mouth to protest.

"I can't control it, Bo," Gwen says sympathetically. "We have to go."

"But."

"You really thought we were, like, special, didn't you?"

I stare at the flames. I try to pull them back through time. You can kill a fire if you take away the oxygen; I want to take away the time it took to burn.

"I get it," Gwen says. "If I could choose my own reality, I'd choose the one where I had powers. Where I had Sofía."

I look at the bed again. The fire has spread. It's in the walls now.

Sofía told me a story once, about how there was a family that had wolves in the walls. They hid behind the drywall and ate the family up at night, all because no one believed the little girl when she said there were wolves in the walls. It was a picture book for children.

I am alone in the room. Smoke boils on the ceiling.

Where did Gwen go?
When did Gwen go?

I'm losing time.

It's always about time.

Ringing. Screaming. An alarm.

I step out of Sofía's room, coughing, choking for air. I have to get out of here. I'll die if I don't. *I'll die like Sofía died.*

No. Not like Sofía. *Sofía died in the cold.*

No. NO. Sofía's not dead.

Smoke billows down the hallway; the flames have spread to other rooms.

You can't control fire.

I close my eyes and think of the timestream. If I could just go back—just a little jump, just a few minutes ago, I could stop the fire from starting.

You can't control time.

I throw my arm in front of my face, and I stumble-run down the hallway toward the stairs. As I pass a window, I see people fleeing, escaping the burning building. There's a thumping sound, and sobbing, and it's coming from the walls. *Wolves in the walls.* One of them knows my name.

The fire has jumped the hall, spreading over the wood paneling of the ceiling. Ashes and embers fall like rain. The carpet singes and smokes, black holes ringed with red, burning my bare feet as I run.

The fire alarm is going off. Sprinklers too.

But it's all too late. Nothing will stop this fire. It will burn until there's nothing left to burn.

I skid to the landing, barely stopping myself from tumbling down the steps into the foyer. People are streaming out the door—the cooks, the nurses, the other teachers. And I see the Doctor there, standing in front, waving his arm as if that'll make people move faster.

The entire world around me dances in light and heat.

"COME ON!" Dr. Franklin shouts, and I race down the stairs. He pushes me through the massive front door. One of the other unit leaders, Ms. Grantham, stops me from falling, and she doesn't let go of my wrist, pulling me down after her with a viselike grip on my arm. "Go to your unit," she yells at me when we reach the driveway, already running toward her own cluster of students, who've gathered in their designated fire area.

I run to Gwen and Ryan, still choking from the burnt air. Smoke billows from the windows and open doors, just like in the house where I saw Sofía trapped when I was falling through time.

That never happened, my brain tells me, but I don't believe it.

Gwen clutches her arms around her chest as tears stream down her face, her mouth gulping at air. Ryan grabs my arm as soon as he's close enough and pulls me to the side.

"Don't you dare tell one damn person what just happened," he snarls at me.

"About the fire?" I say stupidly, not sure how to react to his vicious tone.

"Don't be a dumbass," Ryan says, his voice still low and menacing. "I don't care how much of a schizo freak you are, don't you dare even think of telling anyone what we did. You hear me? We didn't do *anything*." His hand squeezes tighter around my arm.

Behind me, the walls of Berkshire howl like wolves, baying to the flames rather than the moon.

Dr. Franklin rushes up to us. "Have any of you seen Harold?" he asks, breathless, panic in his voice.

And that's when I understand what Ryan meant.

We left Harold. We left him locked in the closet.

To die.

CHAPTER 61

Ryan drops my arm, and the blood tingles back to my fingers. Immediately, my hand goes to my pocket, to the old iron key that rests inside it. I don't pull it out, but I feel it, and I know that Harold's salvation lies in the palm of my hand.

I didn't even think of him.

I let him die. Ryan locked him inside, but I could have unlocked the door. I could have freed him. But I didn't. Because I forgot. Because I'm that selfish. Because in the end, when the flames licked at my heels, I thought of only my own escape.

I drop to my knees, staring up at the burning building. I can hear sirens blaring down the island—the fire trucks are coming.

It's too late. I passed the library. I saw the wooden walls catch flame. The room is filled with old books, musty tomes of paper that will ignite with just a spark.

There's movement by the big front door, still wide open though all the students—all but Harold—are safe outside.

A boy stands there, steaming. His body is drenched in water, but the fire sizzles on his skin, wrapping him in misty clouds. But I can still tell who it is. Carlos Estrada.

"No," I whisper.

He nods. *Yes.*

If I'm seeing Carlos, then maybe all hope is not lost. Carlos comes from another time, slipping from the pool that killed him through the timestream to me. He is proof that the timestream is real, that my powers are real. I stand up shakily, the iron key in my fist. I stare, hard, at the burning walls of the academy.

Ryan sees the key in my hand. He grabs my arm and spins me around. "Don't even think about telling on me," he growls.

I slam my fist right in his face.

For a moment, I allow myself to feel deep satisfaction at the way that his nose crunches. I hadn't planned it, but the fist that struck him still held the iron key inside, and blood streams down his cheek from where the metal cut him. Ryan staggers back, clutching his nose, too shocked to speak. Gwen's sobbing stops as she stares at us.

I ignore them both—I ignore everything: the Doctor rushing to Ryan's aid, the scared cries and whispers of the other students gathered on the lawn, the shouts of teachers to remain calm and to stay put—and turn back to the building.

Fire doesn't melt bricks, but it's melting Ryan's illusion. It falls away like ash, and Berkshire is far clearer than I've ever seen it before. Everything's clearer. Dr. Franklin and Gwen and Ryan look more real, like the difference between a photograph and an actual person. I look down at myself, holding my hands out in front of me. *I* look more real.

And so does the iron key.

There's a thread connecting the key all the way into the academy. Just like the threads of fate that make up the timestream. I touch the thread gently, and it's hot, burning my fingertips. But in that moment of connection, I also see, for just a flash, Harold. His body is slumped inside the closet, one arm still raised as if beating against the door, but it's motionless. He's entirely still. His eyes don't even blink as the smoke swirls around him.

For as long as I've had my power, for as much as I've tried to understand it, I've considered some laws unchangeable. There are moments in time that I cannot prevent. I could no sooner change Harold's fate than I could change the sinking of the Titanic. That is the rule of time.

But I don't care about the rules anymore.

I wrap my hand around the thread connecting Harold to the key. It burns like hot wire melting through my palm, slicing open the thin skin between my thumb and forefinger. I grit my teeth and wrap tighter, pulling it, straining against time itself, begging the universe for the power to finally make a change to the pattern of history.

Even though it feels as if the thread has maimed my hand, when I blink, I can tell that this is an injury no one else can see. Ryan's still clutching his face, and the Doctor's shouting into a phone that there's a kid inside the building. Gwen's watching me, a slight frown on her face. She can't see the thread. She can't see how close I am to breaking it.

With a mighty heave, I *pull*.

The thread snaps.

And now time itself can be altered.

I don't waste a second. I move like a puppet master, grabbing handfuls of threads from the timestream, sifting them through my fingers. I know exactly where I need to go, because I have already been there.

I go back to a few weeks ago. There's a past version of me sitting in front of the old Salem ruins. It's starting to piss rain, the clouds dense and dark. And Harold—still alive, still well— is walking up the path toward me.

Before he rounds the corner, I step in front of him. In moments, he's going to go to the ruined brick fireplace and talk to me about darkness and voices, and then we're going to go back to the academy together. But first, I stop him here.

"I want you to have this," I tell him, handing him the iron key.

Harold looks at me in surprise, but he accepts it.

"Keep it with you all the time," I say. "You are definitely going to need it in the future."

He keeps his head down, staring at it. His fingers wrap around the metal, and he starts to lift his head to speak to me, but I'm already gone.

I'm back in the present, in front of the fire, my eyes on the door. Carlos Estrada is no longer in front of me, framed by the flames. Instead, it's Harold staggering through the smoke, coughing, the iron key in his hand.

CHAPTER 62

I saved him.

I went back in time. I gave him the key. *I saved him.*

My power is *real.*

"Harold!" Dr. Franklin yells, abandoning Ryan so abruptly that he drops to the ground. The Doctor falls to his knees in front of Harold, clutching his shoulders, running his hands along his sides, looking for injuries. One of the teachers—the science tutor, Mr. Glover—passes over a bottle of water, and Harold chugs it, sputtering through a sore throat.

"Where were you?" the Doctor says over and over.

"I was locked in the book closet in the library," Harold says in a weak voice. He raises his arm, pointing to Ryan. "*He* left me there."

"How'd you get out?" Mr. Glover asks.

Harold shrugs. "That lock was really old, and I guess with the heat, it sort of snapped. I'm sorry, I totally broke it."

The Doctor sob-laughs in relief and hugs Harold tightly.

I creep closer, searching Harold's eyes. Does he really not remember using the key I gave him? Or is he pretending not to know because he still doubts the Doctor, as I do?

I look at his hand.

No key.

Above us, the windows burst, shooting out shards of glass followed by bright red-orange flames. Several students on the ground scream and dash even farther away.

"Where are the damn fire trucks?" Mr. Glover asks Dr. Franklin.

One of the windows that broke was to Sofía's room. And while I don't see Sofía's face, I see the outline of a girl in flames. An invisible girl, trapped in the fire.

I move forward without thinking.

The illusory world Ryan created—the one where he made me think I was crazy, that Berkshire Academy was for kids with special needs instead of kids with special powers, that Sofía was dead—has broken away. The fact that Harold is still alive proves that.

As I walk closer to the burning academy, I bring up the timestream. It comes to me easily. All those stutters before, they were all just growing pains. I'm in control now. I understand now. This is not something I need to fear.

The power is mine for the taking.

It washes over me in a glorious wave. I have never been in such control before. I have never felt the power this way. I finally have *complete* control. The power courses inside my body, filling me with a firm knowledge: *I can change time. I can bend it to my will. I am its master.*

The timestream is tantalizingly in my reach, and I can see with perfect clarity exactly how every thread is placed, how every moment in history rests within the palm of my hand.

And I know. I can change it all.

The image of Sofía in the window—I know it was her, I *know* it—it's a sign. I can go back. I can go back to before she went missing in time, before my powers crumbled, before Ryan could manipulate them and me. With this power, I can stop tragedies long before they happen. I can save not only Sofía, but also the Doctor and Berkshire. I can save Ryan from himself. I can bring it all back to the way it was before.

I don't see everything laid out in front of me in chronological order, but that doesn't matter. I can see the first step. And the first step is to go to that image in the window—to the outline of the girl I know is Sofía—who's waiting for me on the second floor of the academy despite the fire, despite the mess I've made of the present.

"Bo?" Dr. Franklin's voice calls out. "Bo!"

I glance behind me just in time to see the Doctor running for me, one arm outstretched. He's still in Ryan's control, still believes he's just my doctor, not my mentor and teacher in understanding my powers. He wants to hold me back. He wants to stop me.

I put my hand up, palm flat.

Time stops.

The Doctor is launching toward me. His frozen face is full of fear and anguish.

I turn back to the academy. The flames look somewhat paler now, but they still move ever so slightly. Or maybe it's just my perception that they're moving as I walk closer and closer to the burning building—I can't tell. The light flickers in and out, playing peekaboo with my eyes.

I mount each step slowly. Even though everything is stopped, I can still feel the heat radiating from the fire.

A moment of fear seizes me, and my control falters. For just a second, the flames lick out and the smoke engulfs me, and I choke.

But then I see the girl in the flames, her shape perfectly cut out of the raging fire, and I am in utter control again. Time is stopped, ready to serve my whim.

The timestream stretches out before me, but I am only looking for one specific thread. The red thread, the one that connects me to Sofía.

And there it is. Leading me through the burning academy.

Clouds of smoke obscure my vision, and I blow, watching as they gently disperse.

It's strange to see the static fire, caught in the process of eating the school like a voracious monster. The crisp black edges of the wallpaper and carpet and wood paneling glow red. The flames lick out from all around, impossibly slow, as if they're inviting me to dance.

I can't help myself—I reach out and scoop a tiny ball of flame from the wall by the door. It has no weight at all; it glows in my palm. It's almost like a hollow shell of light, the orange-red wisp curling around nothing.

"BO!" a voice shouts through the silence.

Several things happen at once. A roar fills my ears, crackling and popping, the timbers overhead creaking as the fire comes alive once more. The smoke billows around me, cascading over my body, and the tiny ball of flame I held in my hand scorches my skin, blisters bubbling up across my palm. I scream in pain. My hand is not empty—it holds the iron key that I went back in time to give to Harold, but now that key is red hot and branding my palm. I cry out, dropping the key to the floor.

How did it get in my hand?

The Doctor runs up the outside steps toward me.

"Bo!" He screams my name again. "What are you doing? Come back!"

I retreat further into the fire. The Doc stops—not because I've stopped time, but because he's afraid of chasing me deeper into danger. His eyes are wide and filled with terror.

"I can control this," I say, my voice just loud enough over the sound of the fire. "Go back to the others. I can handle it."

"Bo." His voice is sobbing now. "Bo, you're sick. You can't see reality. The building is on *fire*. Please, please come back."

The burn on my hand aches and stings, but I shake my head. "You don't understand," I shout, backing further into the foyer. "I have control now. I can go back. I can change it all. I can stop this from ever happening."

"This is suicide!"

His words make me pause. Suicide? This has nothing to do with that. This is about *saving* everyone. I can't die.

I'm in control. I know what I'm doing.

I'm going back to Sofía.

"Bo, please!" the Doctor shouts. "Come back out! This isn't the answer! You *will* die in there!"

The pain in my hand is sharper than any I've ever felt before, but it hadn't burned when I held the fire, only when the Doctor pulled me from the timestream.

"It's okay!" I shout back at him. "I know what I'm doing!"

Before he can protest again, I stop time. I need to stop the burning. The pain in my hand instantly goes away, and the flames slow to a wavering dance. The Doctor freezes, his raised arms immobile, reaching for me.

I turn away from him. Away from the exit.

I make it to the second floor quickly, but I have to hop over a part of the stairs that's been damaged by the flames. The hallway for our unit is in worse shape than any other area, which isn't much of a surprise, since the fire started in Sofía's room. I creep forward, careful to avoid the giant flames that swirl up the wall, creating a beautiful pattern of destruction. I want to touch them, to hold fire in my hand the way Gwen does, but I worry that when I restart time, it will burn me like it did before. So I'm careful.

I see wet footprints on the carpet.

I tread over them, fitting my feet into the tiny prints. Carlos is leading the way for me, showing me the path I should take.

I wonder why Carlos has become this touchstone between Sofía and me, the guide leading me to my full powers. I know why he was important to Sofía: He was the first person she ever saw die. Death leaves a mark.

Maybe that's why Sofía's important to me.

Time erupts around me with a violent roar, the flames shooting out, the heat and smoke choking me. I drop to my knees. "No!" I shout to the fire. "NO! I have control!"

The flames mock me.

Through the haze, I see the flicker of an outline of a girl, running across the hall into Dr. Franklin's office.

I don't have control anymore.

But I can have Sofía.

I bend my head, pushing further into the fire. It's hard to breathe. The smoke burns, the air burns, my lungs burn. I stumble forward, my arm over my nose and mouth. My hair feels hot on my head; my clothes feel as if they are made of embers.

Just a little further.

A little further.

CHAPTER 63

Phoebe

I pick up the phone on the third ring.

"Hello? Hello?" a panicked voice calls out from the other end.

"Hello?" I say.

"Who's this?" the voice demands. "Phoebe, is that you?"

"Yeah?" I reply warily.

"I need to speak to your parents! This is Dr. Franklin, at Berkshire Academy. I have to speak to your parents right away!"

In the background, I can hear a siren.

"Dr. Franklin? What happened?"

"Your parents!"

"They're not here."

Yes, that's definitely a siren. And . . . a beeping sound. People talking. What's going on?

"There's been an accident—a fire." Dr. Franklin's voice is weary.

"A fire?"

"Have your parents call me right away!"

"Is Bo okay?" I ask, my heart catching in my throat. I never wanted this, I never thought the idea that he could be gone would hurt this way, a deep, sharp pain that crackles under my skin, into my bones, burning away the air in my lungs.

The line goes dead.

CHAPTER 64

I can feel something—someone—pinching my nose, forcing air into my mouth. I feel my chest rise with someone else's breath, I feel my ribs pushed down under someone else's hands.

It's foggy, and I'm alone. The timestream has been a tapestry, spreading out like a blanket over the world, but it's not that way now.

Right now, it is only two threads, hanging limply in my hands.

"We're losing him!" a voice shouts. Someone cuts my T-shirt right in half and pulls it apart, all the way down to the hem. Something sticky is pressed onto my skin.

I hear sounds in the dense fogginess of this world where I exist now. A heart monitor, drowning out all other noise.

Beep ... beep ... beep ... beep ...

• • •

Two threads.

Two choices.

A radio crackles. They're taking me to a hospital. I can feel the needles in my arm and hand. I can hear the first responders talking in hushed voices. The Doctor is here. He's telling them I don't have any allergies, he's calling my parents on his cell phone. *Please*, he says, *please save him.*

I see the girl. I know her immediately.

She's not tall, but she's not short. Average. Her hair is to her shoulders, her face is round, her hips are round, her arms long and straight at her sides. Her eyes search mine, a question there, suspended over their brown depths.

She is at the end of one of the threads in front of me.

She does not flicker this time.

She does not disappear.

She is not tantalizingly out of reach.

Instead, she steps forward, her fingers trailing along the thread leading to her. She's barefoot and silent, her steps like a dance.

On the other thread, there is a sound.

Beep . . . beep . . . beep . . .

I know what two threads mean.

Other people may not see their choices, but I do. I see the threads of fate. I control them. I have two threads in my hand. All I have to do is let go of one and hold on to the other. The one I keep will become my reality, the only truth I know. The one I let go of will be nothing more than a faded dream, an opportunity I never took.

Time is giving me a choice between which reality I want to live.

I look down at my hands.

In my left hand is the red thread connecting me to Sofía. If I choose that life, I have powers. I have adventure. And I have Sofía.

In my right hand is the black thread connecting me to the sound of my heartbeat. To the Doctor. To Berkshire. To Phoebe and my family. To Ryan and a world where I'm sick, where I don't know who to trust, where my life is hollow and bitter.

But it's still my life.

And it's still my choice.

EPILOGUE

Phoebe

One year later

My gown is made of cheap polyester, and the zipper is already broken.

I love it anyway.

"One more!" Mom says, adjusting her camera.

"Come on," I whine.

"Just one more," she promises. When she doesn't lower the camera, I stand up straighter, turning to the lens and smiling, making sure the tassel over my graduation cap is on the left side. Mom darts forward and adjusts the medal hanging from my neck—the award for highest AP scores in math—and then dashes back to snap the picture.

"Okay, *done*," I say. Jenny and Rosemarie are nearby, both of them humoring their parents with more pictures too. Rosemarie's little brother, Peter, keeps trying to steal her graduation cap.

"Want me to take one with your whole family?" Jenny's mother asks me.

"Yes! Please!" Mom says, grabbing Dad and dragging him to the fountain, where I'm standing.

"You said this was the last picture," I say under my breath.

"*This* one is." Mom kisses my cheek.

Dad stands up straight and tall beside me. He looks uncomfortable in his suit, even though he wears one every Sunday. He's very aware of the camera Jenny's mom is pointing at us, as if whether or not the picture turns out good rests entirely on his shoulders.

"Wait a minute!" I say before Jenny's mom can click a picture with Mom's fancy camera. "Where's Bo?"

Mom frowns. "He was just here a minute ago . . ."

"Here I am." My brother runs forward. "Trying to cut me out of the family picture?"

I drag him beside me. Without thinking, I'd grabbed his bad hand, the one injured in the fire. It doesn't hurt him, but his skin feels unnaturally slick beneath my touch, and the scarring on his palm feels weird. I drop his hand as soon as I realize, but I bump his shoulder with mine, looking up at him and grinning.

"Okay, everyone, this way!" Jenny's mom calls. "Ready? One, two, three!" She snaps the picture, then holds the camera out to Mom for approval.

"Glad you could make it," I tell Bo as Mom gets Dad to take a picture of Jenny's family for her.

"Glad to be here," he says, but there's still a little distance in his voice, as if he's not really here, not all the way. His eyes are on Dad, drinking in the dark suit and carefully knotted tie. Bo's not dressed up. He's wearing a plain shirt with no holes in it, though, so I guess that counts for something. But the difference between Bo and my dad is far greater than the way they dress.

I want so badly to ask Bo if he's happy now. He came back from the fire at his old school different, but I've never been able to decide if that difference was good. He's steadier now, but is that really better? Sometimes there's a hollowness in his gaze, a melancholy twist to his smile. I think about the blank pages in his notebook. I'm sure they're still blank.

I shake my head. That's Dad's way of thinking. Bo isn't a before-and-after picture, he's just the same Bo. And even though he's different now, and even though I cannot read the difference, he's still my brother. Asking him if he's happy now is moot. *Happy* is too definite a word to describe Bo. He's alive. He survived. And when we talk about the future, like we did that morning over cereal, the conversation now includes what he wants to do and be.

"These are new," Bo says, tweaking my navy blue cat-eye glasses.

"I'm tired of contacts," I say. "And they're not that new."

"New to me." This is the first time I've seen Bo in over three months. The new school he attends is in upstate New York, and even though it's just a few hours' drive, the program there is more "rigorous," as Dad describes it. Mom and Dad get monthly reports from the school, detailed analyses and charts all mailed in a giant manila envelope. They talk about Bo's medication and how it's more stabilized now, and they include schedules of therapy and courses, as well as charts that track grades and progress, both academic and psychological. Every envelope includes a note saying that the purpose of Bo's therapy is not to "heal" him, but to help him cope with his illness and navigate a somewhat normal life. One day. In the future.

He does look better, though. But there's still a part of him that isn't quite here. His body's present, but maybe there will always be a part of his mind that's not. Ever since Sofía died and the academy burned, there's been something about Bo that's more absent than before. He's like a man who lived through a battle but isn't quite sure whether or not he left the war.

"Well," I say. "I'm going to go hang out with my friends." I lean down and pick up my purse from the ground, rooting around inside it for my phone. My parents got their pictures; now it's time to get mine.

"Hey," Bo says, reaching for me.

I pause, surprised, half thinking he's going to pull me into a hug, which he has literally never done before. Instead, his hand goes to my face. He brushes my hair away.

"You're about to lose that earring," he says, touching the diamond.

My hands go immediately to my ears. He's right; the back is loose. I tighten it, then check the other one.

"How did you even notice?" I ask. The graduation cap and several bobby pins hold my hair in place, covering my ears.

"Lucky guess." Bo smiles at me. "I'd hate for you to lose one."

"Yeah," I tell him, my voice choking with unexpected emotion. "These really mean a lot to me."

"I know," he says.

I fiddle with the earrings, checking them again. I'm surprised that Bo would pay enough attention to notice that one was loose, to remember that they're important, to even recognize that these were Grandma's earrings before they were mine. Maybe I'm not as invisible to him as I thought.

"Only for special occasions," I say, imitating Mom in a high-pitched voice.

Bo cracks a smile. "Yeah, well, life is a special occasion."

The words surprise me, coming from him. But for the first time in a long time, I feel like maybe everything's happening the way it's supposed to be happening, and that it'll all be okay.

"Go on," he says genially. "I'm sure you want to take pictures with your friends." I turn to go, but he calls out to me: "Pheebs?"

"Yeah?"

"What school did you pick?" He shuffles his feet. "I mean, the last time we talked about, you know, your future, you seemed a little . . . undecided."

I grin at him. "Don't tell Mom and Dad," I say, leaning toward him and lowering my voice. "I did get accepted to NYU, and I'm going there, undecided major for now, but . . ." I draw out the last word.

Bo waits, his eyebrow cocked in anticipation.

"But I'm going to defer a year," I say. I look behind me, making sure our parents haven't overheard. I'll have to tell them eventually that I plan on waiting a solid year before going back to school, but they can't do anything about it. I've already submitted the paperwork and finalized it all. It's my decision to make, and I made it.

"What are you going to do for that year?" Bo asks.

A grin spreads across my face, an immediate reaction that I'm not sure comes from joy or relief or something else entirely.

"That's the best part," I say. "I have no idea."